More Praise for

Touch

A Barnes & Noble Discover Great New Writers Pick

"[An] eerie, elegiac debut. . . . The rugged wilderness is captured exquisitely, as is Stephen's uncommon childhood, and despite a narrative rife with tragedy, Zentner's elegant prose keeps the story buoyant." —*Publishers Weekly*, starred review

"I cannot lie, I completely fell under the spell of Alexi Zentner's debut novel. It is difficult to be objective when a novel impresses to such an extent. . . . Zentner's flawless, fluid execution allows central moments of life, death, and love to layer into a haunting accumulation." —*Library Journal*

"Calling up both the brutal conditions—the snow almost becomes another character in the story—and the tough men who wrestled with them, Zentner tells a lyrical tale conveying both the beauty and the danger of the wilderness."—*Booklist*

"Reminiscent of Per Petterson's *Out Stealing Horses* in its detailed descriptions of life in a mill town, Zentner's is ultimately a novel to be read for its gorgeous renderings, its evocative language, its vignettes of life in a forgotten land." —Courtney Tenz, *Bookslut*

"[A] haunting multi-generational story with mythical overtones, reminiscent of the work of Canadian literary great Joseph Boyden." —CBC

"Zentner fills his novel with arresting, unforgettable images. . . . As dazzling as the snow that fills its pages, *Touch* marks Zentner out as a talent to watch." —*The Times* (UK)

"Sometimes a debut novel reads like a debut novel and sometimes a debut novel reads like a work of art. Alexi Zentner's falls into the latter category. . . . *Touch* is a haunting, beguiling and beautifully imagined story." —*Winnipeg Free Press*

"A stunning and provocative debut. Zentner mines the human heart to blend humor with tragedy, myth with reality, addicting his audience to a world as uplifting as it is brutal." —Téa Obreht, author of *The Tiger's Wife*

"An affecting debut from a major new talent." —Philipp Meyer, author of *American Rust*

"*Touch* is full of a sinister magic straight from the tradition of the Brothers Grimm. . . . Such savagery, however, only illuminates the deeply human love in the marrow of this novel, which Zentner achieves with incredible grace and greatness of heart." —Lauren Groff, author of *The Monsters of Templeton*

"[T]his book is enchanted with fables, full of images so beautiful and strange that they are haunting. *Touch* more

than delivers on the promise of its title: long after the last
page, you will still be in its grip."
                                        —Josh Weil,
                          author of *The New Valley*

"*Touch* brings to life a lost world, or maybe just a world we
wish was real, in prose as seductive as gold dust. It's a sublime
haunting, a ripping yarn, and a killer debut."
                          —J. Robert Lennon, author of *Castle*

"One of those rare novels that takes hold of your imagination
and your heart and does not let go. . . . It's a gem of a book"
                          —Aryn Kyle, author of *The God of Animals*

W. W. NORTON & COMPANY

NEW YORK   LONDON

Touch

a novel

Alexi Zentner

For information about permission to reproduce selections from this book,
write to Permissions, W. W. Norton & Company, Inc.,
500 Fifth Avenue, New York, NY 10110

For information about special discounts for bulk purchases, please contact
W. W. Norton Special Sales at specialsales@wwnorton.com or 800-233-4830

Manufacturing by Courier Westford
Book design by Barbara Bachman
Production manager: Anna Oler

Library of Congress Cataloging-in-Publication Data

Zentner, Alexi.
Touch : a novel / Alexi Zentner. — 1st ed.
p. cm.
ISBN 978-0-393-07987-6 (hardcover)
1. Clergy—Fiction. 2. Domestic fiction. I. Title.
PS3626.E445T68 2011
813'.6—dc22
2010053554

ISBN 978-0-393-34239-0 pbk.

W. W. Norton & Company, Inc.
500 Fifth Avenue, New York, N.Y. 10110
www.wwnorton.com

W. W. Norton & Company Ltd.
Castle House, 75/76 Wells Street, London W1T 3QT

1 2 3 4 5 6 7 8 9 0

For my wife, Laurie,

the reason why everything I write is really about love,

and for my daughters, Zoey and Sabine.

Touch

ONE

Touch

THE MEN FLOATED the logs early, in September, a chain of headless trees jamming the river as far as I and the other children could see. My father, the foreman, stood at the top of the chute hollering at the men and shaking his mangled hand, urging them on. "That's money in the water, boys," he yelled, "push on, push on." I was ten that summer, and I remember him as a giant.

Despite his bad hand, my father could still man one end of a long saw. He kept his end humming through the wood as quickly as most men with two hands. But a logger with a use-less hand could not pole on the river. When the men floated the trees my father watched from the middle of the jam, where the trees were smashed safely together, staying away from the bob-bing, breaking destruction of wood and weight at the edges. The float took days to reach Havershand, he said. There was little sleep and constant wariness. Watch your feet, boys. The spinning logs can crush you. The cold-water deeps beneath the logs always beckoned. Men pitched tents at the center of the jam, where logs were pushed so tightly together that they made solid ground, terra firma, a place to sleep for a few hours, eat hard biscuits, and drink a cup of tea. Once they reached Havershand, the logs continued on by train without my father: either south for railway ties or two thousand miles east to Toronto, and then on freighters to Boston or New York, where the towering trees became beams and braces in strangers' cities.

I remember my father as a giant, even though my mother reminded me that he was not so tall that he had to duck his head to cross the threshold of our house, the small foreman's cottage with the covered porch that stood behind the mill. I know from the stories my father told me when I was a child that he imagined his own father—my grandfather, Jeannot— the same way, as a giant. He never met my grandfather, so he had to rely on the stories he heard from my great-aunt Rebecca and great-uncle Franklin—who raised him as their own after Jeannot left Sawgamet—and from the other men and women who had known my grandfather. My father retold these same stories to me.

I had my own idea of Jeannot well before I met him, before my grandfather returned to Sawgamet. And meeting him, hearing Jeannot tell the stories himself, did not make it any easier for me to separate the myths from the reality. I've told some of these same stories to my daughters: sometimes the true versions that Jeannot told me, sometimes the pieces of stories that made their way to me through other men and women and through my father, and sometimes just what I think or wished had happened. But even when I tell my daughters stories about my own father, it is hard for me to tell how much has changed in the retelling.

It is more than thirty years past the summer I was ten—
my oldest daughter has just turned ten herself—and I would
like to think that my daughters see me the same way I saw my
father, but it is hard to imagine that they do; my father worked
in the cuts taking down trees, and he ran the water when he
was younger, poling logs out of eddies and currents and breaking jams for the thirty miles from Sawgamet to Havershand. I,
on the other hand, have returned to Sawgamet as an Anglican
priest, coming home to live in the shadows of my father and
my grandfather in a logging town that has been drained of
young men headed off to fight in Europe for the second war
of my lifetime.

So many years I've been gone. I left at sixteen to Edmonton
and the seminary, and then went across the Atlantic, a chaplain
for the war. I came back in June of 1919, getting off the ship
the day the Treaty of Versailles was signed. My mother would
have liked me home, but with Father Earl, Sawgamet did not
need a second Anglican priest. I ended up in Vancouver, with
a new church and a new wife of my own. I've come back to
Sawgamet to visit—infrequent though that has been—but
now I have returned, at Father Earl's request, to take over the
Anglican church from him. He asked me to come even before
it was clear my mother was dying, but still, I almost arrived too
late. Soon enough—tonight, tomorrow—my mother will be
dead and I'll have to write the eulogy for the funeral.

I've had enough experience with telling others the tired
homily that God works in mysterious ways, to know that
there is no making sense of the workings of God. Though, if
I were to be honest, I would admit that I think of my father
and grandfather as gods themselves. I do not mean gods in a

religious sense, but rather like the gods that the natives believe preceded us in these northern forests. In that way, my father and my grandfather *were* gods: they tamed the forests and brought civilization to Sawgamet, and in the stories passed down to me, it is impossible to determine what is myth and what is the truth.

There were only the last few weeks of sitting at my mother's side, knowing she was preparing to die, and trying to sort out the truths from the myths. I talked with her and asked her questions when she was awake, held her hand when she was asleep. And yet, no matter how many times my thoughts returned to the winter I was ten, no matter how many questions I asked my mother as she lay dying, no matter how many stories I have heard about my father and grandfather, there are still so many things I will never know.

For instance, I never knew how my father felt about his mangled hand, and as a child I was afraid to ask. He did not talk about the dangers; the river was swift and final, but it was out in the cuts, among the trees, when each day unfolded like the last—the smooth, worn handles of the saw singing back and forth—that men's minds wandered. Men I knew had been killed by falling trees, had bled to death when a dull ax bounced off a log and into their leg, had been crushed when logs rolled off carts, had drowned in the river during a float. Every year a man came back dead or maimed.

When I was not quite eight, on the day of my sister Marie's fifth birthday, I had asked my mother about my father's hand. That was as close as I was ever able to come to asking my father.

"I was thankful," she said. We sat on the slope by the log

chute, looking out over the river, waving uselessly at the black-flies. My father had taken Marie into the woods, the preserve of men, a present for her birthday.

"You were thankful?"

"It was only his hand," my mother said, and she was right.

That summer morning, Marie had carried her own lunch into the cuts, all bundled together and tied in a handkerchief: two slices of blueberry bread; a few boiled potatoes, early and stunted; a small hunk of roast meat. My father let her carry his ax, still sharp and gleaming though he had not swung it since his accident, and as they walked away from the house, I argued that my father should take me as well, that other boys helped their fathers on Saturdays and during the summers. I was old enough to strip branches, to help work the horses, to earn my keep.

"You've been enough," my mother said, though she knew that I had been only twice, on my birthdays. "It's too danger-ous out there." I knew she was thinking of the way the log had rolled onto my father's hand, crushing it so tightly it did not begin to bleed until the men had cut him free. I must have made a face, because she softened. "You'll go again next month, on your birthday."

They returned late that night, the summer sun barely drowned, Marie still bearing the ax and crying quietly, walk-ing with a stiff limp, spots of blood showing on her socks where her blisters had rubbed raw, my father keeping a slow pace beside her. My mother stepped off the porch toward Marie, but my sister moved past her, climbing up the three steps and through the door. My father shook his head.

"She wouldn't let me carry her."

"Or the ax?"

"I tried."

"And?"

He kissed my mother and then shook his head again. "It's a hard day for a child. She'll go again next year, if she wants." My mother nodded and headed inside to see to Marie's blisters, to give her dinner, to offer her a slice of pie.

The next week, Charles Rondeau, bucking a tree, did not hear the yells from the men, and Mr. Rondeau had to carry his son, Charles, bloodied and dead from the bush. Charles was only a few years older than I was then, and a month later, when I turned eight, my mother gave me a new Sunday suit, hot and itchy, and my father went to the cuts without me.

DESPITE CHARLES RONDEAU'S DEATH, the season that I turned eight was a good one, the cold holding back longer than usual. My father kept the men cutting late into October. There had not even been a frost yet when they started sending logs down the chute from the mill into the river.

When the last log was in the water, my father waved to us from the middle of the jam, and Marie and I ran along the banks with the other children for a mile or two, shouting at the men. My father, like every man that year, came back from Havershand laughing. They all had their coats off, their long, sharp peaveys resting on their shoulders, and small gifts for their wives and children tucked under their arms. Even the winter that year was easy, and when the river did finally freeze up in December, the latest the ice had ever been, Marie and

I had our first new skates. There was still tissue paper in the box. Christmas had come early.

⟵

EVEN THOUGH WE wanted to be with my father in the cuts during the summers, the winters were better, because at least then we had him to ourselves. School days, he took to the mill, filing blades, checking the books, helping the assistant foreman, Pearl, tend to the horses, but he was home when we were, sitting at the stove at night, listening with us as my mother, a former schoolteacher at the Sawgamet schoolhouse, read from her books. He carved small wooden toys for Marie—a rough horse, a whistle—using his destroyed hand to pin the block of wood to the table. Mostly, though, he told us stories.

I know that out in the cuts he was a different man. He had to be. He kept the men's respect and, in turn, they kept the saw blades humming through green wood. While their axes cut smiles into pines and stripped branches from fallen trees, while they wrapped chains around the logs, my father moved through the woods, yelling, talking, making them laugh, taking the end of a saw when it was needed. He pushed them hard, and when they pushed back, he came home with bruises, an eye swollen shut, scabs on his knuckles. He made them listen.

At home, he was gentle. At night, he told us stories about his father, how Jeannot found gold and settled Sawgamet, and then the long winter that followed the bust. He told us about the qallupilluit and Amaguq, the trickster wolf god, about the loupgarou and the blood-drinking adlet, about all of the monsters

16

and witches of the woods. He told us about the other kinds of magic that he stumbled across in the cuts, how the sawdust grew wings and flew down men's shirts like mosquitoes, how one tree picked itself up and walked away from the sharp teeth of the saw. He told us about splitting open a log to find a fairy kingdom, about clearing an entire forest with one swing of his ax, about the family of trees he had found twisted together, pushing toward the sky, braided in love.

Our favorite story, however, the story that we always asked him to retell, was about the year he finally convinced our mother to marry him. The last time I remember him telling the story was the spring before I turned ten.

"Every man had been thrown but me and Pearl Gasseur," he said.

"Old Pearl?" Marie giggled, thinking of Pearl as I thought of him, riding the middle of the float with his close gray hair bristling crazily from his scalp, yellowed long underwear peeking from the cuffs of his shirt.

My father had told the story so many times that Marie probably could have recounted it word for word by then, but like me, like our mother, she still laughed and clapped.

"Old Pearl? Old Pearl?" my father roared, his teeth flashing. "Old Pearl wasn't always old," he yelled happily. "Old Pearl could sink any man and would laugh at you while he spun the log out from under your feet."

"And Mrs. Gasseur was happy to tell you about it," my mother said. "She was happy as winter berries watching him dunk the boys." My mother smiled at this. She always smiled.

Logrolling in Sawgamet was a tradition. Every year the entire town came down to the river the day before the float.

They carried blankets and baskets full with chicken, roasted onions and potatoes, bread, blueberry pies, strawberry wine. My father—and before him Foreman Martin—would roll out a few barrels of beer, and the men took to the water. They spun logs, a man on either end, turning the wood with their feet, faster and faster, stopping and spinning the other way, until one, or sometimes both, pitched into the cold water to raucous cheers from the banks.

"Pearl won ever since I could remember," my father said. "He'd never been unseated, but I had to win." He slapped the worn pine table with his mangled hand and winked at my mother. "Oh, your mother was a clever one." He stood up from the table and hooked his arm around her waist, pulling her close to him and looking over her shoulder at Marie and me. "She still is."

He kissed her then, and it surprised me to see my mother's cheeks redden. Before she pushed him away, she whispered something into his ear and he reddened as well, pausing a moment to watch her take the plates from the table.

"Papa," Marie said, demanding more.

"Oh, but you know all this already. She married me," he said, turning back to us and waving his hand, "and here you are."

"Papa," Marie said again, shaking her finger at him like our schoolmarm.

"Tell it right," I said.

He smiled and leaned over the top of his chair. "She wouldn't marry me."

"But Mama," Marie asked, "why didn't you love Papa?"

My father stopped and looked at my mother. This was not part of the story. "Why didn't you love me?" he said.

"You asked every girl in Sawgamet to marry you," my mother answered.

"But I only asked them once," he said, turning back to Marie. "Your mother I asked every day. All of the men had asked her to marry them, even some of the ones who were already married, but I kept asking. Every day for three years I called on her at the boardinghouse, and every day I asked her to marry me."

"And she always said no." Marie reached out and cupped the withered fingers of my father's bad hand in her two hands. He sat down next to her. "Mama," she asked again, "why didn't you love Papa?"

"I always loved him, sweetheart," she said, pouring hot water from the stove into the dish tub. She leaned in toward the steam, letting it wash across her face. "I just didn't know it yet."

"So I kept asking her to marry me, until one day she didn't say no."

"What did she say?" Marie could not stop herself.

"She said the day she'd marry me was the day I got Pearl into the water."

"I thought it was a safe bet," my mother said. "Your father never could seem to stay dry."

My father was leaning back in his chair now, staring at the moon through the window. He had taken his hand back from Marie, and he rubbed the fingers of his good hand across the back of the bad, as if it ached.

I wanted to hear about his triumph, how that was the year the log had spun so fast he could not see his feet, and how it was not until he heard a splash, and a roar from the banks of the river, that he knew he had finally dunked Pearl Gasseur. I wanted to hear him describe the feel of the cold water when he dove from the log and swam to the bank, the river dripping from his clothes as he walked to my mother. I wanted to see the wink he gave us when he said that our priest, Father Hugo, was asleep with drink at the barrels of beer. I wanted to hear how Father Earl, who had arrived from Ottawa only the day before and who was Anglican and younger than my father, performed the wedding right then and there on the bank of the Sawgamet. But before he could tell us that, before he could tell us how he had to leave the next morning for the float, and how he ran home all the way from Havershand, running to his wife, I asked him, "Do you miss it? Do you miss the float?"

He looked at me for a moment, as if he had not heard my question, and then my mother spoke. "You and Marie wash up now, get ready for bed."

As I rose from the table, he stopped me. He raised his ruined hand, the fingers curled like a claw. "I miss it," he said.

He did not tell many stories for the next few weeks, and then when the snow finally melted enough for the men to take out their saws and axes and get into the woods, my father pushed them terribly, as if he knew how bad the coming winter would be. He kept them working from dawn to dusk with not a day's break until the first of September, when the trees were stacked and lined beside the mill.

THE LOGS HAD TO RUN the river, of course, for the money to come in, and the winter that Foreman Martin had misjudged the weather and waited too long, the river froze with the logs still in it. That had been a hard winter, with money tight and credit long. When cutting started again in the spring, snow still on the ground, my father crushed his hand the first week, and then later that month Foreman Martin died when the errant swing of an ax caught him across the back of the head. The company gave my father the foreman's job.

The year that I was ten, ice clung to the banks of the river on the morning of the float, and the men glanced appreciatively at my father, knowing that the freeze-up would not be far behind. The winter was coming early and fierce, troubling even for the few men who remembered the original rush and the year that Sawgamet had turned hard and lean; the boomtown had gone bust and rumors of desperate men eating their mules to stay alive through the snowed-in winter had been overshadowed by whispers of their eating more pernicious meat than what came from mules.

My father pushed the men to send the logs down the chute, screaming at them, adding his weight to the poles when needed, and by supper, Father Hugo and Father Earl had both blessed the float; the men were gone, the logs gone with them.

The men came back from Havershand in the snow, cold but laughing, flush and ready for a winter of trapping and hunting, a chance to file saw blades and sell a few furs. But by the end of October the cold ate at us, wind pulling tears from our eyes, solid on our cheeks in moments. Men stacked firewood three rows deep outside their houses, the thump of axes a constant sound. Mothers kept their stoves burning all day, the dishwater they threw out the door freezing as it hit the ground.

The river froze inward, flat and even near the banks at first, but by November even the fast-moving water at the center of the river, the dangerous meeting of the Sawgamet and the Bear Rivers, had iced over. Daylight fading, we skated on the river after school while shoreline bonfires raged, giving us a place to warm our hands. Girls played crack the whip while the men and boys played hockey on the broad run of ice swept clear of snow.

Sundays, before dinner, we usually went down to the river. That Sunday, however, my mother stayed in the house to finish her baking, so only my father came down with us, carrying his and Marie's skates slung over the hockey stick he rested on his shoulder. With the cold, which had shattered the schoolhouse's glass thermometer the week before, even my father wore a scarf over his face to protect him. My mother had swaddled Marie and me with so many layers of clothing that we had trouble with the steps. Still, the cold seeped through the layers like water, and we were eager to skate and warm ourselves a little.

Down at the river, we sat on the packed snow at the banks, and my father helped Marie with her skates. He tied her laces and sent her off on the river. As he tied his own laces, she skated slowly toward the tip of the channel, pushing away from us with timid steps, like a newborn moose with shivering legs. The sun was already setting, and I could feel the temperature falling away and getting colder, if such a thing was even possible.

I had my head bent down over my skates and was pulling the laces tight, eager to take my stick and join the other boys playing shinny, when my father suddenly jumped from the snow along the bank, one skate still unlaced. He screamed Marie's name, skates chewing the frozen water, flying toward the thin ice at the confluence of the two rivers. There was just a dark hole where Marie had broken through the ice and disappeared.

Other men raced behind my father, but he was the first to the open water, screaming her name. For a moment he stopped at the edge of the fissure. Suddenly we saw her—we all saw her—gasping, bobbing, taking a last breath at the surface of the water, too cold or too scared to even scream, and as I reached the water, I saw my sister's eyes lock on to my father.

He dove into the water.

And then they were gone.

I hesitated at the edge, staring at the water, surprised at how smooth it was. Pearl grabbed my shoulder roughly. "No," he said, as if he were holding me back, and I realized that I had not even thought of following my father in.

The black water in the hole that Marie's fall had opened up started icing even as Pearl held my arm. The men yelled for rope, but then, not willing to wait, they linked arms, Pearl the first one into the breach. I could see the shock on his face at the first touch of the water. It was a minute at most before the men hauled him back from the water, the skin on his hands gone white from the cold. He could not stand when they took him out, his legs shaking uselessly beneath him.

The sun seemed to have fallen from the sky, pulling the temperature down with it. In the dark, I could barely see the hole in the ice freezing back over, like a mouth that had briefly yawned open and was now closing again. Even though it was too late, another man, and then another, went into the river, reaching beneath the water to feel for my father and Marie. As the last man was pulled from the water, the ice almost sealed shut around his legs, as if the river wanted one more.

It was Father Earl who brought my mother down to the river, and she found me sitting around the bonfire on the bank, near the men with the blue chattering lips. Boiling sap in a burning pine log popped, sending up a shower of sparks; a few embers floated out over the river before dying in the night.

Later, there were the other wives and mothers, quiet murmurs, Pearl sitting beside me, changed into dry clothes but crying, and then, finally, my mother and I turning home.

I HAVE TOLD MY daughters—the two oldest, not the baby—this story, though perhaps not every moment of it. Even now, years later, I can still picture the way my sister looked skating out toward the tip of the channel, her legs wobbling, and I know that as we settle into Sawgamet, as the snow comes and the river finishes freezing, I'll have to watch my own daughters trembling across the ice. A small mercy that the winter has come late to Sawgamet this year, giving me a few precious, extra weeks of knowing that my daughters have been safe on mud and dirt and rock. Still, after nearly two decades in Vancouver, I welcome the snow.

Up here, in my study—what used to be my stepfather's study—I can look out the window and see down the streets of the village. The chromium lights of the train yards leak over the tops of the trees and the buildings three streets away; they are working into the night to load wood to be used for the new war. Every man too old, too young, or too infirm to join the Duke of Connaught's Own Rifles regiment doing his part for the boys across the ocean. There are some women out there, too, in the train yard, working the cuts, driving trucks, handling horse teams. But it's not the machinery of war calling my attention. Rather, I'm staring at the snow drifting down from the sky, held harsh against the artificial lights.

The snow is starting to stick, making the woods and the village appear fresh. There had been snow enough when we lived in Vancouver, but it usually stayed in the branches of the trees, or congregated as slush in the gutters, and even then only for a day or so. Much of the time it came simply as rain rather than snow, and that was a miserable dampness that I never learned to enjoy. Even with a coat and fingerless mittens I struggled to write my sermons during the dampest part of winter. The branch-snapping cold here, the sort of chill that takes all moisture out of the air—too cold to snow sometimes—is preferable to the barely freezing wetness of Vancouver. But I suppose I should be careful what I wish for: the cold in Sawgamet can break you.

The winter that Marie fell through the ice was that sort of winter. What little warmth there had been in October and November dropped completely away from us, and even with a constant fire in the stove, my mother and I took to wearing our overcoats in the house, hats and mittens to bed. Though there were no bodies, there was a funeral, and afterward my mother spoke little to the women who brought plates of food, little to my great-aunt Rebecca and great-uncle Franklin, my aunt Julia and her husband, Lawrence, their daughter, Virginia, little to Mrs. Gasseur, to Pearl, little to Father Hugo or to Father Earl, who visited us even though we were not in his flock. She did not speak to me, even when I lifted my father's ax from the wooden pegs over the stone lintel of the doorway and took it out behind the house. I split wood every morning, and the sound of the ax on the wood seemed to linger, floating through our house long after I had returned from school. Every evening I sharpened the blade, the rasp of the stone on metal making my mother shiver.

The winter punished us into December. Snow fell hard, our roof creaking until angry winds beat the white dust onto the ground. The same winds cleared a great swath of snow from the Sawgamet, until finally, between Christmas and New Year's, the sun came out and the men and children, bundled against the cold, took their skates down to the river again. Except for the whip of the wind and the crackling of wood in the stove, our house was quiet.

The knock on the door sounded like a shot.

Pearl led us to the river, helping my mother down the snow-crusted steps cut into the hill next to the log chute, holding her arm as we walked across the ice to the small circle of men. The ice was smooth and clean after a month of scouring from the wind.

The hands were not touching. Even through the plate of frozen water covering them, we saw clearly that little more than the width of an ax blade separated my father's two hands from my sister's one. His mangled fingers on one hand, the smooth, alabaster fingers on the other hand, all stretched toward Marie's small hand. The ice, like glass above their hands, thickened as we tried to look further out, to see the rest of their bodies and their faces. The lines blurred, only shadows, dark shapes.

There was talk of axes, of chopping at the ice, but my mother forbade it, as if they had suggested pulling my father and Marie from their graves, and then the men left, gliding away from us on their skates. Pearl touched me on the back and headed toward the bank, leaving my mother and me over the ghosts of our family. As the sun dropped below the peak of the hill, we turned from the ice and trudged back up the steps, holding the side of the log chute for balance.

THE NEXT MORNING, when I woke, my mother was sitting in her chair by the stove, rocking slowly, staring at the fingers of flame that showed through the gaps in the metal. I dressed slowly for church, waiting for her to pin back her hair, to put on her gray Sunday dress. But she stayed in the chair.

After a little while she looked up at me. "Go on, then."

I thought about taking Communion, the wafer melting in my mouth like a chip of ice, the wine, diluted by Father Hugo, more water than blood. Then, instead of going to the church, I walked down to the river, the ice and snow screeching under my boots. In the sun, the winter felt like it had flown away, and I began to sweat during the short walk.

I knelt down above them, waiting to see them move. I put my hand on the ice above my father's fingers. I wondered if Marie had known how close my father's hands had been to hers. I waited for something to happen, for my father to reach out and bridge the gap separating him from Marie, but neither of them moved. Finally, as I heard the first yells of the other children rushing down to the river after church, I rose and returned to the house.

My mother had not moved from her chair by the stove. She kept shivering, even with the blankets wrapped around her, even with the surprising heat of the day, so I fed more logs into the fire. And then, as the screams and laughter drifted up from the river, the slaps of sticks on ice, my mother startled with every sound. My skates hung from their laces on a rusty nail half driven into the corner post of the mill, and I thought of taking them down to the river, of skating over my father and Marie, of carving the ice above them, but I did not want my mother to ask me where I was going.

I WOKE IN THE MIDDLE of the night, thinking I heard Marie calling me. Out the window, something looked wrong, as if the entire world were underwater with my father and Marie, and I realized that thin sheets of rain were falling from the sky, icing the trees, turning all of Sawgamet into a frozen river. I went to check the fire in the stove, remembering my mother's shivering, and I saw that the ax no longer hung above the door.

The steps beside the log chute were slick, and the mist was star-bright, neither water nor ice—diamonds falling from the sky. When I reached the river, my mother was swinging the ax. The ice shone below her, as if the river had swallowed the moon, and the sound of the ax hitting the ice was ringing and clear, like metal on metal.

I walked closer to my mother and almost expected the river to shatter under the sharp, oiled blade, the ice to cleave beneath our feet. The river would take us and freeze us alongside my father and Marie. Or my father would step from the open ice himself, pulling Marie behind him, holding her hand, the four of us walking to the house, where we could sit in front of the fire and he could tell us stories about fish made of ice.

My mother kept swinging the ax, and between the pings of the blade skittering off the surface of the ice, I heard her crying. She stopped when she saw me and fell to her knees, shaking. I knelt beside her. The ice was still smooth and clean, as if she had never been here with the ax, and when I put my hand flat on the ice it was warm against my palm, like bread cooling from the oven. Then the light beneath the river disappeared, leaving us on the ice, the film of rain covering us.

In the house, my mother covered me with my blanket and kissed me on my forehead. "I'm sorry," she said, so quietly that I was unsure whether she had really spoken or I had only imagined it.

I lay in bed, falling asleep listening to her sharpen the ax, the rhythmic grind of metal on stone.

The next morning, when Mrs. Gasseur, who was, as usual, the first to morning prayers, found Father Hugo frozen on the bench outside the church, she did not realize right away that he was dead.

"I asked him if he had been well during his morning walk," she said, "since I had such a terrible time with the frozen rain, and when he didn't answer, I touched his hand."

I did not see Father Hugo, but Pearl told me later that the old man looked alive under the clear coating of ice, still holding the Communion cup full of the blood of Christ. The men had to build a small fire in front of the church, waiting until the ice melted to pull him from the bench. Pearl said that he thought Father Hugo might have passed before he was frozen, but with the wine he could not tell.

They tried to dig a grave, but even with pickaxes, the ground was too hard. Father Earl said prayers over the body, and then Father Hugo spent the rest of the winter in the woodshed behind the church, wrapped in layers of oilcloth.

At night, when the cold left the sky so clear that the stars were within easy reach, sap froze in the trees, breaking them open like the sound of river ice cracking. Many of the days, the men could not trap or even chop wood, the wind burning their skin, hands too cold to hold ax handles. During that winter, Father Earl visited my mother and me frequently and stayed for dinner many nights. He was a small man. He looked like I did when I wore one of my father's coats, and I could not picture him taking down a tree. My mother said he had not seemed so small before his wife and unborn child died, during the winter before I was born.

One night, when I should have been sleeping, I heard him ask my mother what she would do in the spring, when the company took the house back, when they gave the foreman's cottage to Pearl and Mrs. Gasseur.

"I can go back to teaching," my mother said, though we all knew that Sawgamet did not need another teacher, and while we would have been welcomed at Franklin and Rebecca's house, that was not a place we could stay indefinitely.

"I have a house," Father Earl said, but then his voice trailed off. He tried again: "I know it's only been a few months, but if you're willing."

I could not hear my mother's response, but a few minutes later I felt the cold draft of the door and heard the latch drawing shut. And when he visited us later that week, they talked of the weather, of books and plays, of gossip about Father Hugo's replacement, as if Father Earl had never offered marriage.

Sometimes I saw him walking on the river, his hands in his pockets, and once I saw him walk to the clear circle of ice above my father and Marie, stopping to kneel, putting one hand flat on the ice the same way I had the night of the freezing rain.

THE COLD FINALLY left in May, the trickle of water underneath the snow becoming a constant stream, the sound of running water a relentless reminder in our house of the coming breakup. The river groaned, and the sound of shifting ice replaced the clattering of skates and sticks.

The morning the river opened, I pulled the ax down from above the doorway.

My mother looked up from her sewing, pulling the needle and thread through the cloth of my father's pants, mending the rips that she had not had time to attend to while he was alive, setting each pair aside for me as if I would wear them when I was older. "Where do you think you're going?"

"To the cuts." I waited for her to speak, but she stayed quiet. "We need the money."

She kept sewing, not looking at me. I wanted to go. I had to go. Pearl and Mrs. Gasseur had not said anything, but this was the company house. This was their house now.

"You're not going," she said finally.

I ran my thumb across the blade of the ax and then

turned my hand over and scraped a white shaving from my thumbnail.

"You can't stop me."

She stood up and walked to me, and without a word, she slapped me. Then, carefully, she took the ax and placed it above the door again.

I turned and walked out the door.

At the cuts, Pearl looked at me for a moment and then handed me his ax. I bucked trees and stripped branches, the ache in my arms familiar from a winter of chopping firewood. At lunch, Pearl gave me a few biscuits and shared some water.

The next morning, my mother told me to wash and put on my Sunday suit, and after the wedding, instead of going into the cuts, I helped my mother and Father Earl—my new stepfather—carry our belongings to his tidy house.

The furniture belonged to the company, so there was only our clothing and my mother's books, pots and pans, drawings, the toys my father had carved, my skates and stick. My mother left my father's mended clothes. "For Pearl," she said, though I knew that Mrs. Gasseur would not keep the clothes of a dead man. After three trips, when all that was left were some jars of summer berries in syrup and a few bundles of clothes, Father Earl reached over the door to take down my father's ax.

"No." He stopped at the sound of my voice, his hand almost touching the handle. He moved aside as I stepped past him. The ax felt heavier than it had the day before. When I pulled it down, the blade struck against the lintel stone, the sound ringing and clear, like the sound of my mother chopping at the ice.

But the last sound I heard in the house was that of my mother's voice. "No more to the cuts," she said.

THAT WAS THE SUMMER that my grandfather finally returned to Sawgamet. He was too late to see my father, of course— and I thought of him a little bit like a sinner trying to repent only after he was already burning—but that wasn't what had caused him to return to Sawgamet.

And maybe because I did not ask my father how he felt about his hand and lost my chance to do so, I asked my grandfather why he had returned. He had been in the house less than five minutes, clearly weary from traveling. When I think about it now, it is almost funny: the picture I have of him in my mind, sitting at the table in my stepfather's house, is that of an old man, though he would have been not much past fifty. Here I am, past forty years myself.

My grandfather kept his hat in front of him on the table, and he alternated between running his thumb around the brim of his hat and occasionally picking up his cup of tea and blowing on it before putting it back down without taking a sip.

I gave him a moment, and when he did not answer, I asked again. "Why are you here? Why did you come back?"

He spun the hat around once, and then did it again. "Do I need a reason, Stephen?"

I felt my mother put her hand on my shoulder and then she reached past me to put a plate of warmed biscuits on the table. "Your son grew into a man and then had a son of his own. It's been nearly three decades since you left, Jeannot. And just now you come back, asking if you need a reason? You've missed him. You're too late. Your son is gone," she said, and then she paused only slightly as she put a jar of preserves on the table, before going on. "And my daughter's gone." I recognized the jar of preserves. I had carried them down to my stepfather's house from the foreman's cottage.

"I'm sorry," my grandfather said. He said it firmly, but he dropped his head like he could not look at my mother, and for the first time I decided that I liked him.

I felt like I knew him already. I'd heard so many stories. I still hear the stories, even now, when they are just things that have been handed down. When I was a child there were men and women in Sawgamet who had known Jeannot—not in the beginning, of course, not when it was just Jeannot and his dog, when Sawgamet was simply an idea, an uncleared swath of trees waiting to be created by my grandfather—but men and women who had known him after that, in the early days, before the gold gave out, before the land started trying to reclaim what had been taken from it.

Even with all of these stories making him a part of my life well before he returned to Sawgamet, as I watched my grandfather sit at my stepfather's kitchen table, Jeannot was a stranger to me in all of his flesh and blood. But the way he said, "I'm sorry," so simple, so clear, made me feel like he *was* sorry, not just about my father, not just about my sister, but about all of the things that had driven him from Sawgamet.

And then, in the next instant, he looked up and his face transformed, and I could see that however deeply those sorrows weighed upon him, no matter how deeply he wished he could change what had happened, he had not come back to Sawgamet in sorrow. He had not come back to mourn my father, to mourn Marie. He had come back with some thought that all of the things that had happened—the deaths and the destruction—all of the things that he had thought he could leave behind by leaving Sawgamet behind, were now things that he could change.

I think my mother saw it, too, saw the same transformation in his face, the same hope, because, like me, she was still, silent, almost holding her breath to wait for him to speak.

Of course, I say this now, with the weight of the years sitting upon me. I speak as if I *knew*, as if I, not quite eleven years old, really knew what had brought my grandfather back to Sawgamet. I understood grief, but even then, parts of my sister and my father had started to fade forever away from me, and I had yet to learn what it meant to carry that loss with me year after year after year. Still, I want to think that with all of the stories I had heard, I knew of Sawgamet both as a place and as an idea, and I knew that my grandfather had returned with some sense of the magic that the woods still contained and all of the possibilities that entailed.

My grandfather lifted the cup of tea, blew on it again, and stared at it. We were waiting for him to speak, and like any good storyteller he savored the anticipation, letting us dangle for just an extra moment. Finally, he put his cup back on the table, looked at my mother, who still stood with her hand resting on my shoulder, and then looked down to me.

"I came back," my grandfather said, "to introduce Stephen to his grandmother."

"What?" My mother stared at him as if he had lost his mind.

"Revenez à moi et je reviendrai à vous, a dit l'Éternel des armées," my grandfather said. He paused for a moment, looking at my mother's blank face, and when he realized she did not understand him, that she did not speak French, he spoke again. "Return to me and I will come back to you, said the Lord."

"Malachi 3:7," my stepfather said. He stood on the threshold of the house, dressed as he usually was during the week in the same kind of work clothing that the other men in Sawgamet wore. He had been at the church when Jeannot came to our house, and I could see that he seemed a little short of breath, like he had come running at the news of my grandfather's return. I wondered what busybody had gone to the church to find him. "Welcome. I was told you'd come back."

"You must be the boy's new stepfather. Anglican, I hear," Jeannot said. "A priest."

"And weren't you meant to be a priest yourself? When you were a boy?" My stepfather said this with a casualness that even I understood to be deliberate, taking a moment to run his boots across the edged rock we had by the door for that purpose.

"That's how the story goes, I suppose," my grandfather said.

"The story also goes that you left the Bible and all it entails behind you when you came to Sawgamet. I'm surprised to hear you quoting scripture."

"Some things never leave you," Jeannot said.

"*Our* Bible is a little different," Father Earl said. "Perhaps something was lost in the translation."

My stepfather was a kind man. He was always gentle and

giving with me, but I thought he meant this as a rebuke to Jeannot, and I was startled by his coldness. Now, with the benefit of being able to look back as a father, I realize that my stepfather was trying to stake his claim on my mother as his wife, on me as his son. He was afraid of Jeannot. Afraid that my mother had not yet come to love him, afraid that the return of my grandfather might upset the delicate balance in his house.

His house. I would be remiss if I did not point out that his house is now my house. This study in which I am pacing, the study in which I will soon need to write a eulogy for my mother, is the same study in which my stepfather worked for forty years. I still think of the small foreman's cottage by the mill as my parents' house—it was my parents' house—but it was not my mother's only house.

I know that my mother was happy here, in this house, with Father Earl. Still, it startles me, the sudden thought of just how long she was married to my stepfather, how long she lived in this house. This house—as much as the cottage where I was born, and maybe more so—was my mother's house as well. She was married to my father eleven years, but she was married to my stepfather for nearly three times as long.

She lived in this house, she will die in this house, and she remains in this house, at least for one more night. Soon, of course, our own furniture and effects will arrive from Vancouver. I do not know how long it will take before I start to think of this house as my own. But that morning, when my grandfather returned to Sawgamet, it was still very much my stepfather's house.

Father Earl moved fully into the house, shutting the door behind him. "Return unto me, and I will return unto you, saith the Lord of hosts," my stepfather said to Jeannot, and then he stepped behind my mother, putting his arm around her waist. "And I suppose you fancy yourself the Lord in all of this?"

My grandfather looked surprised, and I thought that even though I had just met the man, the look of surprise did not fit his face. He seemed like a man who met everything with a sense of equanimity—something that I remember from my father, and that I have tried to cultivate in my own life as a pastor—but this question had taken him unawares.

"The Lord? No. You have things backwards, Earl."

I saw the glance that my mother stole at my stepfather and realized that he had bristled at the use of his name. It sounded odd to me, the name Earl coming unencumbered by title from Jeannot's mouth. Most people in Sawgamet, even the Catholics, called him Father Earl, or even just Father.

"Well then, Jeannot," my stepfather said, pointedly stepping on my grandfather's name, "what then do you intend?"

"I'd think it was evident in the scripture." I was not sure if Jeannot noticed the effect of using my stepfather's first name, or if he was still surprised at the question, but he seemed to draw back into himself and his voice dropped quieter in the already quiet house. He picked up the cup of tea, and this time took a sip before carefully putting it back on the table.

"Return unto me, and I will return unto you," Jeannot said again, repeating the scripture. "What do I intend? Why have I come back to Sawgamet? Why now? I came back for Martine."

He looked at me. "I've come for your grandmother," he said. "I've come to raise the dead."

TWO

Birds

THE TREES PRESSED DOWN so tightly against the banks of the Sawgamet River that Jeannot had little choice but to turn from the river and climb the hill, following a creek into the woods. His dog brushed past him and ran up through the dappled gloom, stopping once to sniff the air before continuing.

Jeannot was sixteen and had been traveling for long enough that the dark and the woods should not have been foreign and frightening, but even though the wind was still, he could hear the trees moving in rustling whispers that sounded like voices. He thought that if he turned his head quickly enough he might see who was speaking, and for that reason he kept his head down and moved with a furious focus. He wanted to be out of these woods as soon as possible, back again tracing the arc of the Sawgamet, looking for a place to stop and pan for gold. Along with voices from the trees, the young man could hear the dog panting, and as he stumbled through a beam of sunlight, he noticed how lean the dog had become.

And then the shadowed whispering came clear and uncluttered, and he heard someone calling his name.

Jeannot.

⟵

THE YOUNG MAN, of course, was my grandfather, more than sixty years ago. When he was older, Jeannot grew tall and broad, but on that day, the day that he founded what was to become Sawgamet, Jeannot was sixteen, whip-thin, wire-strong, and able to both give and absorb a brutal amount of punishment.

He joked to me that he had fought his way across the continent, that he had been punched so hard and so often in his travels that his nose had barely managed to stay on his face. But he never really told me why he had left the orphanage and his training to be a priest. Just once, when he and my stepfather stayed up late talking in the study, while I was supposedly engrossed in reading a book, I heard him mention a girl whom he had loved, but it is only a guess that this was the reason why he quit his training for the Catholic priesthood, left the orphanage, and traveled across the whole of Rupert's Land; Jeannot only told stories from the moment when he arrived in Sawgamet; none of his past before then mattered.

I think of Sawgamet now, a town of motion, light, and sound, with a train running through, and with the movie theater still playing *The Wizard of Oz*, with telephone wires expected in the next year, houses wired with electricity, and it is hard for me to imagine what it must have been like for my grandfather. There are still parts of the woods where you can lose yourself, though they have become harder and harder to find, particularly for me. I have not traveled as far or seen as much as some men, but I was behind the lines as a chaplain when we took Vimy Ridge and held Hill 70, and the world has changed so much since that first day my grandfather came to Sawgamet that to think of the silence he must have encountered is terrifying, almost unimaginable. I have the stories he told me, and the stories that others have told me, and I know what Sawgamet was like when I was a child, but there are gaps in the history of Sawgamet that I cannot fill with anything other than speculation.

Part of it is that there are things that are peculiar to Sawgamet, something about the cold remoteness of the village, that make it feel like it exists in its own country. Elsewhere, points east and south of us, men float their logs in the spring, taking advantage of the roaring meltwaters, but Sawgamet has its own internal logic to it. It used to be that men could not work the cuts in the winters here—sap frozen iron-hard, men's fingers curling in on themselves, the snow a cumbersome obstacle to traverse—so they floated the wood instead in the fall, trying to push as close to the river's freeze as possible, eking out a few more days of cutting wood. Even with men working the cuts through the winter now, with the railway come to town and engines replacing horses, Sawgamet still feels like something set apart from anywhere else I have lived or been, and despite the years that I've been gone, despite knowing that this will be my mother's last night alive, coming back here still feels like I have come home.

WHEN MY GRANDFATHER came to Sawgamet, before it had
a name, Jeannot was already more than a decade too late
for the Fraser gold rush, but this was still only a few years
after the Civil War to the south, only two years before Brit-
ish Columbia joined the Confederation. Where he walked
was virgin territory, untouched by white men. So when my
grandfather heard the whispering of the trees, heard his
name, "Jeannot," called clearly, as if there were another living thing other than his dog beside him, Jeannot hesitated
and then stopped in his tracks.

He could feel the head of the ax pressing against the top of
his hand, the weight of the rifle in his other hand, and with a
slight horror he realized that by holding both he would be able
to use neither. The woods fell silent. For a moment, just to his
side, he thought he saw a young man, a boy his own age, staring at him with a hungry fear, but by the time he turned, the
boy was gone. He moved in a slow circle, more afraid that he
would see someone than that he would not.

He had been alone too long, my grandfather thought, and it
was too easy out there in the untrammeled woods and mountains to convince himself that he saw and heard something
that was not there. He lowered his head again and continued
following the creek up the hill, thinking that when he crested
the rise he might be able to see the lay of the Sawgamet River.
For the last few days he had been following the river mostly
straight up a wide valley. A chain of peaks and mountains rose
on the other side of the river and Jeannot liked being able to

see the improbable snow that capped the mountains against the midsummer sun.

When the trail led him into the clearing, Jeannot risked a last glance into the trees, but with the afternoon's brightness and the dark of the woods, he was able to see only a few dozen paces back, and he still thought there was something in the woods, keeping just past the edge of his vision. While he looked, Flaireur padded up beside him. Jeannot touched him lightly on the head, and then the dog trotted into the middle of the clearing and lay down on the ground near a wide creek.

My grandfather always said that he had stolen the dog from a girl in Edmonton who claimed to be a witch, so when Flaireur—named in anticipation of sniffed-out treasure—refused to move any further that day, Jeannot decided that he, too, would go no further. He had already walked for thirty-nine days since leaving Quesnellemouthe, and he thought that perhaps the dog was right; to travel one more day would be to risk the wrath of God. My grandfather dropped his pack, took his ax, and cut saplings and branches to make a lean-to against a fallen tree. He had learned to handle the ax and to fend for himself during the two years and three thousand miles it took him to reach Quesnellemouthe from Montreal, and when he had finished making shelter, he cut fallen wood until he had more than enough to burn through the night.

After he finished cutting firewood, Jeannot forced himself to walk back through the woods and down the hill to the river, so that he could catch a fish to share with Flaireur for their dinner. When it was finally dark, he unrolled his blanket under the lean-to and listened to the low burble of the creek, and beyond that, the muted roar from the Sawgamet. The sounds of the water and the crackling embers were a comfort to him, as was the slow breathing of Flaireur; the dog had not been willing to move from the spot where he had collapsed earlier in the evening, but he seemed restful now. The wind moved warm across Jeannot's body. He fell asleep quickly and easily.

When my grandfather woke, the fire had died completely, as had the wind. Flaireur stood above him, the dog's mouth open in a soundless snarl. Jeannot had spent countless nights in the dark wilderness during his trek, but today was the first time he had ever felt frightened. He had bedded the witch in Edmonton before stealing Flaireur, and now, with Flaireur standing above him, he thought the witch had come back, first to steal the dog's voice, and then to steal Jeannot's soul. My grandfather could see Flaireur's teeth in the moonlight, and when he put his hand out to touch the dog's neck, he could feel the low rumble that should have carried sound, but all was silent. With a start, he realized that the night had fallen quiet as well. Even the creek had been rendered mute.

My grandfather said that he was never sure if he saw the creature or smelled it first. It was not the girl from Edmonton. It was something worse.

The creature was fish-pale and carried the gagging scent of spoiled meat. My grandfather could not tell if it was a man or a woman, but as it stumbled across the little clearing, Jeannot could see the milk-white eyes that seemed to be searching for him, like the creature knew he was there. Its hair clumped over its shoulders, and its skin was loose and mottled. As the creature's head turned toward him, Jeannot clamped his hands around Flaireur's muzzle, forcing Flaireur's mouth shut and stilling the dog. The creature seemed to pause, and Jeannot felt his stomach turn at the thought that it might see him through its clouded eyes, but it did not stop. Then, as it disappeared into the woods, sound returned. The creek, the river, the rustle of the wind through the trees, everything except for Flaireur. The dog stayed dumb, and Jeannot knew that he had escaped something terrible.

In later years, when he told the story to Pearl and other men, and they told it to each other and passed it around the way that men do, some men argued that Jeannot had simply been young and scared, or that he had been dreaming. That in the moonlight and his tiredness he had mistaken a bear or another animal for some perversion. Other men, particularly men who had spent more time in the woods or who had deal-ings with Indians, men who understood that there were things that they had yet to see, believed him. It was a wehtiko—a man turned into a monster as a punishment for cannibalism—come to eat the flesh from my grandfather's bones. No, it was a shape-shifter, it was the loup-garou, the mahaha, it was an adlet, come to drink his blood.

When my grandfather told me the story, however, he insisted it was none of those things. The creature, he said, was a qallupilluit, a sea witch, who felt the greed for gold running through Jeannot's body and had come to claim him.

Greed did run through Jeannot's body, but though the crea-ture did not return for him that night, he resolved to flee. He was unwilling to break no matter how hard he was pushed, consumed by a burning desire to find gold in the northern cor-ner of this new land, but he had no desire to spend another night under the lean-to, waiting for the creature to return.

He spent the next morning trying to coax Flaireur into

leaving with him. Like the day before, however, the dog refused to take another step. Flaireur stayed near the lean-to and continued to bark soundlessly: his bristly muzzle dropped and snapped without making a noise. Jeannot briefly thought of bashing the dog's head with the back of his ax, but he could not bear to do so. Instead, Jeannot walked down the slope and through the trees, thinking that a fresh-caught fish might work to lure the dog away from his post.

Sitting on the bank of the river, my grandfather thought of the rotted meat smell of the creature from the night before. He would leave even if Flaireur would not accompany him, he decided. He had been so sure of his choice to stop the day before. He thought that Flaireur's refusal to go on was a sign that this was where he was meant to make his fortune. He knew nothing of mining or gold, only that a decade past the Fraser rush he could easily end up like all of the other greenhorns who came late, worked like dogs, and left empty-handed.

Before he left the orphanage and started walking west, the nuns had thought Jeannot would be a priest, and they taught him accordingly, but what he knew about religion when he started walking west was not of much use in the woods. When the creature came to him in the night, he thought that he had read too much into the tiredness of a dog. He did not want to leave Flaireur behind, but as he sat by the creek and waited for a fish to take his line, Jeannot knew that he was afraid of the creature's return: its stench was too close to what he imagined the flesh of his own body would smell like in death.

The line tugged against his hand and he pulled it in slowly. In the still water along the edge of the bank, Jeannot saw that he had lip-hooked a small, bluish trout. Though the fish was putting up a decent fight, it was not worth the effort to pick the little meat from its bones. He was willing to wait for something larger, something that he could split equally with Flaireur. He pulled the trout from the water, slipped out the hook, and tossed both the fish and his line back into the river. Instantly the fish darted back to the empty hook—the grub that Jeannot had used as bait now gone—and hit it hard, swallowing it down. Jeannot decided that, given his urgency to make ground before night fell again, the fish would serve his purpose.

Back at the camp, Jeannot cut off a thin slice of flesh from the trout's back and threw it to the dog. Flaireur caught it in the air, but showed no intention of moving from his guard. The dog barked airlessly, still silent, and Jeannot threw him another piece. He turned the fish over and worked the tip of his knife up alongside the bones, taking off the fillet. He dangled it from his hand. As he swung the piece of fish back and forth, Flaireur's head tilted, tracking Jeannot, but the dog did not move from his spot. Jeannot tossed the fillet through the air. As he did so, a glint of something caught his eye.

At first he thought it was sunlight off his knife, but when he looked down at the scraped carcass of the fish in his hand, Jeannot saw something gleaming from inside the trout. He speared the tip of his knife into the fish's half-split insides and exposed the gold nugget to the air. He fished it out with his fingers and stepped over to the creek and washed it off. When he held the gold up in the air, it glistened in the sunlight. It was solid and misshapen, a damaged acorn the size of the end of his thumb.

He gave what scraps of fish were left to Flaireur, and then he picked up his shovel and a pan and headed down through the woods and back to the river. Damn that sightless creature, my grandfather thought, and damn these woods; they would not drive him off. He had caught a fish with a belly full of gold, and no monsters, no whisperings from the trees would be enough to drive him away from Sawgamet.

MY GRANDFATHER DUG by the banks of the river every day, sifting and panning for gold, first near where he caught the fish, and then further up the river, but he found nothing. At first he tried dragging Flaireur along with him, but no matter how much Jeannot beat him, the dog refused to follow my grandfather down to the river, staying near the lean-to and continuing to bark soundlessly.

Jeannot lost count of the days. He caught fish and gathered berries and nuts, trying to reserve the depleted stores of beans and flour that he had carried with him from Quesnellemouthe. He stood in the river panning until his feet were numb and then he dug along the banks. He looked for gold in the moss and the grasses along the edge of the Sawgamet. He worked until his hands turned to leather and his muscles grew stiff, but more gold eluded him. The same hardheadedness that had allowed him to be beaten but not defeated on his trip west, that had kept him going through cold and hunger and allowed him to ignore the warnings of men who had headed west and returned home empty-handed, kept him digging until well past the time when the leaves had turned and began to litter the ground.

It was not until the first of October when my grandfather

realized what he had done. He was bathing in the river—it was never truly warm, even in the heat of the summer—but as he came naked out of the water, he felt a sudden coldness on his skin, and he seemed to see for the first time the ice that had already begun to cling to the bank. It had taken him one less than forty days and nights to walk from Quesnellemouthe, but he did not have that much time before the snows would be upon him. He had to winter in Sawgamet.

Flaireur still would not move from the clearing, so Jeannot did the only thing he could think of. He dug shallow trenches in the ground around where the dog sat barking noiselessly, marking out where the cabin's walls would stand. He took down trees, limbed them, and stripped the bark, working in haste and barely sleeping. Had Jeannot thought he would need to protect himself for more than a single winter, he would have put more care into footing the cabin, but all he worried about was the simple expedience of shelter and the need to stock food for what he expected to be a cold winter. The cabin took its form quickly, barely to the height of his shoulders. Jeannot decided that once the snows came he could use the enforced leisure of the dark winter nights to dig out the floor, giving himself room to stand. While my grandfather built the cabin, Flaireur stayed in the epicenter of the construction, mimicking the motions of a barking dog, leaving only to relieve himself in the bushes or to drink from the river.

IT TOOK MY GRANDFATHER five days to build the cabin, working late into each night with the poor light of the fire, and as he finished, snow began to settle in. The cabin was crude, the logs only partially stripped of bark because of his haste, barely big enough for him to lie down inside. It was nothing like the neat, securely built homes that Jeannot had been hired to help build in farming communities and mining towns along his journey west, but he did not mind. It was comfortable despite the sound of the wind pushing snow around in the darkness outside. He slept with Flaireur curled against his back.

He spent another two days hauling and fitting flat stones from the river until he had a workable hearth and chimney, and another day hauling enough dead and fallen wood to last him for a few weeks. More pressing than his need for fire-wood—that was something he could take care of even in the cold—was the necessity of packing in food before the last of the game went to ground.

He did not fool himself. My grandfather knew exactly what he was: a young man from Montreal who was, at best, a poor shot with a rifle. He still had some flour, salted meat, and beans left, maybe enough to get him through a few weeks, a month if he did not give Flaireur a share. Snow was starting to pile up against the sides of the cabin, and had my grandfather been a different sort of young man he would have despaired. He would have wondered if he should have risked the snow and headed back to Quesnellemouthe. He could have found a job and a room to rent and spent the winter in a place where he did not have to worry about finding food. But my grandfather was not the sort of young man to look back and question his decisions. Instead, he set himself to the task of procuring food with the same determination that he had brought to the task of panning for gold.

Over the course of two days, he collected as many of the berries and plants as he could find underneath the first coverings of snow, forcing Flaireur to eat a few bites of each variety to ensure that my grandfather would not poison himself. Then, taking up his rifle, he spent several days tromping through the woods, unaware that the few animals that had not gone to ground as the snow built were well warned by his heavy step.

He did not take a single shot, but he walked for miles and miles, from first light until dark, searching for something to aim his rifle at, and finally he was tired. It had been a week of building his cabin, and then a week of tromping through the snow in a fruitless search for food, on top of the thirty-nine days and nights of walking and three months of working the river for gold, and my grandfather could feel himself worn down. He was aware of his one singular strength—his ability to ignore pain and discomfort and to keep working and pushing until his body collapsed under some weight that he did not recognize—but this moment of weakness, this sudden fragility, terrified him. He did not understand the simple signs of tiredness, of having gone beyond the limits of his endurance, and for the first of many times throughout his life, my grandfather, Jeannot Boucher, thought with absolute certainty that he must be dying.

Clearly, of course, my grandfather was wrong. He lived long enough to leave Sawgamet, and then to return and tell me about it. And yet, when my grandfather told me this story, he did not smile when he said that he thought he was dying, and I can imagine the sense of isolation he must have felt: thousands of miles away from his birthplace, surrounded by an unforgiving wilderness, worn out from all that he had endured to get to Sawgamet, and with an isolated winter ahead of him.

Though it was early in the afternoon, he built a small fire in the hearth of the cabin. He lay on the ground, too exhausted to even sleep. As if he knew something was wrong, Flaireur rose from his normal spot in the middle of the floor and ceased his soundless barking long enough to gently lick and nuzzle at Jeannot's face. Jeannot reached up and shook the scruff of the dog's neck gently and said, "You've been a good dog. When I die, maybe then you'll be free to leave this spot."

And then Flaireur began to sing.

For the first time in months—since the creature had passed them by in the night—sound came from the dog's mouth, and it frightened Jeannot. He thought that the dog was calling for Death himself. Though my grandfather was so fatigued that even his bones were tired, he reached for his rifle. He would put up a fight. He was not going to let Death take him unscathed.

As Jeannot rose to his knees, he watched Flaireur sing. The dog kept his haunches firmly on the dirt floor, his muzzle raised into the air, eyes closed, and in the dog's haunting voice, Jeannot, for the first time, recognized the lupine qualities of this dog that he had stolen from a witch.

Suddenly there was a knocking at the door, an uneven and constant beating that called to mind the legions of the dead that the nuns at the orphanage had always told my grandfather he would join when he went to hell.

Thuds attacked the door and then the walls and the roof. He could hear the flap of wing and some terrible cawing that covered even Flaireur's desperate song. Jeannot crouched under the low roof of the cabin, his hands shaking. He thought that Flaireur was calling for Death to come and seize them. The walls began to shake, and he was afraid that if he waited any longer the door would rip off from the hinges he had whittled from tree stumps, the roof would be torn asunder, and whatever monsters waited outside would destroy him. With his rifle in hand, hoping that Flaireur would cease his singing in order to rip at the Dark Angel's throat, Jeannot opened the door, prepared to conquer Death and the legions of the damned that he had brought with him.

He was immediately knocked to the ground by a flurry of beating wings, beaks and claws tearing his clothing and ripping at his eyes. In the commotion, he fired his rifle into the ground before dropping it in order to cover his eyes. After a few seconds of confusion, my grandfather had the presence of mind to slam the door of the cabin, and then to latch it shut in order to keep the hundreds of birds—blue grouses, chickadees, ravens, jays, ptarmigan, even an out-of-season thrush that he spotted for a moment among the flapping hordes—from finding their way out of the cabin as quickly as they had been sung in by Flaireur. As he kept his hands pressed tightly over his eyes, he tried to look through the slits between his fingers, but the flying birds made him fear for his sight. He groped for his spare shirt and then quickly wrapped the cloth around his head.

Wings beat against his head and his arms, and he felt the sharp spear of a bird's beak digging into his side, and the sudden wetness of blood. He placed one hand tightly over the wound and then pulled his knife from his belt. The cabin was so thick with birds that he could not see his slaughter. He stabbed his knife into the air repeatedly. Flaireur, too, joined in the carnage, stopping his singing and opening his mouth to tear and bite. Feathers were in Jeannot's mouth. The floor of the dirt cabin was slick with the blood of the birds, but after an indeterminable time of stabbing into the darkness, the sound of fluttering wings began to slacken, and he dared to pull the shirt off his head so that he could join Flaireur in tracking down the few birds that had managed to elude fang and blade.

Outside of the cabin, my grandfather cleared snow from the ground and then dug until the ground was too frozen for him to go any deeper. His side throbbed from where the bird speared him, but he did not want to let any of this bounty go to waste. He loaded the storage hole with the birds that he had killed. He packed the hole with snow and then fashioned a lid of sorts from a flat stone that he found near the riverbank. That night, confident that he had enough food to last through the snows, Jeannot roasted a dozen birds and blew on them until they were cool enough to feed to Flaireur. The dog lay quiet again, and Jeannot saw to the scratches and gouges that his dog had suffered, pressing moss and snow upon the larger cuts. It was only when he rolled Flaireur onto his back in order to treat a bloody gash in the dog's belly that Jeannot noticed the small bullet hole in the dirt floor.

At first my grandfather thought it was a trick of the light, the fire reflecting off some last vestige of bird blood that had pooled in the dirt, but the glow was something else, something substantial. Jeannot dug with his hands, not even thinking to reach for his shovel, and within moments had pulled a nugget of gold the size of a dinner roll from the ground. He was stunned at how heavy the chunk was. He guessed it to be ten pounds, and as he held the nugget in one hand, he ran the fingers of his other hand through the coarse fur on Flaireur's chest. The dog looked at him and opened his mouth like he was going to sing again, but then he went to sleep in such a restful manner that Jeannot wondered if in Flaireur's unceasing vigilance, his refusal to take another step, he had known that the gold was beneath his paws the entire time.

IN THE SPRING, once the snow broke, my grandfather returned to Quesnellemouthe and used the gold he had found that night in the cabin to hire two dozen men with packs and canoes to carry supplies back to Sawgamet for him.

Jeannot was seventeen by then, and he did not think of what the news of gold would do. The hired men left off the beans and flour and rice and salted meat, the pots and pans, the crate of books, the cloth and the barrel of nails outside of Jeannot's cabin, but they did not return to Quesnellemouthe. Like the hundreds of other men who had jumped at the news of gold, the hired men stayed to seek their fortunes, staking claims and panning for gold on the banks of the river. Every day, dozens more joined the men already there, and soon a colony of tents lined the flat plateau above the river.

Some of the men knew what they were doing, and before my grandfather had even finished unpacking his supplies, a Russian man—the miner looked like he needed to find a strike so that he could buy food, his skin pulled tight against the bones of his face—had already panned out a nugget of gold the size of a bullet. Everywhere Jeannot looked he saw men standing in the water or digging on the banks and up the slope, panning for gold. Though my grandfather was unable to find even a whisper of gold, every hour or so another man would yell in excitement, and those men working nearest to that man would also cheer.

Men continued to stream into Sawgamet in search of gold, and soon enough they began to return to Quesnellemouthe with their bounty and tales of earth so rich with gold that you could not touch the ground without making your fortune. From Quesnellemouthe, the word spread south to Vancouver, and then further south to San Francisco, and from there east to Ottawa and Montreal, to Chicago, New York, and Boston, and it was like an earthquake shook the land, so many feet came stomping through the woods. Women came, too, of course, and one of those was my grandmother, Martine.

THREE

Home Building

THIS MORNING, BEFORE SCHOOL, MARTINE—my middle daughter and my grandmother's namesake—brought her sums into my study. We went through them together. She had them all correct save one. She has taken to school well, and would be content to sit with a book all day if we let her. I am not sure how much Martine follows after her great-grandmother, but she is my wife's daughter in every sense. Send Martine into a blueberry stomp in her Communion dress and she'll come out white and crisp and fit for church.

Marie—my oldest, and named after my sister—takes after me in coloring and in manners: Marie can hardly make it from her bedroom to the hallway without getting herself dirty. And like me—like my father—school seems to itch at her. She reads and does her sums well enough that I cannot argue at her for not doing her work, but she is happier in the woods or playing with the boys down by the river than she is in the schoolhouse or helping her mother in the kitchen. I would like to hope that school is something she will learn to enjoy, as I did, but that remains to be seen: I did well in Edmonton at seminary, but my father refused to return to Vancouver after only one year at school there.

As for the baby, we'll have to see whom she takes after. She's named Nathalie, after my mother, though today I would say that her closest relative seems to be a bear with its paw caught in a trap. She is still wailing away downstairs because we would not allow her a second helping of dessert after her supper.

After I checked Martine's sums, I helped her and her sister get their boots and coats on, hats, mittens, scarves, and then walked them to the schoolhouse. Thankfully, we are past the early-season mud. The ground is hard and frozen. This first snow tonight will stay and give fresh cover to a Sawgamet that I don't think my grandparents could have imagined when they first settled here.

There's the sound of the train whistle. The cars will be stacked and chained down with timber. We've already had a dozen boys come home in boxes on that train—Tommy Miller was the first, killed at Dieppe—and I worry that the trains will leave Sawgamet and come back with heavy loads. My wife tells me it was the same in Vancouver during our first war in Europe: every train met with trepidation. I spent the bulk of that war overseas. For the first year I was a chaplain's assistant, and then, after that, a chaplain myself.

The train sits hard beside what people still call the new mill, though the old mill burned down only a few years after my father and sister died, before I left for seminary. The chute and the stairs are still there, and I wonder what a stranger to Sawgamet would make of those orphaned structures, if he would be able to divine their provenance. My father and Pearl built the chute and stairs the summer that my father was sixteen, and sometimes I go out there and sit at the top, reading a book near the charred remains of the old mill and the foreman's cottage, thinking of who and what are no longer with me.

THAT FIRST MORNING that Jeannot returned, after an uncomfortable breakfast with my stepfather and mother, I followed him out of the village and up to where the mill and the foreman's cottage stood, where I had so recently lived. We spent a few minutes standing at the top of the chute, but he gave it only a glance, instead staring out over the river. He touched a post on the mill and then closed his eyes for a moment. "No," he said, and I knew he was not talking to me, "I don't suppose this will do."

He had told me to bring my father's ax, and when I took it with me out of the house, my stepfather seemed to make a point of not looking up from his reading. My mother had glanced at me from where she stood washing dishes, but I did not meet her eyes.

As we walked, Jeannot did not make any motion to carry the ax, his hands occupied with his own rifle, so I held the ax over my shoulder, striving for the certain casualness that a boy nearing eleven can never hope to achieve. I remember wanting my grandfather to think that the ax was something that I often carried, that I was the sort of boy—the sort of man, is what I really thought—who belonged out in the cuts. He had not said where we were going or why he wanted me to bring the ax. I think he had become so used to his own company that it did not occur to him that he needed to explain. He simply said to my mother, "I think I'll go for a walk now and take Stephen with me," and that was enough.

I followed him to the mill, and then further out into the woods. Jeannot stayed a few steps ahead of me. He did not turn around to check on me, but he kept his gait slow enough that I was able to keep pace. He walked away from the cuts, into the woods and toward the meadow that led to more woods and braided creeks and rivers where men trapped during the winter. As we continued to head uphill and in the direction where I knew the real climbing began, the weight of the ax started to hurt my shoulder, and I envied the loose manner in which Jeannot carried his rifle.

He asked me a little bit after my mother, how she and my father came to be married, but as I started the story, we stepped out into the clearing and I realized that Jeannot's attention was occupied with something else. The mountains seemed suddenly to be on top of us; I felt dizzy at their closeness and height. A chickadee swooped low and fast in front of us, and Jeannot stopped in his tracks. I was so intent on the mountains that I almost stepped into him.

Jeannot shifted the rifle up from where it dangled in his hands and pressed it against his shoulder. There was something urgent in my grandfather's movements, and I wished that I had my own rifle—or rather, my father's rifle—with me, but all I could do was hold the ax in front of me.

I could see my grandfather's head move back and forth, looking for something. I took one hand off the ax long enough to touch his back. "What is it?" I whispered.

Jeannot glanced back at me and said, very quietly, "The mountains. They're too close."

I almost laughed. That morning had been full of uncertainty: my grandfather returning to Sawgamet after an absence of thirty years, the tension between him and my new stepfather, a walk through the woods in search of something that Jeannot felt no need to explain, and now this. My chest started to pound with urgency. I was thinking of all of the things that might lurk—the dangers of the woods: bears and wolves—but I had not expected it to be something as innocuous as the mountains that always loomed above. The mountains appeared close, but the morning light always changed the way things looked, the sun bouncing off the scree and dirt where the trees gave out against the angle of the slope.

Jeannot kept the rifle to his shoulder and surveyed the meadow, but then, slowly, he lowered the gun. "Nothing, I suppose," he said, but then, at the sound of dirt underfoot, he pulled it to his shoulder again and swung around, nearly hitting me in the head with the barrel.

"Easy, there, Jeannot," the man said, stepping out of the trees.

"Uncle Lawrence," I said.

He smiled at me and gave a little wink. His rifle was safely hanging on a strap over his shoulder, and though he was shirtless, I noticed a thick sheen of sweat on his forehead. He was an Indian, and his skin, normally dark, had begun to take on the even deeper color that came with the summer's sun. "Why don't you lower that rifle, Jeannot?" he said, though he did not appear ill at ease from having the gun pointed at him.

I reached out solicitously and put my hand on the barrel

of my grandfather's rifle to push it away, but I needn't have bothered. Jeannot was already lowering the muzzle to point at the ground.

"Lawrence?" my grandfather said. He blinked slowly and let out a breath that I could hear. "Horace's boy? You were just a little one, Stephen's age, when I left." Lawrence nodded and then Jeannot stared at me for a moment. "Did you call him your uncle?"

"It's been a while, Jeannot. Things change," Lawrence said. He reached out and tousled my hair, though he knew it was something I did not like. "Julia and I are married. Franklin's girl. We have a girl of our own, too. Virginia."

Jeannot smiled and then extended his hand to the Indian. "Well, I guess you're family, then. Sorry. I didn't mean to give you a fright with the rifle. You know how it gets out here."

"Seeing things?"

Jeannot laughed and pointed back to the mountains. "They seemed so close, like they'd been dragged in during our time in the woods. Thought maybe an ijirait was near."

Lawrence shook his head. "A shape-shifter wouldn't come upon you with the boy like this," he said, motioning to me. "Only when you're alone." He stepped around Jeannot and then me and out into the sunlight. "Besides, my father liked to say that they aren't always going to bring harm. Sometimes they carry a message that you need to hear."

"That's not what your father said when he first told me about ijirait," Jeannot said. "But perhaps he's seeing things differently now."

Lawrence stared at my grandfather, his eyes flashing red from the sun, and then he shook his head. "No more. He went over more than fifteen years now. Before this one," he said, pointing to me, "was a thought. But yes, he started seeing things a little differently. What with the way things change, with the new, he said, the old couldn't stay the same, and he began to think that the old ways might have changed as well."

"So I shouldn't worry anymore if I encounter an ijirait?"

Lawrence grinned. "Well now, that's not exactly what I said. But if you do encounter one you'll know because you'll quickly forget about it. Or"—and he grinned again, but this time in a less friendly manner—"they might bring you a message."

Jeannot laughed. "Well, that's not particularly helpful," he said. "But I'll keep what you said in mind. A message, huh?"

"A message," Lawrence agreed.

As we watched Lawrence tromp off across the clearing and disappear into the woods, Jeannot turned to me and said, "Ijiraits are evil beings no matter what Lawrence says of it." He swung his rifle back onto his shoulder. "Let's head out ourselves."

DURING THE LAST FEW WEEKS, as my mother has wasted away, there were times when the house felt like it was closing in on me. I left others to sit with my mother—my aunt Julia, Virginia, my stepfather, my wife—so I could take to the woods like I had as a child. Sometimes I, too, felt like I was seeing things. Except that I wasn't seeing the places where the trees became dark and dangerous, where monsters lurked, but rather I was seeing where all those places no longer existed.

On one of the walks, my eldest daughter came with me. I

told her about Xiaobo, the Chinese miner turned servant to my great-aunt Rebecca and great-uncle Franklin. I told her how half of his body had been burned: the right half a mass of knotted scars, the left half as unblemished as fresh snow. We walked near Rebecca and Franklin's house and I pointed to a tree behind the house. I told my daughter how my father had fallen out of the tree and broken his arm, how Xiaobo had set the bone. My father said that Xiaobo's scarred hand felt hot and burning, as if it were still engulfed in flame, while the other hand felt cool and calming as springwater.

"This tree?" my daughter asked. "This is the one he fell out of?" I nodded and helped her reach the lowest branch, pushed her feet as she hoisted herself up, but even as I did so, I realized that I was wrong. The tree was too low to the ground; it was certainly no older than I was.

The tree my father climbed and fell from had been cut down decades ago. But it did not matter to my daughter. To her, this was my father's tree, and as I watched her lower herself until she hung from the tree, for at least a moment the tree *was* my father's tree.

Sawgamet has changed. The darkness driven away. But, I tell my daughters, there are still parts of the forest that remain secret, places where the mountains can loom close upon us, where shape-shifters fly past us in the dark.

MY GRANDFATHER AND I veered away from the mountain, taking a loping circle around the village, always staying in the woods. As we walked, my grandfather told stories, telling me how after he left Sawgamet he went as far east as he could go, past Montreal and toward Halifax, lobstering and then working as crew on a fishing boat for a season, nearly dying from hunger he was so seasick. "May I never go to sea again," he said, holding his hand up. He told me how he worked his way west again, across the plains and mountains, laying track and cutting tunnels on new rail lines, before finally coming back to Sawgamet.

"Why now?" I asked.

Jeannot took a few more steps and then walked over to a small creek. He knelt down and cupped his hands in the water, drinking twice before finally rocking back onto his heels and looking at me.

"The woods," he said, and then he trailed off. "The woods," Jeannot said again, but as his voice started to go silent a second time, I nodded as if I understood, and then he stood up fully. "Sometimes the woods ask things of a man."

There was a small natural clearing where we had stopped, a large plateau of rock and grasses, starting only a few feet away from the creek. Jeannot stared at it and I remained silent. Finally he let out a sigh and then leaned against a tree, still surveying the clearing.

"I killed a man. Did you know that?"

I stayed quiet. I had not known that, and I did not know what to say. But no answer seemed necessary. Once again I wondered if my grandfather was talking to me or to someone else.

"Actually, I killed him twice."

"Twice?" The sound of my voice startled me.

"The first time he wouldn't stay dead, but when I killed

him the second time, I made sure to keep the bones and carry them with me." He laughed, a short, barking laugh like a wolf's howl. I thought of the shape-shifter, the ijirait, and the idea thrilled me that my grandfather might be one, that he might be able to transform into a wolf. I imagined some sort of wrenching change, skin buckling, my grandfather turned into a brutish, menacing animal with stained teeth. But no transformation took place.

"Have you got them with you now?" I eyed the odd bulges of his pockets, but could see no way for him to be carrying a man's skeleton.

"It's funny how little the bones of a man weigh," he said. "Kept bound in cloth, they've been the only thing constant that I've carried with me these past thirty years." He was silent for a moment and then he glanced over at me. "No. I don't have them with me anymore. Sounds odd, I suppose, but I can't know how much you'll understand at this age, Stephen. So I'll tell you this: I kept his bones because it was the only way I could make sure that he stayed dead. Turns out he was a man, after all. But I was afraid to let those bones out of my possession; afraid he would come back here and come after your father. And then it was time, and I knew it didn't matter anymore. I knew I could put the bones to rest in the ground, that I couldn't protect your father anymore. The woods and the river claim their own in the end."

He took a step into the clearing. I heard some echo of a soft voice float through the air. I realized that we had circled up and around the village. We were past my stepfather's church, but not quite on the trail that led to the cuts. A ten-minute walk or less from my house if done straight and true.

"And how did you know it was time," I asked, "that you could bury the bones?"

"Your grandmother," Jeannot said. "She came to me in a dream. Said to be done with it, to bury the bones, to come find you." He turned to look at me, and I realized that he had tears in his eyes. "She didn't tell me about your sister, Stephen, didn't tell me about my son."

"A dream?"

"Sometimes it's as simple as that," he said. He wiped at his eyes with his fingers, and then he leaned his rifle against a tree. "This will do," he pronounced.

"For what?"

"For a home site. I'll need a place to sleep come winter."

"You're staying?" I asked.

"I mean to," Jeannot said, "at least for a while. There's two ways of seeing your grandmother. One's in you," he said, and he looked hard into my face. "You look her grandson more than you look mine. You're ten? Eleven? So that might still change, but for now it's one way for me to see a piece of what I lost." He stopped talking a moment and then patted me gently on the cheek. "You know, there was once a time when I didn't care if I ever came back. I didn't care if I ever saw your father again."

He stared at me expectantly, and I did not know what to say.

I DON'T KNOW when my father stopped expecting my grandfather to return to Sawgamet—or if he ever did stop expecting it—but I know that the stories about Jeannot were something he held on to. He lived with my great-aunt and great-uncle and their daughter, and though Franklin and Rebecca treated him like a son, my great-aunt told me more than once that every knock at the door, every footstep in the distance, every person who came out of the dark who was not Jeannot, was like a splinter in my father's heart.

When school wasn't in session, and when he wasn't helping Franklin in the store or at home, my father spent much of his time with Pearl. My father loved Franklin and Rebecca, but he was made for the cuts, and after that first year away at school in Vancouver, he said he would not leave Sawgamet again.

The summer after he returned from school, the summer that my father and Pearl built the steps and the chute beside the mill, my father was stunned at how soft he had become in only a single year away. He had turned sixteen while in Vancouver, but back in Sawgamet he found himself spent before midday.

First he and Pearl cut and planked the stairs down from the mill, an arduous process that left my father's hands raw. Sixteen was young enough, however, that the extra flesh on his body melted quickly, and he turned hard and lean working with Pearl. By the time they finished digging and driving the pilings, my father had come to enjoy the work, and he was disappointed that the chute was nearly finished.

There was more to it than that, of course. Pearl and Mrs. Gasseur had not had any children of their own, and there had been a time when my father had studied Pearl's appearance with great care, hoping to find some truth to the idea that he might be Pearl's son. By the time he was seven or eight, however, my father knew with certainty that Pearl was not his father—from looking in the mirror and from what little my great-uncle Franklin had been willing to speak of Jeannot— but one summer afternoon he asked Pearl anyway.

They had canoed across the Sawgamet and taken the fork up the Bear River, paddling an hour or so before beaching the canoe on a shaded gravel bank that Pearl promised was rife with fish. This was something, my father told me, that he and Pearl had done most Sunday afternoons that he could remember, gone off into the woods together, snow or sun, to fish or hunt or just for him to have a chance to get away from his aunt and uncle for a while. Occasionally Franklin's daughter, my father's cousin, Julia, came along with them, but mostly it was just Pearl and my father together. Usually Mrs. Gasseur packed something for them to eat, always thinking to include something that my father—or, for that matter, any boy of seven or eight—liked: shortbread, a few slices of fruit bread, jam-filled scones.

Pearl had been right about the fish, and in short order they caught enough to fill the creel. Pearl set his rod aside and leaned back on the shore, tipping his hat over his eyes to block the sun. My father kept casting idly, carefully pulling the hook out of the mouth of fish he caught and then gently lowering their twitching bodies back into the cool water. When I was a boy and fished with him, he told me that he loved the way the fish stayed in his hands, hovering in the water for a moment after he released them, how when they darted away they were like streaks of gold flashing in the water.

He let one go and then he finally turned and asked if Pearl was his father. Pearl touched his hand to his hat but he did not uncover his face. "You know I'm not your father, Pierre."

That was all he said then, and though my father might have hoped for more—for Pearl to say that he wished he *had* been his father—he did not ask again. Later that day, as they let the canoe drift lazily down the Bear River, in no hurry to get to the confluence of the Bear and the Sawgamet and the edge of the village, Pearl told my father a new story about my grandfather. It was not much of a story, and my father knew it was an exaggeration—Pearl told of how Jeannot had once spent the better part of an hour trying to cut a board and cursing a saw's dullness before realizing that he was holding the saw upside down—but it was a start.

After that fishing trip, Pearl began to tell more stories about Jeannot, stories that my father had not yet heard. In some ways, my father realized, people in the village had been afraid to tell him stories about Jeannot, convinced that by talking about my grandfather they made his absence more notable for my father. This trickle of stories—it could hardly be called a flood, coming from Pearl—was a relief of pressure that my father had not even realized existed. Pearl was the sort of man who was quiet except for when he was not, and there were times when he liked to tell stories about the woods, about the first few years of Sawgamet, how my grandfather let a tired dog choose the location of the village. Sometimes Pearl even told my father about what he himself had done as a younger man, the way he had worked his way from New York to San Francisco and then north. He was the one who taught my father how to track game, how to shoot and how to clean his kills, things that Franklin could not do for my father.

So even at sixteen, as my father grunted and pressed his shoulder against the final board of the chute, digging his feet

into the shifting bottom of the river, he was already nostalgic for
what they were about to finish, wishing that the forced company
of this project was not about to end. The water was up to his
waist and the current carried strong enough to make it difficult for him to keep his place, but none of that seemed to bother
Pearl. The older man sat comfortably on the chute and eyed the
nail, wiggling it against the wood before finally giving it a few
solid whacks with the hammer. He scooted over, placing three
more nails home, and then looked up at my father with a grin.

"That ought to about do it," Pearl said. "You can ease off.
I'll throw in a few more nails and then it's time to give this
contraption of ours a whirl."

My father ducked his head into the water. His legs had
already gotten used to the cold, but the water running down
the back of his neck and dripping from his hair came as a
small shock.

"We're sending logs down?"

"Of course not, Pierre. They'd just float away down the
river, and I don't think the men would fancy us letting their
work go to naught like that. I've something a little different in
mind." He gave the sort of grin that thrilled my father.

Despite Pearl's appearance of maturity, my father always
said when he was a boy and spending time with Pearl, that
Pearl could be counted on for a certain amount of mischief,
usually of the sort that neither Uncle Franklin nor Pearl's wife
approved of. Not to say that Mrs. Gasseur was an unpleasant
woman, but I think that at times she felt as if she needed to
be more careful than other women to keep up appearances.
Even I have heard the whispers that Mrs. Gasseur was once
less proper in her manners, that she had come to Sawgamet

during the boom to work, not to marry, but Pearl brought the sort of respect and fear that made men unwilling to openly tell stories about his wife's past.

Pearl walked a fast clip up the stairs beside the chute, not looking back, and my father found himself lagging behind. Though he had just turned forty, Pearl's hair had already turned white while my father was in Vancouver for school, and at least on the surface, Pearl looked like a hard man.

At the top of the stairs, Pearl moved off to the sluice and turned the wheel enough to start sending some of the diverted creek water down the chute. "Not so much to start," he said, grinning at my father. "Just enough."

"Enough for what?"

Pearl looked surprised. "For us, of course."

My father watched the water rush down the chute and swiftly hit the river. "You first."

They rode down the chute on greased wooden trays for more than an hour, until neither one of them could face the trip up the stairs again. Each of them was bruised and their throats were tired from whooping. My father had gained a few splinters and Pearl had torn his pants at the knee and bloodied his cheek a bit, but he said it was worth the pain. "Now, not a word of it to the wife," he said with a wink as they walked between the homes and the shops, past the saloon. "And best not to say anything to your uncle or aunt, either."

MY STEPFATHER HAS TOLD ME that even now, daring boys still ride down the chute during the summer, soaping the rails of sleds or trays jury-rigged for the express purpose of taking the swooping plunge into the river. Though the chute wobbles, and I'm sure that sooner or later it will simply collapse, the boys emerge from the river none too much the worse for wear, with only splinters and bloody knuckles from bashing against the side of the chute. Michael Keeny broke his wrist riding it a few summers ago.

As we stood in that clearing, however, my grandfather staring at me, I was not thinking of riding the chute, but rather of my father building the chute with Pearl, of my father's desperation to know Jeannot as more than a story, and I was thinking of what my grandfather had just said, that there was a time when he didn't care if he ever saw my father again, and the anger must have shown on my face.

I understand now what Jeannot was waiting for when he stared at me. As a priest, I am all too familiar with this look, have seen so many members of my church stare at me with the same hope: that I would somehow absolve them of their sins. But even if I had the power to do so with Jeannot, if I, as a ten-year-old boy, could have forgiven him, I did not want to. I did not want to forgive him for leaving Sawgamet, for returning too late to save my father, too late to keep Marie from falling through the ice. If anything, I wanted to drop the ax I was still holding and smash my fist against his face.

"You probably want to hit me, huh?" Jeannot said, as if reading my mind.

"A little bit, yes."

"Go on," my grandfather said, stepping closer to me and leaning over. "Hit me if it will make you feel better."

So I did.

I was surprised at how easy it was to hit my grandfather, and how Jeannot's head snapped back and then his body seemed to follow. I looked at my grandfather on the ground, and then I could not help myself: I started to laugh.

"Dammit," Jeannot said. He had his hands covering his face, and I could see blood already dripping down his chin. "My nose."

And for some reason that made me laugh harder. "You didn't think I'd do it, did you?"

Jeannot shook his head, and then gave an odd half-smile that made me again think of him as a shape-shifter, as a man who could also be a wolf. "No, Stephen, I can't say I really thought you'd do it. Guess I deserved it, huh?"

I thought about it for a second, but then I shook my head. "No. I understand. You didn't want to be burdened," I said, and I was stunned by the pained look in Jeannot's face, the way my grandfather's hands fell away and the blood, already slowed to a trickle, left a mark on Jeannot's shirt.

"Burdened? No. God, no, Stephen, I didn't think of it like that. I knew Franklin would take care of Pierre. I wanted him to be safe. I couldn't be sure that the woods were done with me, or if there was still more to pay." He wiped at his nose and then shook his head. "And I thought if I came back that maybe it would be too hard, that maybe I didn't want to see any part of your grandmother if I couldn't have all of her again."

"So you've come back to find her?" I could not help the eagerness in my voice, and my grandfather heard it. "But she's dead."

Jeannot regained his feet and stood next to me. Slowly and deliberately he put his hand on my shoulder. "I can't do anything about your father, about Marie." He dropped his hand from my shoulder and with an exaggerated cheerfulness he started pacing around the clearing, stopping at a large hillock. "Here," he said. "This is a fine site for a cabin. We'll dig it out and build it into the hill. It will keep the winds at bay some during the winters, make it warmer. We'll cut the wood and strip it before we touch a shovel to the ground."

He walked to the edge of the clearing and we spent nearly an hour marking out the trees that he planned to take down, aiming for trunks that were straight with as little taper as possible. Once or twice Jeannot turned down trees that I pointed to, saying they were too big for the two of us to handle without a horse team, but mostly my grandfather nodded his assent at whatever I chose. Finally, when we were ready to cut, Jeannot reached out his hand to take the ax from me, but I did not give it over.

"You left yours at the house."

Jeannot raised his eyebrows and laughed once. "The ax you're holding was mine well before you were born."

"And you left it when you left Sawgamet," I said back evenly. "Had you really wanted it you would have taken it with you."

Jeannot looked at me, and at the tightness in the way I gripped the handle of the ax.

"Just because I left it behind doesn't mean I didn't want it," he said. He held up his hand so that I could see the shiny, scarred flesh on his palm. "That ax left a mark on me the night your grandmother died. But if you help me take down these trees, then I'll say you've earned it."

I grinned and held the ax in front of my chest. "And I'd say you don't have much choice in the matter anyway, unless you want me to hit you again."

"I'm not enough of a fool to try to fight a boy who is holding an ax when I've not mine. Besides, you seem like you take after me in your unwillingness to yield. We might be here all day beating on each other. Let's save our blows for the trees, shall we?"

"Jeannot," I said, and both of us cringed at the sound of the name. "Sorry."

Jeannot sighed. "I guess I can't expect to have you call me grandfather after all this time. Jeannot will do."

"What's the second way?"

"The second way for what?"

"You said you came back so you could see my grandmother, and that there were two ways to see her. One was to look at me. What's the second way of seeing her? What did you mean when you said you're going to raise the dead?"

"Well, I don't mean that I'm going to raise the dead, exactly."

I let out a little breath, not even realizing that I had been holding it. "Oh."

"I don't need to. She's already out here, your grandmother, in the woods. All I have to do is find her and bring her home."

FOUR

Boom

AFTER MY GRANDFATHER'S NUGGET of gold started a rush, the fervor brought miners and landgrubbers, dance-hall girls and gamblers, and it brought my grandmother and her brother from the Red River. They came across the prairies, and all the way to Sawgamet, where they set up a general store.

My grandmother, Martine DeBonnier, stayed in the small cabin behind the store, baking and cooking, while her brother, Franklin, twenty-two and four years older than her, sold tin pans and beans and hatchet blades to the miners. Sometimes, when her brother needed to lie down from the headaches that were visited upon him, she put on his white apron.

She had not wanted to leave the Red River and had been angry at Franklin the entire journey—the shriek of the dust-clogged wooden axles grinding on wooden wheels still seemed to ring in her ears—but now that they were in Sawgamet my grandmother was willing to admit that she had been wrong. Before they left, Franklin had talked to Red River men who had joined the Cariboo gold rush at the start of the U.S. Civil

War nearly a decade earlier, and aside from food, clothing, some tools and supplies to live on, the only merchandise Franklin brought with them was tin pans. Ordinary, fifteen-cent tin pans. Every tin pan he could buy or have made before they left the Red River, more than four hundred in all. Martine had asked him if they ought not to bring shovels or cloth or nails or something other than tin pans, but Franklin had said, "Never you mind, Martine." He had smiled smugly in the way that he had taken to since their parents died three years previously, and then, in a happy singsong, "Tin pans is tin pans is tin pans is all we need."

Franklin had been right about the tin pans. So many of the men who streamed into Sawgamet in search of gold—walking north or taking steamships from San Francisco and then hiking inland—came ill-prepared. Some of them had even less knowledge of how to find gold than my grandfather. They brought food and clothing and shovels, tents and whiskey and the news that gold was there for the taking, but not enough of them carried tin pans.

For her part, my grandmother was curious as to why a man would pay eight dollars for a simple pan, and she made Franklin go down with her to the river one day. They had to walk for nearly an hour to find a stretch of water that was not already claimed. Franklin rested on the bank, sitting wanly in the sun, reading a book, but my grandmother stepped into cold water and mimicked the gentle swirling motion that she had seen men doing. Her skirts got wet and dragged heavily as the current pulled at the cloth. Franklin occasionally shaded his eyes from the sun and looked up at her, clearly impatient and ready to return to the store, but she ignored him. After an hour or so, she had found only a single glimmer of gold, and that was when she decided that it was simply easier to sell the pans than to use them.

And they did sell, even at eight dollars a pan. Men continued to pour into Sawgamet, and as the miners pulled the gold from the ground, some of it always stayed in the hands of my grandmother and her brother. They sold all of their pans in a few days and then hired men to bring in dried beans, shovels, bullets, flour, and always, more tin pans. Martine baked bread and Franklin sold it for a dollar a slice, two dollars with butter. The pies she baked were nine dollars. Seventeen if the miner wanted to keep the pan that the pie came in. Franklin kept the prices high, yet there seemed to be enough gold in Sawgamet—at sixteen dollars an ounce—that men paid what Franklin asked.

After he sold his first load of tin pans, Franklin bought a ramshackle cabin and then hired my grandfather to saw and build a solid, handsome store in front of the cabin.

As for my grandfather, by then he had already stopped trying to use his own tin pan. While gold seemed to leap from the ground for other men, my grandfather had not found even a glint of the metal since digging the nugget from the floor of his cabin. Instead, my grandfather worked the trees, providing lumber to miners. By the time he was finished building the store for Franklin, Jeannot had more than a dozen men whipsawing for him up the hill. Whatever wood he could produce was spoken for before the sawdust settled: the miners needed to build sluice boxes and flumes.

My grandmother and her brother spent their first winter in the rickety cabin behind the store, and though it was not

a particularly cold winter—certainly no colder than any they
had experienced on the Red River—for Martine, the cabin felt
like penance for a sin that she had not committed. Franklin
did not mind that the cabin was small and let the wind leak
through it. He spent most of his time in the store, weighing
gold dust and sending for more supplies by sea from San Francisco or by land and river from Quesnellemouthe; it was Martine who spent her days trapped inside the hovel, baking goods
for her brother to sell, the poorly vented stove sending choking
smoke against the low ceiling. At least she was near the fire,
she sometimes thought, because she could never seem to keep
warm, and the flames gave off more light than the one small
greased-paper window let in.

The wind blew constantly that winter, but the snow held
itself. Only a few inches stuck to the ground—not enough to
stop men from working—and by the spring, ten thousand
men had transformed Sawgamet into a dirty, noisy, bustling
boomtown. Jews, fishermen, Indians, farmers, Chinamen,
Londoners, Irishmen, Russians, bankrupt men needing a fresh
start, former slaves and former slave owners, beat-down sol-
diers, dreamers, adventurers, and even honest-to-God miners
boiled over the landscape, and with them came saloons and
whorehouses, but never enough dressed lumber or tin pans.

WHEN MY GRANDMOTHER realized that the winter had
passed but that she still could not get warm, she marched
fiercely into the store and demanded that her brother build her
a proper house.

My great-uncle looked up from the counter and blinked at his sister, as if Franklin were not sure whom the angry young woman was. "I'd no idea," he said. "Why didn't you say something earlier?"

"Franklin," Martine said, "I did say something. I said something every morning and every night. Even my bones said something while I was sleeping. Did you not hear me shivering from across the room?"

Franklin rubbed at his temples. My grandmother watched him pressing on the side of his head, as if the bright sun that streamed through the large windows in the front of the store pierced his eyes. She wondered if he still thought of her as simply his younger sister. He was certainly capable of looking at her and not realizing that she was eighteen and attractive, one of the few unmarried women in Sawgamet who was not a whore or worse. They ought not to be sharing a single-room cabin anyway.

"Franklin." She was careful to make sure that her voice did not sound angry, though she was insistent, and Franklin nodded and reached for the ledger book under the counter. She did not know why he bothered to reach for the book: he well knew how much gold they had earned.

"I'll order you some dresses," he said, and she thought of silk and beads and swiss waists and buttoned shoes that were more appropriate for an opera than for the muddy streets of Sawgamet. "And books. I know you'd like to have some more books, and they're something we could sell once you've finished them."

My grandmother smiled and reached out to pat her brother's hand. He meant well, but sometimes she wondered if he thought much beyond the gold that passed through his hands. He seemed so odd to her sometimes. She asked for a house and he offered her dresses and books. "We'll not be heading back to the Red River, will we?" she asked.

Franklin let her touch his hand for a moment and then he took it off the counter. She watched him pretend to look down at the ledger book and felt a sudden stab of love for him. He had done the best he could with her since their parents died. He had taken her west with him when it would have been so much easier for him to simply leave her to her fate on the Red River. She would have married somebody. She could have scratched out her life as a farmer's wife.

"No," he said. "We'll not return there."

"Then let's not live as if we will," Martine said. "It's thoughtful of you, Franklin, but I don't need new dresses and I've nowhere to wear them anyway. What I want is a house, something with walls and real floors rather than swept dirt, with enough windows—glass windows, not greased-paper—to let in the light, and a properly built stove. I want something that feels more like a home than a coffin. You've given the goods that you're selling a better home than you've provided for me."

"Well, they cost a pretty penny more than you do," he said. "I only had to bring you from the Red River, and you walked some of that way on your own." He waved his hand out toward the shelves and then touched her nose. "Some of this I had to have shipped in from San Francisco."

She swatted away his hand, and then, with a mischievous look, yanked the ledger book out from under his hands. She knew he hated her touching it. She slammed the ledger shut with a flourish. "Lord knows you sell those damned tin pans for enough that you can afford to build me a proper house."

"Lumber is hard to come by right now," he said. "I was lucky to get enough to build the store." He reached out and gently pulled the ledger back from her. "My little temple of commerce." He slipped the book under the counter. "Jeannot can't keep up with the demand," Franklin added, "and now some of the men are starting to work pit mines, so he's making props, too."

At the mention of my grandfather's name, Martine felt a coldness move through the store. The last hum of winter, she thought, and she pulled her shawl over her head and wrapped her arms around herself.

"Are you all right?" Franklin, usually so self-absorbed, so busy with his books and his wares, sounded concerned.

"You see, even in here I can't get warm."

MY MOTHER HAS SHIVERED like that for the last few days. We kept her covered with blankets, the fire burning, the furnace turned up, and still she shivered. Her hands were cold in mine, and I rubbed at them, trying to put the chill at bay.

"The winter they fell through the ice," I said, "you shivered then, too."

"I wasn't dying then," she said. I flinched at the words, and my mother squeezed my hand. "Stephen. You're a priest. You've sat by the bedsides of enough mothers and fathers."

"Never my own mother," I said. "Besides, experience doesn't make it easier."

"I was cold that entire winter. I felt like I'd gone through the ice myself. You were a good son, though. You kept the fire stoked, kept chopping wood for kindling." She nodded at the fireplace. "I still like a good fire, but it's easier now. Turn the dial and the furnace does the work. Same with the stove. Unimaginable luxuries, and all you have to do is turn a knob." She shifted onto her side to face me, letting out a small grunt. Her bones had been hurting her. "Can you put a pillow behind my back?"

Her body was hard angles. She was so thin and small that it was hard to believe she had once carried me. I adjusted the pillow and I heard her suck in her breath. "I'm sorry," I said. "I'm trying to be gentle."

She nodded but closed her eyes, and in a few minutes she was sleeping.

I stared at my mother while she slept. The logs burned in the fireplace, and it was at that moment, watching the fire, that I knew there was nothing I could do to stop her from dying.

A child should never be allowed to watch his mother sleep.

THE NEXT AFTERNOON, Martine and Franklin walked through the forest and up the hill. In the clearing, three large frames held logs off the ground. Each frame featured a sawyer standing underneath with another above, the men taking turns pulling on their ends of the eight-foot-long saws. The blades tore at the wood and sent shivers of sawdust floating down onto the men who were below. A few men hauled a straight, bucked tree into the clearing, while off to the side another man stacked a small pile of rough-cut boards.

Across the meadow, a thin man who seemed no older than Martine stepped out of a squat, crooked cabin. He stooped over to rub the muzzle of a shaggy gray dog that lay near the door, and then he looked up and appeared to see Franklin and Martine.

Martine had seen my grandfather when he and his crew built the store, but she had not talked to him before. In some ways, though, she felt that she knew a lot about him—she had heard men in the store talk of the young Frenchman who had first discovered gold in Sawgamet but who had found himself more lucky cutting trees than along the river—but she was surprised by the accommodations he kept for himself.

"That's his house?" she asked.

"First one built in Sawgamet," Franklin said. "Wintered here alone with that dog."

"It looks a little . . ." She paused, searching for a word. "Forlorn."

Franklin laughed. "He's eighteen and without a wife. What does he need more than that for?"

Jeannot wiped his hands on a cloth as he walked across the clearing, the dog trotting behind him at close attention. Martine was struck by the way that my grandfather carried himself, and how, when Franklin said, "My sister's wanting a house," Jeannot only glanced sideways at her, like he was afraid to look at her directly.

The thought almost made my grandmother laugh—and both my grandfather and my great-aunt Rebecca did laugh when they told me their versions of this story—and I can understand why. My great-uncle Franklin was not the sort of man who usually inspired concern, and my grandfather, though not a large man, had the sort of face that made it clear that he did not mind settling disputes with his fists.

Jeannot turned and looked at the gang of men working for him, seeming to consider something, and then he turned back. "I'm sorry, Franklin," he said. "I've been selling it for one hundred fifty dollars for a rough-cut thousand feet."

"I can pay," Franklin said quickly. He glanced at Martine. She had the distinct feeling that he was for some reason afraid she might suddenly turn on him if he did not get her what she had asked for. Franklin had his coat off and his sleeves rolled, and she could see sweat building at the top of his forehead, but my grandmother shivered a little, as if she had never known the touch of the sun. "And I'll hire you on to construct it if you're willing."

"I'm willing, but I can't," Jeannot said with a sigh. "I'd be happy to sell it to you, Franklin." He paused, gave a little cough, and, still not looking at my grandmother, added, "And to your sister. But it's not mine to sell. The wood is already spoken for through September, even at these prices. I don't pretend to understand all of it that the miners need—if I knew about mining, I'd still be working the river myself—but there's sluice boxes and rockers and props, and even more, there are men who are worried that next winter won't be so mild. You aren't the only one looking to build a house. These forests have good, strong, straight trees. Like nothing I've ever seen. A man could spend a lifetime cutting in these woods and never touch the end of it. But every time I get one man trained, another one decides he'd rather try to find his own mother lode. If I were a smarter man, I'd have you bring me in blades and I'd build a mill over the creek."

"The next three months' wood may be spoken for," Martine said, and though she had begun to shiver even more despite the sunlight, her voice was clear. "But the lumber that you and your men will be cutting in October is not."

Finally Jeannot looked at her, and when he did, Martine felt the cold strike through her. It seemed to her like they stared at each other for hours until she heard her brother's short laugh.

"She's a shopkeeper's sister, all right. Striking deals runs in the family," Franklin said. "Shall that be it, then? October? And will you run a crew to build it?"

Jeannot smiled and shook Franklin's hand. "If your sister wants a house, I'll build her a house. Would you," he said, dropping Franklin's hand and turning to my grandmother, "like to see how the boards are made?"

"I'm not sure what there is to see that I haven't already seen," Martine said. She suddenly felt both hot and cold, and when my grandfather laughed at her words, she could not decide if she was going to freeze or burst into flames.

WHEN MARTINE AND HER brother left, my grandfather told me, he surveyed his men, gave a few instructions, and then went back inside his small cabin. When he had settled Sawgamet he was burning for gold, had suffered through a winter alone for it, had suffered many other things, but now that other men had come to Sawgamet, it seemed like whatever magic had led him here in the first place had also decided that he would have to make his gold another way.

He was happy enough with the work, and he was making

more gold selling lumber than he likely would have digging it from the ground, but now that he had the gold there was little use for it. He had food and books and new clothes brought in already, but he was nearly eighteen and without a wife. He lay down for a while and thought of Martine. He had noticed her before. It was hard not to.

There were not so many women in Sawgamet, and she was a handsome woman. And her pies. That was something he had spent his money on. My grandmother and my great-uncle Franklin charged enough for those pies, but that did not stop men from wanting them. My grandfather touched a small furrow on the side of his forehead and smiled. Men sometimes came to blows over who would be the one to pay their sweat-earned gold for a pie. He was sure their desire for the desserts would not have been so frenzied had Martine been a less attractive woman, though he was almost certain that she was unaware of the commotion that her pies caused.

To me, Jeannot joked that he might have just mistaken hunger for love, but that afternoon, lying there thinking about Martine and having to face another winter in his cabin alone, my grandfather resolved to walk down to Franklin's store and talk to him about Martine.

I'VE HEARD TWO STORIES of this encounter. The first from my grandfather himself, in which he was funny, charming, and commanding, and in which he spoke openly of his love for my grandmother. In this story, he asked for her hand in marriage, she accepted, and when she came to the marriage bed it was in all of her virginal glory. But the other version of this story, told by my great-aunt Rebecca, the woman who raised my father and who was never known for bowing to social pressures, is the story that I believe to be true.

When my grandfather entered the store he was momentarily taken off guard when he saw Martine behind the counter rather than her brother.

"May I help you find something, Mr. Boucher?" Martine said.

"Where's Franklin? I mean, thank you, Miss DeBonnier, can I help you with anything?" He winced as he heard himself speak, and he felt an unaccountable urge to bow to Martine, as if she were royalty.

My grandmother laughed. "As it's my store, shouldn't I be asking if I can help you? But if you want to help me with something other than building a house, you could put another log or two in the stove," she said, nodding toward the corner. "It's better in the store than in the cabin, but I've a sudden chill."

Despite the warmth of the day and the almost stultifying feel of the store, my grandfather fed wood into the stove, taking the opportunity to settle himself. He stirred the fire with the poker and then turned back to Martine and pulled a book from his pocket, Dickens's *A Tale of Two Cities*. "I thought you might like to borrow this." He saw her hesitate and rushed on. "I have a few other books as well if you've read it."

Martine made no move, so Jeannot, absentmindedly touching his crooked nose, placed the book on the counter. "It's good," he said, and then he half-smiled and looked down at the book. "Nights are long here in the winter and it's this or spending my money on drink, I suppose."

"How do you know I can read?" My grandmother had to bite her lip as she watched Jeannot suddenly redden. His mouth opened but nothing came out. "I'm sorry. You just seem so solemn," she said with a laugh. "I can read, and I appreciate the gesture. Books are hard to come by here." Then she touched her fingers to the cover just as Jeannot did the same. Their hands touched and my grandmother let out a gasp.

Jeannot glanced down at his hand, at Martine's hand, at the book, and wondered if her gasp was something else he would not understand, but when he looked up again, Martine was already standing and backing away from the counter. "You'd best leave now, Mr. Boucher," she said. "You can come back another time, when my brother is here."

Jeannot did as he was asked, and as he walked up the path and through the meadow, past the men who were still sawing boards, he thought about the high blush that had come into her cheeks at the touch of his hand. It must have neatly matched his own.

According to my great-aunt, my grandmother thought of the sudden rush of heat that came from Jeannot's hand, the surge that had run through her and broken the coat of ice that seemed to cling to her, how for the first time since she had come to Sawgamet she had felt warm. Finally, after a while, she locked the store and went back to the small cabin, where her brother slept with a wet cloth on his forehead. She woke him gently, and when he sat up, she said, "I think I'm ready to be married."

Franklin stared at her and then held out his hand to reclaim the wet cloth. He lay back down and closed his eyes. "There's a needle pushing into my head. Something sharp and burning."

"Yes," my grandmother said, "that's what it feels like. Will you talk to him?"

But before Franklin was able to finish buttoning his Sunday suit, Jeannot knocked on the door.

Martine waited anxiously in the cabin while her brother and Jeannot talked in the store. She handled the thin gold chain around her neck that her brother had given her for her eighteenth birthday, and she tried to read the book that Jeannot had left, but everything she touched felt like it had come directly from the fire.

When Franklin came back to the cabin, he was alone.

My great-uncle took his time, carefully unbuttoning and hanging his jacket, lighting an oil lamp against the dimness of the cabin, pouring himself a cup of water from the metal pitcher. Martine waited until he sat down on the rocking chair that she usually occupied and then she snatched a wooden spoon from beside the stove and stood over her brother. "I swear, Franklin, I will whack you so hard," she said.

Franklin looked up at her with his insufferable grin and took a sip from the cup of water. He opened his mouth to speak but then, with a barely smothered laugh, took a second drink instead. "This water is really almost sweet-tasting. Remarkable."

Martine rapped the wooden spoon on his head. Franklin hunched down and rubbed his head. "I didn't really think you'd hit me."

"I'm about to do it again," she said. "Harder."

Franklin reached up to grab the spoon but she pulled it away. "Very well," Franklin said. "I told him he must build you a house first."

"Pardon?" My grandmother let the spoon drop down.

"A house. You asked me for a house, but if you're to be married to him, then he'll need to build you a house. I'll help to pay for it. I'm not sending you into your wedding with nothing," Franklin said.

"A house? But he said that he won't have any lumber until October."

Franklin's voice turned strong and proud. "I told him that if he wanted to marry you, the men who had a claim on his lumber could damn well wait until he'd built you the house that you wanted."

He stopped and looked at his sister. She stayed quiet, and Franklin stood up and stepped over to her, placing his hand on her shoulder, and waited until she looked up at him. "You've just met him. Are you sure?" She nodded. "It's good that he has to build you a house," Franklin said. "It will give you a chance to spend some time with him. Perhaps he can begin to take dinner with us."

"Franklin," Martine began, but then she looked down and let her voice fade. Her legs felt weak and she let herself sit on the bed.

"You'll be happy with him," Franklin said softly. "He's a good boy." He laughed. "A good man, I should say. I'm not nearly old enough to be calling him a boy. But some of the men here . . ." He did not finish his thought. "I suppose I'm happy that you've chosen him and not made me find a match for you on my own. Jeannot is a good man. He's spoken highly of, and he's made something for himself. Something real, something more than all this scratching in the dirt. We talked about what he is going to do in the future, what kind of a life you can expect, and I'm going to bring in some blades for him, a wedding present of sorts, so he can build a proper sawmill. That will give him something to keep with after all of this plays out," he said, waving his hand.

"And you?" Martine said quietly.

"You know me," Franklin said. He sat down beside her on the bed. "I've got the store. That's enough for me for now."

"Is it?"

"Well, I wouldn't say no to you inviting me over for Sunday dinners and bringing me a pie now and then."

AND HERE AGAIN, according to my great-aunt Rebecca: That night, well after Martine heard the deep steadiness of Franklin's breathing across the room, she could not sleep. She had buried the fire under ashes and cracked the door of the cabin, but still she was hot. She sat up in bed and pulled her sleeping gown away from her body. It was covered in sweat— she thought she could wring it out and turn the dirt floor to mud—and her hair matted around her shoulders like she had just come from the river. First she could not stop shivering, she thought, and now this. She stepped out into the night, seeking relief from the oppressive heat that was consuming her.

Outside, the stars seemed so close that they were dripping from the sky. She looked at the quarter moon, its tip brushing against the mountains that rose up on the other side of the river, and for a moment she thought she felt waves of heat coming from the moon's buttered glow. The tents and houses were silent, and as a light rain began to fall, Martine let her gown slip from her body, thinking that in the unseen darkness between the cabin and the store a cool breeze might take away the growing sense that she was on fire, but each drop of rain sizzled and seemed to smoke as it hit her body, and she felt like something pulled her toward the slope and the forest.

If she had not been burning with such feverish intensity, my grandmother never would have walked naked through the sleeping village, but with every step she became hotter and hotter. The moon and the stars cast enough light for her to follow the path, but she could have walked blindfolded, so strong was the scorching feeling on her skin. When she finally came into the clearing, she saw my grandfather standing outside of his cabin.

He was turned away from her and his shirt was off, his back glistening from sweat and rain. He swung his ax heavily and swiftly, hacking at firewood like summer was already fading instead of just greeting Sawgamet. He had not been able to sleep, either, though the sensation of heat had not seemed to bother Flaireur. If the night would not let him rest, Jeannot resolved, it would not be wasted. But as he brought the ax down, my grandfather felt suddenly as if his back had been thrust into burning coals. He turned to face my grandmother.

Jeannot stood dumbly, unaware that he was still holding the ax, watching Martine come across the wildflower-strewn field toward him. At first she simply appeared to be trailing a cloud, but just as he realized it was smoke, she became enveloped in flames. He did nothing, simply watched, unable to understand what he was seeing. The fire did not seem to bother the girl, and after a moment, she stepped from the flames unscathed, empty-handed and naked except for the gold chain that circled her neck.

My grandparents made love in the grass and the flowers of the field, and wherever they lay for more than a moment, the ground scorched beneath them. Afterward, Jeannot smoothed his hand over her body, and touched her neck and her breastbone with wonderment: the necklace had sunken into her skin. It had melted and become part of her, and it stayed part of her even after she died, even when the rat-eyed farrier who also served as the undertaker broke three knives trying to carve it from my grandmother's body.

FROM THAT NIGHT THROUGH the next few months, as my grandfather hired more men to cut and mill wood and to build a two-story house near where his small cabin already stood, both Jeannot and Martine slept easily and separately. Jeannot took his dinners with Franklin and Martine, and on Sundays they brought picnic lunches down to the banks of the river. For the two lovers, it was like the night in the meadow was only a dream, an imagined moment of abandon, one not to be repeated until their wedding night.

The house rose quickly—and beside it, a new mill on the creek—and Jeannot furnished the house with Franklin's help, ordering glass windows, a bed, dressers and nightstands, settees and a table with seating for twelve. Franklin, unexpectedly easy with his gold, ordered china and silverware and a crystal chandelier for the house, saw blades for the mill, all of which had to be carried in from steamships off the coast.

By the time the house was finally finished and furnished, and the young Catholic priest, Father Hugo, married Martine and Jeannot, it was mid-September. They were both eighteen and they found that the first and only time they had made love was the way it felt every time. They were young enough that for the first few weeks of their marriage they did little more than luxuriate in each other's company several times a day.

When they finally felt the need to leave the house it was to a summer that had lingered well beyond what it should have.

FIVE

Into the Woods

THE SUMMER AND FALL of the year that he returned to Sawgamet, my grandfather told me, reminded him of the summer and fall of the year he was married: the heat lingered well past when the snows should have come. He thought the warmth was a welcoming. I thought the warmth was a mockery of the ice and cold and snow of the winter that had just gone by, the winter that had held my father and my sister under the ice.

I helped my grandfather build his cabin in the clearing, though my stepfather had grudgingly offered to let him stay with us. We worked side by side through the bugs and the unaccustomed warmth, but he did not say much during the days. Most evenings he took dinner with us, and it was at those times that he reminded me of my father.

At the end of that first week, my cousin Virginia, who was uncle Lawrence and aunt Julia's daughter and only a year older than me, joined us for dinner. My grandfather did not seem to mind her continual questions.

"But how did the dog—"

"Flaireur."

"Flaireur," Virginia continued, "know where to lie down?"

"Providence," my stepfather muttered, though he had already begun to warm a little toward Jeannot.

"He was simply tired," Jeannot said. "Or it was magic. One or the other."

"Uncle Jeannot!" She shook her finger at him.

I remember that the tone of her voice when she said his name, the good-humored protest, the same way that she shook her finger at him, reminded me so strongly of Marie that I had to leave the house, making the excuse of needing to relieve myself.

And so it was that I missed the grand entrance of my great-aunt Rebecca.

Later, Virginia told me that her grandmother had stormed through the door, not bothering to greet my mother or Father Earl before slapping Jeannot across the face.

"It was a great slap," Virginia told me. "Like kindling broken over the knee, but there was a little wetness to it, and it wouldn't surprise me one whit if Grandma had spit in her hand before hitting uncle Jeannot. And he seemed almost like he was expecting it. He just closed his eyes like he was in prayer and let her hit him. I'd sure like to see Grandma try to slap me like that. I sure as syrup wouldn't just close my eyes and let her," Virginia said, though we both knew that neither one of us—and for that matter, few men in the cuts—would dare to do anything other than turn our cheek to my great-aunt.

I had assumed that everyone in the village knew of Jeannot's plans to find my dead grandmother wandering in the woods. By the end of that first week, it seemed as if most people knew, and they eyed Jeannot with wariness at what they took to be a touch of madness. But only a touch of madness, for anybody who had lived in Sawgamet for any length of time knew that the woods were deeper than they could imagine. Apparently, however, Great-Aunt Rebecca had only heard of Jeannot's plans that very evening, and Great-Aunt Rebecca, alone among the men and women of Sawgamet, seemed outraged.

It was at that point that I returned to the house, having missed the great slap that Virginia later described for me, but arriving in time to see Great-Aunt Rebecca point her bony finger in my grandfather's face.

"I buried your wife's body," she said, her hand shaking. "She is dead and gone to heaven. You can argue that the woods took her from you, but you won't find her out there in the trees. You won't find her other than in a box in the ground in the cemetery."

"She's out there, Rebecca," Jeannot said simply, as though he were used to having women shouting at him as he ate his dinner.

"I carried the stink of burnt flesh in my nostrils for longer than I care to remember," Virginia's grandmother shouted, and she continued shouting until my mother rose from the table and gently ushered her out. There was a moment of silence in the room, and then Virginia began to speak with forced cheer of the elegant cake that she planned to bake for Jeannot's birthday, and how much she looked forward to making it. Despite what had just happened, I had to smother a laugh at the lie. Even now the thought makes me smile. We joined

Virginia for dinner last week; after twenty years of marriage and five sons, she has grown to be a serviceable cook, but as a child, she no more enjoyed spending time in the kitchen than my oldest daughter does.

AS THE WEEKS WENT BY and my grandfather and I finished building the cabin—it was small but light and airy, a serviceable building, tightly chinked against the coming winter—I took to walking in the woods with him, ostensibly helping him look for my grandmother, but mostly just enjoying spending time with him.

Though I was not in school during the summer, my stepfather required me to spend my mornings reading and working on my letters. I think that was the time when I first started to seriously consider his entreaties that I attend seminary; it was certainly the point when I first discovered a facility for books, if not a love for studying.

In the afternoons, once I was done with my letters, on the days I did not spend with my grandfather, I was sent up to the mill to do work for the company. Out in the cuts, boys my age and younger were already taking off branches and helping to shape the fallen trees into something that could be skidded through the woods and stacked near the mill, but my mother had forbidden me to go into the cuts, and that injunction still held, regardless of the return of my grandfather. I would have much preferred the cuts—limbing trees, running tools, cleaning chips, and hitching the chains for the skid teams, even taking care of the horses—but still, I enjoyed the solitary nature of the work at the mill. I suppose I've always enjoyed my own company.

Once September struck, my birthday already come and gone and school begun again, it was only a few weeks before Pearl set the men to sending logs down the chute. When they floated the logs I was left on the banks, watching the men and the wood disappear down the Sawgamet, the first float that I could remember leaving without my father.

The night of that float, a Friday, I spent dinner with my mother and stepfather, but Jeannot, who had not been at the float, either, was absent. Afterward, I took a walk in the woods, stopping by his cabin and then heading toward the cuts, but he was not there nor elsewhere that I could find him. The next morning I rose earlier than I wanted and went to the mill, spending a few hours straightening, cleaning the worst of the wood chips, and placing tools on their pegs so they could be found for sharpening over the winter. I am willing to admit that I swore when I gouged my hand on a saw that had been left carelessly under some stripped branches, but though the blood pooled freely, the cut was not so bad. I fed the horses and mules as I had been asked by Pearl, mucked the stables, and then thought to check the chute to see how it had held during the push of trees the day before.

Then, still unable to locate my grandfather, and with nothing else to do and not interested in spending one of the last fine days of autumn inside with a book, I went to find my cousin. Virginia was a capable fisherwoman, could shoot well enough for a girl, and paid little heed to her grandmother's strictures. All in all, a perfect companion when I was looking to whittle away a few hours.

Virginia was in the kitchen, an unusual enough sight, and I could not stop myself from laughing when I saw my cousin's flour-dusted hair, the smeared mess of her apron, and what looked like a berry stain on one of her cheeks.

"Have you and Aunt Julia been throwing flour at each other?"

Virginia looked up, a smile at the ready. She'd smile at me no matter what I said. She'd been this way since my father and Marie died, and the thought made me feel ashamed for a moment, as if my coming to spend time with my cousin were a sort of charity.

She had put together the semblance of a cake; there was something wrong in the way it slumped in the middle and an ooze of liquid seemed to dribble from the side. "I wanted to make it for special for Jeannot."

I rolled my eyes and theatrically struck my hands to my chest. "If you really wanted to make it special, you'd have left well enough and let your mother bake the cake." She grimaced at this. Aunt Julia had never been much of a baker, either. "Well, she's gotten better," I said charitably, though we both knew it was not true. Only the week before she had forgotten to add sugar to a pie, and then scorched it badly enough that only Uncle Lawrence was willing to eat any.

Virginia tapped the side of the cake. "Your mother told me how, but I've done something wrong. It's collapsing. A disaster. I don't think I cooked it enough, or perhaps I didn't use enough flour. I don't really suppose it can be salvaged, can it? Would you like some bread? We can slather the cake on it as a sort of jam. I've put enough sugar in it to give Mother a fright." She took a knife and sliced four thick pieces of bread and then reached with the knife into the cake and smothered it across the bread. "Do you think Jeannot will be disappointed when he finds out what sort of cake I baked?"

"What sort of cake you didn't bake, really," I said. The cake-smeared bread was grainy with sugar and thick against my tongue, but it tasted good. "I don't think Jeannot much cares one way or another." I saw the way she dropped her eyes, and I hastily added, "I'm sure he'll be pleased that you thought of trying, though."

"Where is he today? I thought you'd be off in the woods with him."

"I haven't seen him. Want to come looking with me?"

Virginia brushed the flour out of her hair and washed her face, and then we took some apples and a hunk of cheese and headed up the woods behind the village. I let Virginia walk in front of me, following her up one of the narrow paths. We passed by the Anglican church but did not see my stepfather. At Jeannot's cabin, Virginia knocked on the door, but there was no answer and no movement behind the windows.

We decided to head up into the trees. For a short while, we were shadowed by a pair of chickadees that flew past us and around us, but mostly it was just Virginia and me, comfortable in the coolness of the tree-shaded path. We walked for nearly an hour, until we came out to the ledge that showed the village and the river below, the flats devastated by logging, and across the way, the rising mountain. I sat with my feet hanging off the ledge, occasionally tossing rocks or pebbles down the slope, and Virginia lay down away from the edge, in the grass near a spot of sun.

At first I thought the flicker that cut between the trees

below was an animal, but then I saw that it was a man. My attention was taken away for a moment by a soaring hawk, but then I saw the movement in the woods again. The man moved back and forth with no apparent meaning, but there was a certain urgency to his movements. I was about to call to Virginia to ask for her to toss me an apple when I realized the man was my grandfather. I kept still, watching Jeannot scramble up the gentle slope. He did not look up to the ledge where I sat, and it was not until my grandfather had already passed that I shook Virginia's shoulder and we started following.

We almost had to run to stay with Jeannot, catching glimpses of him through the thick trees. The hill flattened and the trees thinned, but when we came out into the broad clearing, there was no sign of my grandfather.

"Where did he go?" Virginia said. We were both a little out of breath.

I shook my head. The open field full of wildflowers and thick, matted grasses was still. Jeannot had been in front of us, but not far enough so that he would have been able to scramble across the shallow creek and cover the thousand feet or more into the next section of trees without us seeing him. "He must have turned around somewhere back in the woods," I said.

"What was he chasing?"

"Maybe something was chasing him."

"We were chasing him, Stephen. No. He was after something." Virginia walked forward to the creek and knelt down next to the water, cupping a handful to her mouth. "Cold," she said.

"Think it will be long to freeze-up?" I squatted next to her and took a drink myself.

"A while yet, at least according to my father. He said the other Indians were laughing at the men for the early float. They don't think much of Pearl's ability to see the weather coming."

As she said this, I saw something glint in the water. I fished my hand down among the rocks, wetting my sleeve. I pulled a chain from the water and held it up for Virginia to see.

"That's a pretty chain." She grinned at me. "You should give it to Jeannot for his birthday. He might like it more than a cake."

I splashed some water at her and she scrambled back from the bank. "Here," I said, holding out the chain. "You should have it." She lifted her hair so that I could fasten it around her neck, and as she turned to show me the way the gold lay against her throat, we heard Jeannot's voice.

"Where did you find that?" Jeannot was breathing hard, sweat on his face and tightness in his voice. He moved toward us and reached out to touch the necklace around Virginia's neck. "Where did you get this?" He looked at Virginia and then at me.

"It was in the creek," I said.

"Did you see . . ." Jeannot's voice trailed off and then he sank to his knees. His head bent to his chest, and then he began to shake. I looked at Virginia.

We stayed silent, not moving, letting my grandfather cry. Finally, Jeannot rubbed his eyes with his sleeves. Slowly, like it pained him to do so, he rose to his feet. He touched the necklace around Virginia's neck again, fingering the chain as if somebody else wore it.

"Don't let Franklin see you wearing this," he said.

"Uncle Jeannot?" Virginia looked scared as she spoke. I was scared as well. The sight of an adult crying, let alone Jeannot, was unsettling.

He turned to me and said, "It was your grandmother's. Your grandfather," he said to Virginia, and then looked back to me. "Martine's brother, your great-uncle Franklin, gave it to her. It was buried with her."

"You should have it," Virginia said. She reached behind her neck to unclasp the chain.

"No." He stopped her fingers with his own. "She would have been your great-aunt. She wants you to have it. That's why you found it. I don't know why, and I don't know why she won't let me find her, but when it's time, I suppose she'll show herself."

He did not say anything else. He just turned and walked back toward the village.

VIRGINIA SENT ME the chain a few years ago. "For one of your daughters," she wrote. "It's not something that any of my sons would appreciate."

I wrote back and told her that it was not something that either of my daughters—this was before the baby was born— were of age to appreciate, either. Still, I kept the necklace. It's in a box in the drawer of the desk now; sometimes I'm tempted to pull it out and finger it.

One thing that has been an unexpected joy in returning to Sawgamet after so many years has been the chance to spend time with Virginia again. My wife and Virginia have taken to each other with alacrity, and for me, spending time with my cousin has been yet another thing that brings me back to my youth.

Virginia hasn't changed as much as I would have thought. Or perhaps it is rather that, despite my travels, I haven't nearly changed so much as I thought, either. Physically, she looks surprisingly the same. If I look closely at her hands I can see that she is as worn and old as I am, but her face is that of a much younger woman, and on the several occasions when we have taken to walking in the woods together, I have found myself winded while she gaily carries on her end of the conversation.

I wish that I'd returned to find my mother similarly unchanged.

My stepfather has remarked that it is funny how providence works; all of the details for me to come and assume my stepfather's station as the minister of the Anglican church in Sawgamet had been settled for some months before we even had wind of my mother's illness. But in the few weeks between when my mother first started feeling poorly and we arrived in Sawgamet, she had already taken to bed.

My mother was never a large woman, but she had been cheerfully fed and active, the sort of woman who thrived in a town like Sawgamet. I don't mean to make her sound like farm stock, but neither was she a delicate china doll. She read and sewed and baked and complemented Father Earl in leading the church, but she also hiked through the woods with him, could handle an ax to cut firewood, and other than the winter that my father and sister died, never seemed to mind the cold.

When I finally arrived in Sawgamet, it was to a woman I barely recognized. True, it had been two years since the last time we had seen each other—she came to Vancouver to see the new baby, her namesake—but the changes wrought so quickly were a blow to me. Is that always how it works? That we grow old in the space of a few weeks? I feel as if I should still be a young man, but when I look in the mirror I am greeted by a shock of gray hair that is thinning at the part.

Still, even though I should have been expecting the change in my mother, my first thought was that some imposter had clambered into the bed beside which my aunt Julia sat vigil. Julia—Franklin and Rebecca's daughter—distracted me with the flicker of her hands and the shadows she threw on the wall. Shadow puppets seem like such children's games, but as her hands moved I saw the dance of caribou, hunting wolves, sled dogs, and then, as she turned at the sound of my footsteps, a bird taking flight.

"Stephen," she said, her voice quiet. "How was your journey?"

"How is she?"

"Sleeping," my aunt said, "which is well enough. She's uncomfortable and been sleeping poorly."

As I stared at my mother, I could see some of the familiar features that had begun to sink away. Between the lights from the bedside lamp and the flame in the fireplace, stark shadows made crevices on her face.

I don't know how long I stared at my mother, but I forgot about my aunt Julia until I felt her hand on my shoulder.

"Why don't you sit with her?" she said. "Your mother will be happy to see you when she wakes. Just keep the fire stoked so she doesn't catch chill."

The door closed behind Julia, and I sat in the chair and

took my mother's hand. Her skin had turned so thin, paper-like, that I thought I would be able to see the light pass through it if I held it up to the lamp.

SITTING ALONE IN MY STUDY like this, night fallen hard and the house finally silent, it is no wonder that I might worry about my own mortality. It's still a few hours yet until midnight, but the girls are asleep, as is my wife, and I know that downstairs, in the parlor, Father Earl is resting in a chair beside my mother's bed.

I should be preparing to write my mother's eulogy rather than thinking of my grandfather and grandmother, of my father diving through the ice and reaching out to my sister, of all of the many things that both drove me away and brought me back to Sawgamet. Easier said than done. To write the eulogy is to accept that very soon my mother will be truly and finally dead, that I will be—even though I am past forty—an orphan. Were I more like my grandfather, I would simply refuse to believe in my mother's death. Were I more like my grandfather, I'd believe that even when my mother does die, whether it is tomorrow or tonight, somewhere out there, past the window, past the train yards and the houses, into the cuts and woods, she would still roam.

SIX

The Miner's Angel

WHEN I THINK ABOUT the first winter after my grandparents married, I am prone—as I often am—to think of it in biblical terms. Or maybe it is simply that I am looking for a reason, for something to explain all that happened. I can explain the rise of Sawgamet easy enough: all it took was a few men— my grandfather among them—with instant wealth to cause other men to flock to Sawgamet. The Yankee who gathered enough gold dust from shaking out his clothes that he bought a horse, the Chinaman who walked into town one morning with a nugget the size of a baseball, and Twelve-Foot Pete, so named because in a mining claim measuring only twelve feet by twelve feet, he unearthed enough gold to buy a thousand acres of farmland in his native Ohio. On this, dreams were made.

We are experiencing another boom of sorts in Sawgamet now, with the growing war. The need for lumber—the resilient wood that comes from our forests—has increased enough to return some of the flush to this town, but I know it will not last. Sooner or later, every boom has a bust, though at least there is something tangible in these forests; I can see the trees, walk through the cuts. But gold. Gold is something else. A dream that ends soon enough.

My grandfather would have been familiar with the proverb, "He that tilleth his land shall have plenty of bread: but he that followeth after vain persons shall have poverty enough." But, of course, he and my grandmother were not thinking of gold when they ignored the way that the summer held longer than it should have. They may have been the only people in Sawgamet who were not thinking of gold: the previous winter had been mild enough for the miners to work through, and the summer had been warm and lasted well into the fall, the town growing by the day. But my grandparents were in love. They weren't thinking of the way that empires crumble, the way that people can lose faith, the way that nothing lasts forever.

They expected the summer to last forever, and when they finally woke to frost on their windows near the end of October, it came as a surprise. They had gone to sleep the night before to another unseasonably warm night, but the morning frost was thick on the glass. Sun scattered through the ice crystals and splayed across the room. Flaireur stayed sleeping at the foot of the bed, even as Martine washed and dressed and made her way downstairs to see what Rebecca had prepared for breakfast.

The same Rebecca, of course, that I knew only as my great-aunt, witty and often warm to me and her granddaughter, Virginia, but a sharp-tongued matron who suffered no fools. It is difficult for me to imagine her as the young woman—she was a year or two older than Martine and Jeannot—that my grandfather hired as soon as the house was complete. Rebecca was one of the few women who had come to Sawgamet unwilling to sell her body.

While Rebecca made breakfast—pancakes and bacon, syrup and preserved raspberries—my grandmother returned upstairs. She found Jeannot dressed in thin pants and a light shirt, pulling on his pair of boots.

"Where are you off to?"

"I've been cooped up here long enough," he said, and then he saw the look that flashed across Martine's face. "Not with you. With you I could lay forever," he said, "but I'm used to being outside more. I was thinking of going for a paddle."

"Where?"

Jeannot stood and stepped over to the window. He scratched his thumbnail against the frost on the window. "I think I'm going to go off into the woods a ways." He rubbed on the glass until there was a small square that they could both see through. He nodded at the view over the river and at the hills rising into peaks on the other side. "I've always wanted to know what's further along. Today seems like a fine day for it. Would you like to join me," he said, and with a small smile he added, "or do you have too much to do?"

THEY DID NOT BRING MUCH with them. Rebecca packed Jeannot and Martine some fried chicken wrapped in paper, biscuits, and shortbread, and Jeannot brought his rifle. The sun had already chased away the morning's frost, and my grandparents wore light summer clothing that belied the date on the calendar. They paddled upstream until their shoulders and arms ached. Because of the current, they moved slowly, no more than half the pace of an easy walk, and several times they pulled the canoe from the water and portaged it, carrying it past whitewater and then launching it again when the river widened. After a few hours, they stopped for lunch, beaching the canoe on a gravel bar. They set aside some shortbread and gave the rest of the chicken scraps to Flaireur. After eating, the dog fell asleep in the sun.

The river moved slowly and sang quietly. Jeannot sat on the gravel, leaned back against the canoe, and closed his eyes, but Martine stripped off her clothes and swam in the river. She let herself float in the current, her long hair trailing behind her. Three times she drifted down the river, swam to the side, then walked back to Jeannot. He watched her, noting the way that the sun seemed to burnish the gold chain embedded in her skin, and finally, after she called to him, he, too, joined her in the cold water.

They played, dunking each other under the water, swimming down to touch the bottom, letting themselves be carried along by the gentle pull of the wide, lazy river. Though Jeannot told me they just swam, I'd imagine that after a while the playing led, as many things do for newlyweds, to kissing, and the kissing to making love. Jeannot standing in the river with the water midway up his chest, holding Martine in the slow sway of the current. Even with muscles sore from paddling, she would have seemed weightless, and when they were finished, they remained still, Martine wrapped around him, Jeannot's head on her shoulder.

Whether they were just swimming or something more, my

grandfather told me that as he held his wife in the river, she started to fall asleep until she heard him let out a small gasp. She started to speak, but my grandfather's hand darted from the water and touched lightly on her lips. Silently, she turned and looked out on the bank.

Flaireur lay sleeping, curled near the canoe, even though a caribou stood only a few paces away from the dog. The caribou was enormous. From where my grandparents were entwined in the river, the caribou seemed to stand nearly six feet at shoulder height, easily a foot bigger than any caribou either of them had seen before. He was heavy, as well. Perhaps because of the delay in the cold, the rutting season had not begun, and this bull had not lost his stores of fat. More striking than his size, however, was that he seemed to be made of solid gold. Had he not taken a step forward at that moment, both Jeannot and Martine would have been willing to believe that he was some sort of misplaced statue.

The caribou hovered over Flaireur, but the dog did not stir. The sun reflected off the caribou's golden coat, his antlers, his feet.

"Even his bones must be made of gold," my grandfather whispered to Martine. His words broke the stillness that had come over the couple. Gingerly, Jeannot lowered Martine to her feet, and then he slowly began to ease his way out of the water, his eyes flickering from the rifle that lay in the canoe to the golden caribou that stood only a few paces away from the boat.

The caribou looked up at Jeannot, but the animal showed neither surprise nor fear as my grandfather steadily advanced upon him. As Jeannot moved forward, the caribou turned and

took a few steps toward the woods before stopping and looking back. Jeannot froze, expecting the animal to bolt, but the
golden caribou shook his head and then took only another two
steps before pausing again.

Jeannot reached for his rifle, but Martine, who had crept
behind him, touched his wrist lightly, and instead he took her
hand in his. Together, carefully and slowly, still naked, the
water glistening on their bodies in the midday sun, Jeannot
and Martine walked after the caribou. As they headed into the
woods, Jeannot glanced back and saw Flaireur still sleeping
peacefully.

My grandparents followed the caribou through the forest.
At first they were tentative and solemn, but soon it became
almost a game. By the time they were deep enough into the
forest that the light had become diffuse—as if they were walking in the moonlight—they had forgotten any need to be quiet.
The path that the caribou followed was wide and twisting,
and the fallen leaves and dirt stayed soft underneath their feet.
Jeannot noticed that the tree trunks and bushes near the trail
glittered with gold dust, and they wondered if the forest grew
its own gold, but then they came to realize that the caribou
seemed to be shedding gold as it walked. The air was thick
with it, and the few beams of light that came cleanly through
the forest canopy appeared as spears of gold.

The caribou walked in front of them, slow enough that
they could follow, but fast enough that no matter how much
my grandparents called to him, he kept out of reach. They did
not try running after him. There was something in the hush
of the woods—broken only by the clicking of the caribou's
feet—that made them reverent. After a little while, they began

to forget why they had started following the caribou. Hand in hand, they began to speak of children and the future, subjects that neither of them had spoken openly to the other of before, and neither of them noticed the change in the light or the sudden cold stillness in the air until they had already come into the clearing.

Ahead of them, the caribou waited. The trees formed an almost perfect circle around the glade. The sun, past its height, still shone heatlessly down, and its light bounced brilliantly off the giant boulder that occupied the middle of the clearing. The caribou watched Jeannot and Martine emerge from the trees, and then he turned to the boulder and began grinding his antlers and his shoulders against it.

At first neither Jeannot nor Martine understood what they were seeing, but after a moment it became clear. The caribou was not made of solid gold. Rather, it was covered in dust from vigorously rubbing against the golden boulder. The boulder stood several hands taller than the caribou, and it seemed so substantial and large that both Jeannot and Martine thought they could hear the earth groan beneath its weight.

They kept still, unable to move, enthralled and awed by the sight of the powerful caribou pushing and grinding against the golden boulder. With every push of his antlers or scrape of his side, gold dust sprang into the air. The glade was full of the floating dust, and in the light, Jeannot and Martine thought they had found some sort of fairy kingdom, each fleck of dust a sprite.

The caribou finished rubbing against the boulder, and then he pawed at the ground. He stopped and looked up at the watching couple, and then he scraped the ground again.

Martine dropped Jeannot's hand, and as if she could not help herself, she took the dozen steps that separated her from the caribou. Hesitantly, she reached out and touched him, running her hand up his muzzle. A cloud of gold burst from his coat and settled around her. She tried to pet him again, but the caribou stepped back and then tilted his head and showed the kind of stillness that always augurs flight in animals. My grandfather moved forward and grabbed my grandmother's elbow, suddenly worried about the thought of malevolent spirits. He glanced at the boulder, knowing that nothing ever really came without cost.

But it was no creature of the woods that bothered the caribou, only the sound of Flaireur's barking. The sudden sharp pitch of the dog's voice moved through the trees, and after shivering for a moment, the caribou tensed and then bounded into the woods, disappearing so quickly that all he left in his wake was a small puff of gold.

Flaireur came bursting into the clearing, stopping short at the sight of the golden boulder. It was like the dog did not even see Jeannot or Martine. He crouched low, his hackles suddenly rising, his tail tucked between his legs, and he let out a thick, rumbling growl. Flaireur bared his teeth, showing the leather-colored stain at the roots of his fangs, spittle dripping from the sharp tips.

Jeannot and Martine felt a cold prickling on their bare skin and the rise of gooseflesh on their arms. Jeannot reached out to touch the golden boulder, and as he did, Flaireur's growl pitched even deeper. It was then that Jeannot realized the sensation of cold was not simply that of fear: a new, winter-carrying wind had started to cut through the clearing. At that moment, the sun fled behind gray clouds, the shadows in the trees turning darker. Jeannot took Martine's hand and tried to turn her toward the woods, in the direction from which Flaireur had just come.

"What about the gold?" Martine said, unwilling to turn.

"We're earning plenty enough from sawing wood," Jeannot said, and then he placed his hands forcefully on her shoulders.

Martine stared at him, rubbing her arms with her hands, seemingly unaware of her actions. "But what about . . ." she said, trailing off and looking at the boulder.

"It's the winter," Jeannot said. "It's coming. Now. We have nothing to start a fire, we don't have our clothing with us, and what we do have at the canoe won't see us through a night in the woods. I'll mark this spot and we'll return." He whistled to Flaireur, and the dog broke off his growling.

Jeannot held Martine's hand, pulling her after him through the trees and following Flaireur, and they were both surprised when, after only a few hundred feet, they emerged onto the gravel shore by their canoe. Jeannot took his knife and marked a pair of trees on the beach.

"We'll be able to find the clearing easily enough," he said. "Better to return properly dressed tomorrow, or even to wait until spring. It will be there waiting. Gold's not of much use to us if we freeze to death."

NAKED ON THE SHORE, they felt as if they had been suddenly dipped into winter. The frost on their windows that morning had not been inconsequential, but a warning that summer had overstayed its welcome. Whatever the miners and the settlers of Sawgamet wanted to believe, the cold was coming. The temperature fell by the minute as my grandparents dressed in their light clothing. They launched the canoe, Flaireur sitting regally in the middle, like he was accustomed to being ferried along the waters of the Sawgamet. Jeannot dug his paddle in the water with a fierce urgency, but Martine turned to look back on the shoreline, and as she did, she thought she saw a flash of gold, the caribou's rack moving through the edge of the woods.

Even as the beach was still in sight behind them, the first few flakes of snow began to fall, fat and heavy in the air. Had Jeannot and Martine been dressed for the cold and closer to home, they would have delighted in the soft cleanliness of the falling snow. As they paddled, the wind picked up its pace, moving them faster but also whipping up the water and making them colder. Jeannot saw Martine's hands begin to blanch in the cold.

It was, my grandfather said when he told me this story, like canoeing through a dream. The wet snow hung heavily in the air, seeming almost suspended, and for Martine and Jeannot, it was like they were passing through curtain after curtain of whiteness, the snow opening in front of them and then closing behind them. Flaireur was quickly covered in snow, and as if he were a statue rather than a living dog, he remained still, letting the snow stick to him until he turned to marble. Jeannot and Martine's vigorous paddling kept the snow from accumulating on them as thickly, but the flakes were more water than ice, and with each stroke of their paddles it was like a bucket of water poured over them. Martine's teeth began to clatter from shivering.

The snow gathered in the bottom of the canoe, and Martine occasionally stopped paddling to clean out the boat as best she could. They paddled for more than an hour, and as Martine moved more and more slowly, Jeannot drove even harder. He had done little that required any real effort since they had married, but he felt the strength flowing back, as if what Martine lost came to him. He would not slacken, would not tire until he had returned her to safety. His paddle dug at the water and the canoe seemed to move so swiftly with the wind and the current that it barely touched the water. Distance that had been hard-fought in the morning passed quickly.

And then, Jeannot knew that all of his struggles had been in vain, that he need not paddle any longer. He and Martine were already dead. Angels floated around them.

The muffled light began to fall away into darkness and the wind settled. Jeannot stopped paddling, letting the canoe drift through the clouds and curtains of snow. Martine slumped into her seat, seemingly unaware of her own demise, but Jeannot looked out at the angels that had appeared beside the canoe. He had not expected to go to heaven, but as long as he was here, he thought he should show some reverence and marvel at the miracle before him.

Each angel they passed seemed like it was dancing methodically, reaching down and then up, pushing and pulling, or swinging its arms in gentle circles. He could see such a short distance ahead of him, and the current caused the canoe to pass each angel so swiftly, that Jeannot was unable to make out more than a little detail: the way the angels' robes seemed like they were made from snow, a lack of wings or halos, a preponderance of beards.

It was only when the voices came through his wind-touched ears that Jeannot realized he was not seeing angels, but rather miners in rubber boots standing in the river, panning for gold despite the onset of snow. They were nearly home.

He picked up his paddle and brought them around the bend and then up to the banks. He did not even bother pulling the canoe onto shore. Flaireur jumped out of the canoe, a splash and a happy bark, and then disappeared in the whiteness, while Jeannot simply stepped into the shallows, not noticing or caring about the icy water soaking through his boots. He picked up Martine and, cradling her in his arms, began to run for the house. Behind him, the canoe, lightened of its load, drifted away into obscurity.

Darkness had fully descended, and with the snow that still came hurrying through the trees, Jeannot had to trust the path and the sound of Flaireur barking up ahead. The trees were close and threatening, and Jeannot's feet felt heavy with cold fire. He stumbled a few times. He thought he caught the whiff of rotted meat, and despite the cold, he felt a prickling heat on the back of his neck, as if animals watched him from the dense underbrush. Martine was unbearably light in his arms, but still he labored up the slope from the river. He had begun to sweat from his exertion, but Martine was painfully cold against his body. Her lips moved, like she was talking, but he could hear nothing other than the sweep of the snow.

When he came into the clearing there was a sudden stillness, a break in the snow. The house stood before him, glowing so brightly that for a moment he thought it was on fire. In each of the windows that he and Martine had purchased so dearly and had shipped to Sawgamet, Rebecca had placed an oil lantern, and it appeared as though she had lit every candle in the house. On another day, perhaps, Jeannot would have stopped to take in the burning brilliance of the house like a beacon in the snow, like standing in the midst of salvation, but with Martine in his arms, Jeannot did not pause. He burst through the door and ran into the house, not even acknowledging Franklin, who sat beside Rebecca on the settee. He carried my grandmother up the stairs, stripped off her clothes, and then slipped naked into bed beneath the covers with her, his body a torch to reignite her.

I TRUST THAT YOU will forgive me if I digress for a moment. I should like to speak of many things—of the way my aunt Julia's first fiancé perished in the forests, his body found ravaged by animals, of Xiaobo, the Chinese servant who once worked for my grandparents and then my great-aunt, of my stepfather and his first wife, of the year that birds covered the ground in Sawgamet like snow—but for now, I'll follow my great-aunt for a moment.

Rebecca had seen Jeannot run though the parlor carrying my grandmother. She followed them into the room just in time to catch a spare glimpse of Jeannot's body as he slid into bed. She did not say anything to Franklin, but she thought of Jeannot's naked body pressed against Martine's as she prepared hot tea, stoked the fire, and helped to rub the blood back into Martine's hands and feet. Later that evening, after Martine stopped shivering and fell into a deep sleep, Rebecca watched Jeannot's soft breathing as he, too, slept, his arms wrapped around his wife, as if it were only his grip that kept her from floating away from him. Rebecca sat in a chair by the fireplace in the bedroom, occasionally stoking the fire or adding a piece of wood, and as she looked through the window at the fluttering whiteness, she wondered how much longer it would be before Franklin held her in the same way.

In the morning, Rebecca woke with her neck sore, slumped over in the rocking chair, the fire banked and still spreading warmth to the room. She heard her name floating softly toward her, "Rebecca, Rebecca, Rebecca," and with her eyes still closed, she said, "I'm here, Franklin."

"Rebecca." The voice was louder, insistent, and Rebecca sat up to see Jeannot, already washed and dressed, staring at her.

My grandfather told me that had he not been so concerned about his wife, he would have smiled at his servant. His servant. It is still difficult for me to think of my great-aunt in that fashion, to believe that she ever allowed any person to order her about. I wonder how long into her marriage it was before Franklin recognized the steel in his bride.

As Rebecca woke from her dream, Jeannot said that he recognized the tone of her voice, the half-dreaming warmth in the way she said his brother-in-law's name. He had seen the way that Franklin lingered over Rebecca, and the way that Rebecca tended to the dishes and cooked with a special care on the nights when Franklin joined them for dinner, but he had seen all of that without truly seeing it. He knew that for many people being in love meant seeing love everywhere, but for him, with my grandmother, the focus of his love was such that he could not conceive of any love or desire that was outside of his own, and it was only that moment that he realized Rebecca had fallen in love with Franklin.

"Something's wrong with Martine," he told Rebecca. "She's no longer cold, but she's complaining that she's tired and feels unwell. I'd like you to heat some broth for her."

THROUGH THE WINDOW in the kitchen, Rebecca marveled at the thick flakes of snow that kept falling. It had lightened some since the night before, but had not stopped. She could see across the meadow to where the trees wore the whiteness like a coat. The new mill stood starkly in the field of snow, piles of lumber beginning to be covered over, and Jeannot's old cabin had drifts pushed halfway up the walls already.

She fed a larger piece of wood to the burning kindling in the kitchen stove, and then startled at the sight of a man's face outside the window. The man did not pause, did not seem to see her, but shortly behind him followed another man, and then another.

She heated some biscuits on the stove and then brought the hot broth up to Jeannot and Martine on a tray. Martine sat up in bed, looking pale and trembling, and though Rebecca had her suspicions—the couple had been married for more than a month, after all—she said nothing as Jeannot sipped from his own cup.

"Winter has come," Jeannot said, glancing out the window. "Here to stay, I suppose."

"The miners are leaving," Rebecca said.

Jeannot turned to her and then put his cup of broth on the nightstand and crossed to the window. Rebecca stood beside him and together they watched another man follow the broken path of snow along the edge of the clearing. His mule, loaded down heavily, tromped behind him.

"Last winter the snow held off, but this isn't that sort of snow," Jeannot said. "They won't be able to work the river. Some of them will stay to set up pit mines or continue with what they have."

They turned at the sound of laughter from the bed. My grandmother took another sip from the broth and sat up straighter. Some color had returned to her cheeks. "If you knew anything about mining," she said, "you'd have been doing that instead of sawing boards."

My grandfather rolled his eyes so that Rebecca could see, but there was looseness in his face that showed he enjoyed his wife's teasing, relief that she felt well enough to do so. "True, but then, if I had known anything about mining I might never have stopped here." He stepped over to the bed and sat down on the edge, reaching over and touching Martine's hand. "Supplies are tight— you can ask Franklin about that." He glanced quickly at Rebecca with the mention of Franklin's name. "Men would rather winter indoors in Quesnellemouthe or further south. There isn't much to spend their gold on here, and what's the point of wrestling it from the earth if there is nothing to spend it on?"

"You may take this, please," Martine said to Rebecca, nodding at the tray and then squeezing Jeannot's hand. "And I have talked to Franklin about it. He said that gold has been coming with less ease from the ground, and sooner or later the men will leave for another rumor of gold somewhere else."

"They'll come back in the spring. And if not these men, then other men will come." Jeannot sighed. "As long as there is gold, men will come to take it."

Rebecca picked up the tray and then stopped in the doorway. "I've baking to start," she said. "Is there anything else you would like?"

Martine shook her head, and as if the motion sickened her, she whitened a little. Jeannot did not seem to notice, however, and there was a light upward tremble on his lips, a suppressed laugh, when he turned to Rebecca. "Sunday dinner. Franklin will be coming. Could you make some sort of a cake? We'll celebrate the fact that I managed to not quite kill his sister. I'm not sure what he likes particularly, but something."

"Rum cake," Rebecca said, and then she quickly spun away from the room.

OVER THE NEXT WEEK, it kept snowing. Occasionally the snow would seem to lighten, and the sky would clear enough that the few flakes that still fell seemed like they had been orphaned by some greater storm, but it soon became clear that each slackening was followed by a redoubled effort. Jeannot cleared snow between the woodpile and the house, and when he was not shoveling he split wood frenetically. Martine, for her part, mostly kept to bed, sleeping like she was one of the animals that had gone to ground for winter.

Rebecca found herself polishing silver and trying to think of excuses to walk down to the tents and cabins on the banks of the river, to Franklin's store. The miners continued to leave, at times an unbroken stream of men and mules passing by the house and smashing down a path through the snow.

After a full week, and after Franklin did not come for Sunday supper, Rebecca told my grandmother that they needed to purchase soap. Rebecca pulled on her woolen underwear, her stout boots and heavy coat, and with mittens and a shawl, she stepped carefully through the snow. Alone in the forest, she kept her skirt hiked above her knees, gathering the trailing fabric so that it did not drag behind her. Beside her, where fleeing miners had not trodden down the snow, it easily would have reached her waist. Even the thought of trying to break fresh trails made her tired. Still, she was cheerful at the excuse to visit Franklin's store. Though it was snowing lightly, it was not terribly cold, and she did not mind the air on her legs. She even began to sing a light tune.

The song fell away from her lips as she stepped out of the woods and saw the swath of beaten-down ground, the ripped and abandoned tents, the shambles that the departing miners had left behind. She had seen the men departing, but she was not prepared for this. Among the snow-packed streets that she could see from the hill, there were only a few dozen buildings of any substance; mostly, what lay before her was empty, flattened parcels of land where thousands of miners had packed their tents and departed only a few days or hours earlier.

The snow was falling slowly enough that it would have been idyllic if not for the desolation that the miners had left behind. Rebecca watched a few clusters of activity on the hill, men ferrying boards and scurrying to create structures that did not quite look like houses. She did not recognize the shaft mines that the men were trying to get started before the snow buried everything, and she instead turned her attention to the other center of activity: one of the few well-built structures in town, Franklin's store.

When she reached the building, she realized that the bustle was not a crowd, but rather a mob of thirty or forty men. They milled on the rutted street, Indians and white and black men and some so unkempt and dirty that it was impossible to tell which group they belonged with. A small group of Chinese stood off to the side, and there were even a few women—whores, by the look of them—mixed in with the mob.

So unassuming was the solitary figure on the porch of the building that it took Rebecca a moment to realize that the voices that were raised in anger were directed at him. Franklin stood with a hunch, like he was still behind a counter, and he had not taken off his shopkeeper's apron. His hands shook as he raised them, attempting to quiet the yelling.

While the shopkeeper's actions had no effect, the booming voice of Dryden Boon did.

"If you want to be alive to spend your gold at the end of the winter, Franklin," Boon yelled, the voices of the mob dropping away almost immediately, "you'll keep your prices where they were when this snow first started falling."

Boon was a large man, his head above most of the crowd. Rebecca felt a sudden tightness at the sight of him. He had tried to pay her before, mistaking her for one of the women who had come to Sawgamet to work in a brothel.

He was well dressed and loud. His black suit and fine hat, his kid-leather boots and his close-shaven cheeks and chin, showed that he was not one of the miners, but someone who fancied himself as more important. He took a few steps forward until he was standing on the bottom of the steps, yet even so, his head was almost even with Franklin's.

"You know me, Franklin, and I wouldn't begrudge you your profit, but there's only so far you can push us. Even the girls," he said, motioning to a pair of immodestly dressed women who stood near the front, "won't stand for it. They'll stab you in your black little heart during the night. And who knows what the Chinamen will do to you?" He turned toward the small huddle of Chinese men standing off to the side, bugged his eyes out, and wiggled his fingers. "Strange magic," he whispered loudly, and at that, a number of men started laughing.

Boon, who had walked up the two steps to stand next to Franklin, turned to face the crowd, though he pretended to address Franklin. "Now, fair is fair, Franklin. Four dollars a pound is already too much money for potatoes, but that's what you charged me last week. Today you want eight?"

"It's the snow," Franklin said. "I'm not sure when I'll next be able to get supplies brought in." He straightened up a little. "And if you don't like my prices, Boon, you don't have to shop at my store. You can bring your own goddamned supplies from Vancouver."

Boon slid his arm around the shopkeeper's neck like they were friends, and then he glanced to the side and saw Rebecca. He showed his teeth and then turned back to the shopkeeper. "Let me ask you, Franklin, if this fine lady over here," he said, now pointing to Rebecca, "needed to buy a length of rope, would you sell it to her?"

Franklin looked over at Rebecca, and as he locked eyes with her, she could see that something seemed to break. He slumped over a little more and his voice was quieter when he responded. "I'm not saying I wouldn't sell to you, Boon, but I'm not making you buy."

Rebecca watched as Boon tightened his arm, making Franklin cringe.

"So you'd sell me a length of rope, then? Because I'm going to be needing it to string you up."

"You'll not threaten anybody, Dryden," a loose-limbed man said as he pushed through the crowd, walked up the steps, and then stepped in front of Boon and the shopkeeper. That man—Pearl—had the same thickened French accent as Franklin's. Rebecca had seen him working at Jeannot's mill, though Pearl had said little to her.

I'd asked Pearl about this incident once, when I was twelve or thirteen, after Great-Aunt Rebecca had told me her version of the story, but Pearl had looked at me as if I'd claimed the ability to fly. Still, despite his insistence that he was not there, both Rebecca and Franklin named him as the man who stepped in.

"You'll get the hell out of here, and when you come back"—Pearl turned to my great-uncle—"Franklin will have decided that the prices he had last week are fair. Franklin?" Franklin nodded.

Boon smiled, and Rebecca thought he gave her a little glance. "Ah, Pearl, and just when I was thinking it might be best to kill him and have it done with anyway." He pulled his arm off of Franklin's neck, ruffled the man's hair, and said, "A misunderstanding, huh, Franklin?" Then he turned to face the crowd. "How about it? I'll stand you all to a drink."

They cheered, and most of them followed Boon down the

street, a few others—Pearl included, despite denying that he had been there—drifting off to their cabins or their mines. Rebecca stayed where she was. Slowly, hesitantly, Franklin looked up at her. He seemed sad, like some conversation had passed between them, but Rebecca did not understand what it had been. She took a step toward him, but he turned away and went into the store.

The snow was packed down on the street in front of the building. That was something good about the cold, Rebecca thought. Instead of rutted mud and precarious boardwalks, she could walk where she wanted without worrying about being sucked into the muck or dirtying her dress. The snow that fell from the sky balled tighter and seemed as if it turned to ice for a moment, pelting her face and stinging her, and she shook herself out of her daze, following Franklin into the store.

He did not look up when she entered, and she stood by the door, unsure what she should do.

"That wasn't something I wanted you to see," he said. His voice was quiet and trembled, but it startled Rebecca a little. She was, she realized, not expecting him to acknowledge his embarrassment.

"You didn't come to dinner on Sunday," she said by way of a reply.

"Would you still have me?"

"For dinner?" She pulled down her shawl and stepped closer to him. Still, he did not look up.

"Not for dinner," he said. "Would you still have me after seeing that?"

"I would have married you already," Rebecca said, "if

you'd but ask." She tried to keep her voice light and warm, as if it would be enough to cause his chin to float up, despite a stomach that felt ready to drop below her, but Franklin did not move. He kept his head down, like he expected a scolding. Franklin had been so proper with her, not taking advantage of her for so much as to hold her hand.

WHEN SHE TOLD ME this story, my great-aunt gave a terrific smile and said, "I decided it was time to risk seeming indelicate."

"Indelicate? Hadn't you just told him you'd marry him if he'd but ask? You don't consider that indelicate?"

"And are you the one telling this story?" she said, but I could tell that she enjoyed seeing me attentive, just as I am now tolerant of the questions my daughters ask of me when I repeat these same stories for them.

Franklin would not look up at her, so Rebecca stepped behind the counter where Franklin was seated and gently touched her hand to his cheek. And then leaned down and kissed him.

As my great-aunt was telling me this—with Virginia sitting beside me and knitting a scarf—my great-uncle came into the parlor and sat beside her.

"And then what happened?" he said, taking her hand.

"And then we were married," Rebecca said. "And then we were buried."

SEVEN

Qallupilluit

I HAD GROWN UP USED to the idea that the float was a time for waiting: waiting for the men to return to the village from Havershand, for my father to bring Marie and me presents, for a last flush of celebration before the winter. But the year I was eleven, the float did not occasion much change in our daily life. I'm sure the men did not return from Havershand any quicker that year, but without having my sister there to ask me daily when our father would return, it felt like it.

When the men came back from the float, the new priest who had come to replace Father Hugo accompanied them. He was young, and handsome, and charming, still carrying a thick accent from the Ireland he'd left only a few years earlier, and I overheard Mrs. Gasseur laughingly tell my mother that some of the women were complaining that the Catholic priest was not allowed to have a wife like the Anglican priest. By this time I had grown used to living in my stepfather's house, the difference in Sunday services between his church and our old one. Likewise, Jeannot's presence in Sawgamet had become familiar, comforting, even with his vain pursuits in the woods.

Life did what life does, and progressed, and I found myself thinking less and less often of my father and my sister. And then came the freeze-up.

The river froze quick and flat and calm, and it was not long before afternoons and Sundays meant skating and hockey as long as there was light. That year, parents were careful to tell their children to stay away from the tip of the channel.

MID-NOVEMBER, MY MOTHER and I walked back to the house after Sunday service, her hand resting lightly on my shoulder. We stopped for a moment and looked out at the children and parents already spilling onto the ice.

"Go on, then," she said to me.

"What?"

"If you want to skate, to go down to the river, you may. I know you'd like to go be with your friends."

One of the children—from where I stood, I could not tell who it was—a girl, perhaps seven or eight, wobbled away from the snowbanks and out onto the ice. She caught up with another girl, and the pair linked arms. The two girls skated forward until one of them fell to the ice, pulling the other atop of her. Their shrieking laughter carried to me.

My mother's hand left my shoulder. "I'll put your skates out for you."

Her footsteps on the snow sounded like sugar crunching, and the two girls on the ice climbed gingerly to their feet. I turned and looked at my mother. She moved lightly across the packed snow in the direction of our house. For the first time I realized that though I thought of my mother as old—and now looking back, already ten years older than my mother was at the time, I shudder to think of how ancient I must appear to my own children—she was still young enough to be a mother again. I knew that my stepfather had been married once, but until that moment I had not thought of the idea of my mother and Father Earl having children of their own. As I watched my mother's back moving away from me, it took me a moment to realize that I was on the verge of crying

I suddenly, desperately, did not want to be alone, but neither could I face the thought of returning to the house, of looking at the skates that my mother was sure to put out on my bed.

I headed back toward my stepfather's church, passing a family headed down to the river with their skates and sticks. When I neared the church I saw my stepfather talking with a few last parishioners, and I ducked behind the old cabin that he lived in when he first came to Sawgamet. The small building's roof had fallen in years ago, and a sapling was twisting its way through where a window had once stood. I could not imagine my mother and me living with Father Earl in such a small house, even if it had stood whole. The house we were in by the village was not luxurious—nothing like the one that Uncle Franklin had built for himself—but it was large enough for me to have my own room, for a study, and even spare bedrooms should my mother and Father Earl start a new family.

After a few minutes I heard footsteps and the familiar voice of my stepfather pass by and then disappear. I hurried across the tramped-down path, past the large rock, the church, and then a little further into the woods until I came to Virginia's house.

To those who came across Julia and Lawrence's house unexpecting, it must have seemed like a mirage. There was a small cabin that had been Uncle Lawrence's before he married Julia, and then, on the other side of the clearing, the stone-built, three-story house that Uncle Franklin had lavished his attention on as a wedding gift for his daughter. The house was elegant and strong, and would not have been out of place on the grand streets of Vancouver. It was much larger than Julia and Lawrence could use with only one child, and there were several rooms that nobody ever seemed to go into. Virginia and I had often played hide-and-go-seek with Marie in the house, though my sister had refused to hide by herself after the time when we forgot to look for her and she accidently locked herself inside a chest in a forgotten room.

I stood on the front porch and hesitated. I had left the river thinking that I could not go home but could not stand to be alone, but the idea of spending time with my cousin was more than I wanted. She was always so cheerful, so full of energy, but what I needed at that moment was someone who would allow me to be alone within their companionship.

I was thinking this—or the simulacrum of this that an eleven-year-old boy thinks—when Uncle Lawrence opened the door.

He did not seem surprised to see me standing there, though I cannot say that I ever saw him look particularly surprised.

"Virginia's out with Aunt Julia." He took a bite of his apple. "Skating." He looked directly at me when he said it, without shame or avoidance. "Want to help me feed the dogs?" He motioned to his old cabin and the kennels that lay behind them.

"No, thank you." I glanced at the kennels and then realized that the dogs were silent. "How come they didn't bark when I came up?"

"I told them not to." He stepped fully out onto the porch and shut the door.

"You knew I was coming?"

"A little bird told me," he said. "I was thinking of taking the dogs out for a run after I feed them. If you want to join me, you're welcome." He stared at me until I looked down. "Unless you just need to get off into the woods by yourself for a while."

Uncle Lawrence had invited me to ride the trapline with him before, but I had always turned him down. There was something about the fierce sharpness of Lawrence's toothed traps that unsettled me, the careful way that my uncle worked through the bloody piles of pelts. I liked the dogs, though, and on another day I would have agreed to help him feed them. Some men's teams were furious and unruly, but Lawrence had a true hand with his "boys," as he called them, even though the lead dog was a bitch.

"Would you like to borrow a fishing pole? You can still find some open water if you pick a stream that gets good sun. Maybe you'll be able to bring something home to your mother. It's inside the old cabin," he said, pointing across the clearing. He swung his hand against the side of my arm and then walked off the porch.

He pushed open the door of the cabin for me and then walked around the side of the building to the kennels, leaving me alone to enter the house that he had lived in before he married my aunt Julia and my great-uncle Franklin had insisted on building him, as Lawrence called it, a castle in the woods.

As I stepped inside I was struck by how neatly he kept it. Lawrence had built the cabin himself, and though it was quite small, the joints were so tight that I could not imagine the wind leaking through. Even the floor was neat; Lawrence had washed gravel and hauled it up from the banks, covering the floor with the fine rocks. He had told me before that he had always planned on putting down planks, but then he had married Aunt Julia and Franklin had insisted that there was nothing to it but to build a house that was fit for his daughter.

The cabin had a slightly musty smell, but still looked ready to live in, as if Lawrence expected guests at any time. The inside was an odd mixture of practicality and unexpected warmth. Brutal, jawed traps hung from pegs, organized by size and looking well oiled, while there was a fussily crafted wardrobe tucked into the corner. The arched doors matched perfectly in the middle, and Lawrence had fashioned a latch out of a stone from the river's edge and carved a wolf in the wood. Two bunks were set against the wall, one above the other, and the small tabletop was a sawed-off round, sanded and polished so that even in the light wafting through the windows, the unlit lantern on its top seemed to have a twin. The two chairs tucked into the table were indistinguishable from each other. I wondered how Lawrence had bent the wood backs so well. Our house was filled with furniture my stepfather had purchased, but this furniture was something different, something that seemed to draw all of the light. That might have been why the last thing I noticed was the pelt hanging from the wall by the door, almost against my elbow. I had never noticed it before, and I touched it warily, like it might still be alive. The fur was incredibly soft, colored gray with two fierce streaks of sunset parading down the length. It was as long as my arm and half again as wide.

I heard footsteps outside and then Uncle Lawrence came in through the door. He looked at me touching the fur, and I said, "What's this from?"

Lawrence pulled the fishing rod from a slot on the wall. "Don't know. Came up in one of the traps last year. Spit and fought and tried to bite me. Couldn't get near the thing. Had to shoot it four times to get the thing to die. Never seen anything like it."

"The woods," I said.

"The woods," Lawrence agreed. He handed the pole to me. "Here. Made the pole myself. Spent a few hours shaping and whittling it. You've got to get it when it's green and know which ones have enough give. It's a fine pole. You won't find grubs in this weather, but I've got some stale bread I can give you, something for the hook. Not sure you'll catch much anyway, least not unless I take you to my secret spot. But if you do catch something, be sure to let your mother know who lent you the rod."

I waited outside of the big house for a moment while Lawrence went in for the bread. When he came back out he handed me a tied handkerchief filled tight.

"Seems like a lot of bread," I said.

"Well, I might have slipped some cookies in there," he said, and gave me a wink that was so large and obvious and slow that I couldn't help laughing. "But there ought to be enough bread in there to see you through anyway. And you'll tell if you catch a fish with a chunk of gold in its belly."

I went away grinning.

THE WOODS THEMSELVES were quiet except for the crunching of my boots in the snow. The birds and squirrels had taken flight at the sound of me, unusual enough that I wondered if there was something else that had passed through the trees recently, a wolf or some other predator. I stayed on the well-worn trail that passed by the abandoned mines and led to the small cluster of cabins where the Chinese lived. Past that I cut my own path through the snow along the banks of the river for fifteen or twenty minutes. I stopped for a minute to catch my breath, and when I did, I heard the voice.

It was a woman's voice, high and floating, and though I could not make out the words, it seemed to be calling to me. I listened for a moment, and then, though I could not have said why, I was suddenly sure that it was my sister, that Marie was calling for me. I started to run, pushing branches out of my way and stumbling across the uneven ground, heading toward the sound of the river and my sister's voice. The voice came louder, growing as I approached the water, but when I burst from the trees into clear view of the Sawgamet, the voice was gone. The sun shone down heavily, the river called, and the whistle of birds returned around me, but I no longer heard Marie's voice.

I stood on the bank, holding the rod and catching my breath, looking out across the partly frozen river, waiting to hear her voice again. For a second, I thought I heard it, but then I realized that it was the sound of the water splashing and running against the ice and the rocks and its own flow, and I began to laugh at myself, at my grandfather, and at the idea that my sister, that anyone dead, would be out in the woods, calling me down to the river.

I had intended to walk a little further, but where I stood would serve for fishing. The river strangled in and ran quickly here, and the fast-flowing water was still only partly frozen despite it already being mid-November, the water burbling and bouncing white. Though I knew better, I put my foot down tentatively on the edge, banging my heel against the hollow-sounding ice, and then eased my weight onto it. I shuffled out a few feet toward a small hollow where the water ran slower in the midst of its fury; the ice cut away into what looked to be a deep, gathering pool of water. The sun angled enough to keep my shadow from hitting the water, and I thought I saw the glistening movement of fish beneath the surface. With the winter coming and the drop of temperature, it would only be another week or so before it was all ice, even the rushing violence of the water in the middle. Past that, far enough into the winter, and I would be fishing again out on the river, huddling on stools over cut holes in the ice with Pearl and my grandfather, hoping to liven up the winter menu of canned and salted meats with something fresh-caught.

The ice creaked a little underfoot, sending the breath out of my body, but it held. I thought of turning to shore—I knew I was being foolish—but I was already firmly situated. I might as well have a few fish to show for my stupidity, I thought.

It did not take long for me to feel a tug on the rod, and the fish that I pulled from the water gleamed in the winter light. It took a few flops on the ice before I smashed in its head with the butt of my knife. Lawrence's joke made me think of gutting it to check for a gold nugget, but I cast the line back in instead. Two more fish came out in quick succession, easy targets for the stale bread and lined hook my uncle had given me. The fish were of size enough that I thought one more would see me well returned home this afternoon. My stepfather would take the fish with no word, but with the little smile he gave me every time he was happy with something I did. He never seemed to know what to say to me, how to tell me he was proud of something, but I could feel it.

A burst of steam came from the surface of the water where I had been fishing, and I watched it carry over the water a ways, and then I dropped the hook back in the river, trying to lay it near the rock where the water slowed a little. Almost immediately the line tugged again and I lifted the fish from the water, watching its scales flash in the sun and letting it hang above the river for a few seconds, enjoying the weight of my catch. When I tipped the rod down and lowered the fish to the ice beside me, it pushed its tail heavily, bouncing and trying to flip itself to the water. The tail sent a loud knocking sound that made the ice creak and reverberated through my boots, making me once again question my decision to stray out onto the ice.

When I reached for the fish I gagged at the stench. I could smell rotten meat and disease, as if the fish had been dead for a day already in the heat of August. As I knelt down and tried to grab the wiggling fish, fighting against my urge to be sick, I heard the ice creak again.

I looked up to see the creature—I could not tell if it was a man or a woman—standing above me, its scaly skin fish-pale and bumped, mottled like it had been submerged under the water for a very long time. It had a large pouch on its back and stringy hair, and despite its milk-white eyes, the creature stared directly at me.

The creature took a step toward me with unmistakable menace; it grabbed my wrist and dove into the water, pulling me after it.

It was like being pulled into the air. Despite the ice and the current, I felt no colder than I had a moment before, perched on the frozen shelf above the river. The creature's hand stayed tight upon my wrist, dragging me down beneath the water, and I was so surprised at not feeling wet that I almost forgot to panic. And then I tried to take a breath.

It felt like someone's hand was clamped firmly over my mouth. Eyes wide, I could see bubbles of air escaping through my nose, and I started to feel a mounting pressure in my chest. I tried to pull its hand away, but the creature did not let go. Though I remained dry, I could feel water coming down my throat, choking me, filling me with liquid instead of the air I craved.

I kicked and pushed but the creature seemed undisturbed. And then I stopped fighting. I realized that I did not want to fight. I realized that if I let this creature keep its hold on me, if I let it pull me under the shelf of ice and drown me, I would be able to join my father and Marie. And I wondered if this was what it felt like for my sister, this combination of weightlessness and burning, as if I were in heaven but had to breathe the sulfurous air of hell.

And then I heard a voice, one that was familiar even though I had never heard it before, and I saw a woman floating in the river in front of me. She was older than me, but I recognized something of myself in her. She smiled at me in a way that made me fear that she would cry if she were not already under the water. She reached her hand out to me but was too far away to touch my hand. Then she turned to look at the creature holding me.

"It's too much," she said. Her voice flooded me, familiar and filled with light. "It's too soon for this, too soon," she said. Her words expelled the water and filled me with a sudden burst of air. This was what it felt like to be held by my mother, to be rocked to sleep, to be comforted and loved, I thought. For a moment it was as if I were above the river again, but then I saw a second creature beside the first, felt another hand grasp my ankle, and then a third creature appeared from the dark of the water, moving closer.

"You've taken enough," the woman said. "Please."

I looked toward the floating woman and tried desperately to touch her, knowing that if I could only grasp her hand I would be freed. But she looked back at me with terribly sad eyes and drifted backward into an inky darkness, the current taking her away. As she disappeared, I felt the rough grip of the creatures' hands on my ankle, my wrist. My eyes bulged and I looked at the creatures, thinking of my father and Marie, thinking of my mother, warm and dry and waiting for me at my stepfather's house, sewing or chopping vegetables, my skates neatly put out on my bed. The creatures looked back at me, and though the crushing weight and burning in my lungs and my throat started to turn everything black, I thought, just for a moment, that I could see something that had once been human in these creatures, a look akin to pity.

And then my head smashed against the ice and I felt the blooming taste of blood and bone. I gasped in the cold air, the sudden relief of being on the surface. For a moment I thought I felt a gentle touch upon my head, the way my mother used to stroke my hair when I was taken with fever, but then the feeling disappeared and I felt the ache of my forehead. I touched my head expecting to see blood, but my fingers came away clean. Beside me, the three dead fish lay neatly arranged, while the fourth fish—the one I had just caught—still danced and knocked against the ice. There was no smell of rotted meat, and my clothing was dry. I must have slipped, I thought, smashed my head into the ice, dreamed a moment of the sea witches bringing me down. I had listened too often to my grandfather and his stories of the woods.

Wincing at the pain in my head, I quieted the fish with the handle of my knife, slipped it from the hook, and then strung all four fish together. As I stepped off the ice and onto the snow-covered gravel, the shelf of ice gave a last, loud creak and then collapsed into the water, a jumble of chunks and sheets. Too late, I realized that I had left Lawrence's fishing pole sitting on the ice. It was gone now.

I had not even turned when I heard my grandfather calling to me. Jeannot came running across the open bank, stumbling a little over the uneven ground. He ran close enough to grab my arm above the elbow, and though my grandfather was breathing hard, like he had run a far way, he gasped, "Away from the river. She told me to take you away from the river."

I nodded and let my grandfather drag me up into the woods until we came across the path that I had cut barely an hour earlier. Jeannot moved quickly, and once or twice I stumbled following, but Jeannot did not relax his grip on my arm until we were already walking back toward the village.

We walked in silence until we were past the abandoned mines, and then I spoke quietly, afraid my grandfather would hear the quaver in my voice.

"It was her, wasn't it? Marie, grown to be a woman," I said, though I already knew that it must not have been.

"Your sister?" My grandfather glanced at me but he did not stop walking. "No," he said, and he gave a moment of pause when he heard me sob. We stood there until I had quieted myself, and then he put both hands on my shoulders while I stared at him.

"I've already said I can't bring your father or your sister back, Stephen. It was your grandmother. She came to warn me. To tell me to get you away from the river, that the qallupil- luit had called you to them."

"Why didn't they take me?"

He kicked at the snow and then started walking toward the village again, a little slower this time, secure in the knowl- edge that he had taken me back from the river.

"There's not an answer for everything, Stephen. I don't know why they didn't take you, just like I don't know what I need to do to get your grandmother to return to me." He stopped again suddenly, and then he rubbed at his eyes. "Didn't know, I should say. I think I know now."

"What did she tell you?"

My grandfather did not look at me, but he answered immediately. "She said it was darker than she had expected. She asked me to bring her some light."

Thirty Feet of Snow

THE ARE SOME THINGS I have to take on faith. A funny thing for an Anglican priest to say, isn't it? My whole life is, in some ways, about faith. And I do have faith in these stories about the history of my family. I would not be back here if Father Earl had not asked me to return, but I have faith that there is a greater reason why I am back here in Sawgamet, raising my daughters in a place that has taken so much from my family and me: I have faith that there is something that I can reclaim. And I do still have faith in the Church, even if it is sometimes shaken; unlike my grandfather, every test seems to reaffirm my faith.

That winter, the winter that Great-Aunt Rebecca and Great-Uncle Franklin were married and then buried under the snow, might have been the last time that my grandfather had faith in a kind and merciful God. It had already been snowing for a week by the time Rebecca walked down to the store and kissed Franklin, and then another week of accumulated snow—some light, some heavy, but no stopping it—before Rebecca and Franklin were married at Jeannot and Martine's house.

Two weeks of snow, and by the day of Franklin and Rebecca's wedding, Xiaobo—the Chinese miner who peddled in herbs and later worked as Franklin and Rebecca's servant—had come and gone from Jeannot and Martine's house, informing the couple of what they already suspected: Martine was pregnant. Facing the loss of Rebecca's services, Jeannot contracted with Xiaobo to come on as their servant the day after the wedding, but by the state of the small man at Franklin and Rebecca's wedding—the last Jeannot had seen of the Chinese man, he had been standing on the piano and singing along to Pearl's playing—Jeannot did not expect Xiaobo to arrive at the house ready to move in and begin cleaning anytime soon.

The morning after the wedding, when my grandfather came downstairs, he stopped for a moment to pick up three half-full glasses on the landing, thinking he would straighten a little. Any thoughts of cleaning were dashed when he came completely downstairs: the dining room table was still littered with empty plates and champagne bottles, and that was not the half of it.

He left the mess on the table for Xiaobo—sooner or later the Chinese man would come back to the house ready to start in his role as hired man—and stepped into the parlor, which was as much of a disaster as the dining room. It looked like the winds had blown through the house unabated.

At the thought, my grandfather looked through the window and was startled to see a solid wall of white. For a moment he believed the snow had accumulated a half dozen feet in the night, completely covering the glass, but then he saw the subtle shifting and movement of snowfall. A blizzard. Though the snow was already waist-deep on the ground, the night before it had begun to slow. There had only been a few flakes falling down as Franklin and Rebecca had bidden everybody a good night—among lots of cheering from the guests—and the moon had shone full and brightly above. Jeannot remembered thinking that the snow was ready to stop. Clearly he had been wrong.

Jeannot pulled on his boots and jacket and stepped out to the porch. The roof sheltered him, and there was only a small drift of snow skittering on the planks, but the snow had piled nearly level with them. If the snow had been solid ground there would have been no need for steps. He could see nothing past the edge of the porch.

It was like somebody had drawn a curtain. Even a few days earlier he would have used the word blizzard, but a blizzard was wind and snow until the sky was emptied and the sun came to blast everything with the kind of light that burned his eyes; a blizzard stops at some point. This was not stopping, though. It had been near two weeks of snow, and every time the snow teased as if it were going to stop, it came again, and this time it was even harder.

Jeannot looked at the small pile of wood that was still left on the porch, and then stepped back inside. He took a spool of ribbon from Martine's sewing box, tied one end to the porch railing, and then stepped out into the whiteness.

As soon as he left the shelter of the porch, he was enveloped. The wind blew through him, sending snow down his collar and biting his face. He closed his eyes against the snow and trudged forward. He took a half dozen steps and then had to rest. He was actually warmer from his waist down; the snow insulated him from the wind. He took another five or six steps, unspooling the ribbon behind him, and then stopped to rest again. He did not bother to look back toward the house. He knew he would not be able to see it.

He did not even see the woodpile until it was within reach of his hand. He reached out to touch the ax. It hung from a peg under the eaves on the side of the cabin. The woodpile had seemed so close and convenient against the side of his old cabin, but with the deep snow and the wind, Jeannot realized he would have to keep a path cleared. His legs already burned from the few steps he had taken. He thought about going inside the cabin for a few minutes to gain respite from the wind, but instead piled a few logs in one arm, keeping a tight hold of the ribbon with his other hand.

Even with the blasting snow, after walking back and forth, his tracks remained clear, and he took a shovel to clean out a path from the porch to the woodpile. It was hard work. The first layers of snow had come down heavy and wet, and he had to cut a wider path than he wanted so that the snow did not simply fill in behind him.

As soon as he put down the shovel, the blizzard began to erase his work, but that did not bother him. He carried load after load of firewood onto the porch, filling it with enough to last several weeks. He decided to bring some more inside, to make a pile in the kitchen so that Martine did not need to venture outside if she did not want to. Jeannot did not like the idea of his pregnant wife outside in this swirling whiteness.

He was about to turn and head inside, thinking that by now Martine would be up and have some tea ready, when he heard a snapping sound. At first he thought it was a branch breaking, but it was too close for that. The snow gusted and turned around him, the roof of the porch seemingly offering no shelter, and he realized that he could see nothing past his outstretched arm. The sound came to him again, a sharp crack that carried over the wind. He could not tell where the sound came from.

The wind pitched high and brittle, and the crack repeated, making my grandfather startle. Despite the cold, sweat trickled down the small of his back. He tried to peer into the impenetrable snow, afraid of what he might see, but even more afraid of what he could not see. One of the Indians had warned him of adlets, they way they would come to drink his blood with their pups, and of noise ghosts, shrieking until they drove men crazy enough to come out into the cold so that they could crack their bones and eat their hearts. In the swirling motion of white, he thought he saw a face, and he leaped backward.

Again, the cracking sound ripped near him, but this time he saw the colored fluttering, and he realized that it was Martine's ribbon snapping in the wind. He felt himself flush and was glad that he was alone on the porch. There was nothing out there. Nothing to be afraid of. He needed to remember that not everything was momentous, that sometimes the wind was just the wind.

INSIDE THE HOUSE, Jeannot discovered that Martine had risen and toasted some bread on the stove. She sat at the dining room table, spread a little jam on a piece of toast, and then slipped it to Flaireur, who sat at her feet. Martine stood up and poured tea into a cup for Jeannot. "We'll be housebound for a day or two, until the snow blows itself out?" she asked. Jeannot nodded. Martine sighed and put the teapot down. "At least we've plenty of food, though Xiaobo doesn't seem to have the same sense of an early start that we do."

Jeannot grinned and gave her a kiss. "I'm sure he'll turn up when the snow lets up and he's had a chance to let sleep erase some of the champagne. He's a little man for as much as he drank." He wife pushed him gently away and he looked up toward the kitchen.

"Smells like you left the toast on the stove," Jeannot said, but as the words left his mouth he realized that the acrid smell was something deeper than burning bread.

When my grandfather told me this story, he had to stop for a minute and collect himself. We were sitting at my stepfather's table over breakfast. I don't remember where my mother was, but I know that Father Earl was already up at the church, preparing for a funeral for somebody who had been taken by pneumonia. My grandfather paused and then got up to pour himself more coffee. I remember thinking how unusual it was that he could not go on. My grandfather told me the stories, but did not editorialize upon them as I am now. I suppose the very act of telling the story was enough for him to help make sense of things. He did not have the same need to turn things over and over again as I evidently do.

As he poured himself coffee, he said, very quietly, "That was the end of things. Do you understand how something so small can be the end of things? It could have just as easily been a candle left unattended, a dropped lantern, it could have been a bird's nest in the chimney."

In our house now, we have a new electric stove, a convenience that my stepfather had installed for my mother only last year. My wife is pleased to have use of the electric stove, and I am pleased that she is pleased. My wife had grown used to an electric stove in Vancouver, and if there is one thing that I have learned in my years of marriage it is that an unhappy cook makes for an unhappy family. Still, I do miss the familiar bulk and warmth of the woodstove, and I wonder what became of the great iron beast that used to lurk in my stepfather's kitchen.

As he spoke, I remember that my grandfather reached out to the stove and touched the stovepipe for an instant before cursing and dropping his hand.

"Stupid," he said. "I know better than that." He sighed, shook his hand, and sat back down at the table. "I don't know if it was embers caught in the pipe or if the flu had been knocked loose during the party, if there was a gap between the metal flu and the planked wood of the ceiling," he said. "But the result was the same. One misplaced spark was all it took."

My grandparents crowded into the doorway of the kitchen. No flames were visible, but a thick, rolling smoke seeped from the ceiling. My grandfather pushed rudely backward, bumping against my pregnant grandmother, and rushed through the front door.

Martine grabbed a bucket of water from the counter and ran up the staircase. She looked into their bedroom, but aside from rumpled blankets, it was calm. She opened the door to the other bedroom with some trepidation, but the doorknob was cool in her hand, and had she not been looking for it she would not have seen the snaking wisp of smoke that curled from the floorboards near the wall. She took a step forward, holding the bucket with two hands, unsure of where she should throw it. The floor creaked beneath her feet and she stopped moving, listening now. Under the sound of the snow pelting the windows and the wind moving outside, she heard something rolling and crackling.

"Martine!" My grandmother nearly dropped the bucket at Jeannot's voice. She had not heard his heavy boots on the stairs. He stepped past her and pushed her back toward the door. He had still unmelted snow in his hair, and he was holding the ax. Jeannot swung the ax over his shoulder and then smashed it into the floor near where the smoke crept into the air.

He unleashed a fury. Flames shot like a magic trick and Jeannot stumbled back, beating his free hand at his face like he himself was on fire. "It's between the floors," he yelled. "More water," he said. Martine hesitated, but Jeannot handed her the ax, grabbed the bucket, and emptied it onto the flames. The water turned to billowing smoke but seemed to have almost no effect on the flames.

"More water," Jeannot said again.

"The water barrel's empty from the last night," she said.

"Snow, then." He stepped around the burning hole in the floor and then pushed the window open. He reached out onto the roof of the side porch with the bucket and started scooping snow in furiously. The snow made the fire hiss and smoke, but it was almost like he had been shoveling sawdust: the flames grew.

My grandfather climbed out onto the roof so that he would be able to scoop the snow more quickly, but it was clear to my grandmother that the snow would not do enough. She ran downstairs and headed into the kitchen, thinking she could at least drag out some of the stored food. Thick dark smoke hung in the doorway of the kitchen. She held her breath and then started inside. She had taken only a step or two before she felt the heat against her face and she retreated, Flaireur following her. She ran back up the stairs. The smoke was thicker, nightmarishly solid in places, and through the door of the bedroom the flames and the smoke made it difficult to see to where Jeannot still shoveled snow through the window.

"Get out," he called to her. "Get to safety."

Flaireur followed her outside, where Martine shrugged herself into the coat she had grabbed as she ran through the house. She looked up, and though the snow beat at her, she could see traces of Jeannot still working with the bucket. Martine screamed to him, calling his name several times until he stopped and looked down at her. He stared at her, and Martine thought he was going to turn back to the fire, but then she heard the shriek and breaking of wood. He stumbled a little, and then jumped off the roof of the side porch.

He landed awkwardly in a billow of snow that would have, at a different time, made Martine laugh. He rose and waded through the snow to her. When he broke through to the path, he stepped gingerly, limping a little.

"My ankle. It's fine," he said, though she had not asked. "You've still got the ax."

Martine glanced down at her hand, surprised to see the ax still in it. She handed it to Jeannot. "I couldn't get into the kitchen."

The two of them looked up at the sound of breaking glass. Through the blowing whiteness, the flames looked like some sort of illusion, and Martine tried hard to believe that they were not real. Soon enough they could feel the heat beating at them, however, and there was no denying the fire. Occasionally the wind would let up long enough for the house to appear before them in all of its burning glory, the snow melting as it touched the flames.

Martine was not sure how long they had been staring up at the burning house when Jeannot turned to her and said, "Xiaobo will be in for quite a surprise when he comes to start work."

Martine could not help herself. She laughed. "That's what you have to say?"

"There's not much else to do, is there? If it was summer I'd be trying to rouse the town for a bucket line, but even if we had the men here right now, there's not water available to us." My grandfather turned and looked through the snow to where the creek would be if it was not already frozen and covered with snow. "We've still got the sawmill and we still have the cabin," he said. "I've got my old worn-down jacket and some clothes still in there."

The sound of burning pitched up a little, and then, with a loud cracking sound, the second story of the house sank in a series of staggering drops, disappearing as if it were sucked into the earth. A cloud of smoke shot up. A mesh of flame drifted up and into the air. Martine recognized it as a piece of lace. The lace burned and swirled up through the falling snow, looking for a moment like it was dancing, and then the flames went out and the lace dropped to the ground; blackened gauze.

A gunshot came from inside the burning house, and then another.

"My rifle," Jeannot said.

Martine turned to head toward the cabin, but Jeannot stopped her and pointed to the flat roof, already burdened with snow. "The mill's better," my grandfather said. "We won't have to worry about the roof collapsing."

"Then let's get out of the snow," my grandmother said, her voice straining over the wind.

Jeannot set himself in motion past the cabin toward the barely visible wall of the sawmill. By the time they made it, they were wet and exhausted and glad to be inside, even though the mill did not offer much shelter. The roof, at least, was solid and slanted enough that Jeannot thought it would shed some of the snow. The cabin, he knew, hastily constructed and ignored since he had built the house, would come down from the weight of the snow soon enough. The mill was built to last, though not necessarily to protect more than the saw blades and the wooden wheels: the walls were made with poorly fitted rough-cut lumber, and in many places my grandmother would have been able to stick her fingers through the gaps if she had wanted. They would be safe, if not exactly comfortable.

A BLIZZARD IN A CITY is a different thing altogether. When I lived in Vancouver we only had one true blizzard—even with the closeness of the streets and alleys, we still could not see from our parlor window to the house across the street— and it was something of a holiday. This was when we only had our first daughter, before she'd turned a year, and the temperature had dropped enough that instead of the wet, aching snow I never became used to, we were covered over in the sort of lightness that I remembered from Sawgamet. The winds threw the snow around and brought drifts against the edges of my church and other buildings, piled around newsstands and in the alleys. I call it a blizzard, but it wasn't much of anything compared to the snow I remembered from my childhood in Sawgamet. Still, it was enough to make Vancouver come to a standstill for half of a day, enough to cover over the dirt and the gutters.

A few days ago, my mother told me that the winters have changed in Sawgamet since I was a child. She said that the snows and the cold had not been the same since I'd left, as if the woods had decided to give mercy to Sawgamet with the last of my grandfather's blood gone. I laughed and told her that I'd finally become old enough to realize that I'd be telling my own daughters that the winters had gotten easier, and they'd tell the same thing to their daughters. "A parent's childhood is always harder," I said.

My mother smiled and started to laugh, but it turned into a retching cough that seemed to tear at her, her entire body shaking in the bed. When she finally stopped coughing there were tears on her cheeks from the pain, and she shook her head. "There was the long winter of your grandfather, and then the cold winter of your sister and father. Everything else has been a mercy." She reached over and touched my hand. "I'm glad you've come back, Stephen. Glad to see you here with your wife, the girls. This is where you belong." Then she closed her eyes and presently I could hear her breath turn into the evenness of sleep.

Tonight, now that it's too late for me to tell her that I, too, am glad that I have come home, I also wish I had told her that she was right about the winters. The winters in Sawgamet have become something that people joke about, something that breaks the spring and fall, rather than something to be endured, to be survived.

I've heard that the men in the cuts work through the winters now. It's not just that the need for the wood is greater with the war, or that they have trucks and portable kerosene heaters, or that they can do some of their work from inside the cabins of their machines. The winters themselves have become lighter, less treacherous. When my grandfather first came to Sawgamet, when my father worked the cuts, men didn't take to the woods because they couldn't. Some men ran traplines, but even that was a different task than standing in the cuts, swinging an ax into the iron freeze of the trees. And that's what I was born into, those sort of winters. It was only when I left Sawgamet that I learned that in other places men floated the logs in the spring to take advantage of the melts, that the winter didn't have to be something to be afraid of.

I'm not scared of the winter now, though. Despite the fact that I expect my mother to die tonight, in concert with the winter's first snows, it's different somehow. I'm no longer afraid of what comes with winter. Or of what is waiting in the woods.

MY GRANDFATHER HAD just lit a fire in the mill's small stove when Flaireur started barking. The dog crouched down in front of the door of the mill and began to growl, the hackles of his fur on end, his teeth bared and a trail of spittle leaking to the floor. Jeannot stepped toward Flaireur to calm the dog, but then the door of the mill swung open. The wind gusted hard enough to make the flames in the stove flare up, and snow pushed across the floor. My grandmother started to stand, but my grandfather stopped her.

"Wait," he said, and then he picked up the ax and stepped to the door. Flaireur stayed behind my grandfather, his growl turned low and constant, stone rubbed on stone. My grandfather peered out into the whiteness, the snow attacking and biting his face, the wind cutting through his clothing. There was nothing, he thought, but as he reached for the door, suddenly the man stood before him.

My grandfather told me that he was so startled—"I had just decided it was the wind, nothing more, no witch from the woods, nothing to be afraid of"—that he almost swung the ax. My grandmother screamed. Flaireur's growl grew stronger.

Then the man moved forward, out of the snow and the wind, coming from nowhere and stepping into the shelter of the mill. And once he was inside the mill, once he separated himself from the vast emptiness outside and entered the building, the man no longer seemed like something my grandfather should be scared of, and even Flaireur—who still seemed wary—let his growl fade away, his canines tucked back into his mouth.

The man gave a wide grin that showed several blackened teeth, tapped his own chest, and said, "Gregory." My grandfather repeated the name, and the man gave a happy yelp. He said it again, "Gregory," with almost a compulsive pleasure, and then said it a third time before lowering his pack. He took out a hunk of bread and bit into it. He was a gaunt man, like he had not eaten for years, and he ate the bread as if every bite made him hungrier.

My grandfather eyed Gregory's lumpy, half-full pack warily. My grandfather thought he must have been one of the miners beating a retreat from the coming winter, a Russian, but the man's load did not seem commensurate with the long distance he would need to cover. Jeannot thought that once the snow broke he would take this Gregory to Franklin's store and buy the man some dried beans and dried meat; he would not want to be haunted by the thought of the Russian starving to death on the trail.

They huddled around the small stove and took turns feeding scrap wood into it. Occasionally the wind gusted and sent snow piling through the gaps in the walls. For a while Martine swept the floor clean of snow, and then Jeannot and Gregory took some of the sawn boards that were stickered in piles and nailed them up against the wall. The mill was not cozy, but despite the high ceiling, by the time they were finished covering the gaps it was more of a shelter than it had been. The wind still touched at them, but the heat from the stove started to keep. Near midafternoon Gregory unpacked a few hard biscuits and they melted snow on the stove. Periodically, Martine, Jeannot, or Gregory would step outside to see if the snow had slackened, but always they returned, shaking their head to let the others know. Alone among them, Flaireur seemed content, curled up around his own tail and sleeping by the stove.

They passed the night uncomfortably, with Jeannot waking regularly to feed the stove, but apart from Martine waking and screaming that the roof was on fire, morning came without incident. It also came without any letup in the snow.

"Two feet since daybreak yesterday," Jeannot told Martine. He held up his hands to show Gregory, and though he knew the man did not understand, he said, "You won't be making it to Quesnellemouthe before spring. Well, we can go into town and bunk with Franklin and Rebecca once the snow slows down enough that we can see our way."

Gregory nodded in vigorous agreement, and responded like Jeannot had asked him a question. He pulled out rolled oats, a small container of sugar, and a blackened pot.

The smell of the food was surprisingly intense inside the mill, and even my grandmother found herself with an appetite despite the morning sickness that she had been feeling for the past few days. Jeannot fashioned a table of sorts out of a log end and some scraps of wood, and after Martine ate her fill from the blackened pot, the miner and Jeannot shared the rest of the oatmeal and then gave the scraps to Flaireur.

By their fourth day in the mill, they had stopped eating Gregory's food with such frivolity. At night the snow seemed to lessen, but with each break of light the wind picked up and they could barely see ten paces in front of them. The snow piled high enough that the path my grandfather dug from the mill toward the house had walls that soon outstripped his height. Jeannot struggled over to the burned-out hull of the house twice, but aside from a stuffed chair that sat miraculously untouched in the middle of the ashes, there was nothing left to salvage, and even the ashes quickly became covered in snow.

MY GRANDFATHER KEPT WAITING for the snow to slow enough that they could see to make their way to the village, but it did not stop snowing. After a week, Gregory kept pointing to the roof of the mill, an anxious look on his face, and finally he hammered together a ladder and went out with a shovel to clear off the roof. When he returned, Jeannot took the shovel from him and dug a tunnel between the mill and the stack of firewood on the side of the cabin, the whiteness now high enough that there were both walls and a roof in the snow.

My grandfather had gotten his old clothes and coat from the cabin on the first day, and by the time he dug the tunnel the cabin's roof had collapsed, but he was glad to be able to bring in the firewood. He did not want to burn up his good lumber if he did not need to. Though he was afraid it might collapse, he carved the tunnel out big enough so that he could stand in it, passing the snow to Gregory, who brought it to the stove so they could melt it down, pouring it into barrels. They worked slowly, with no particular sense of hurry, matching the pace of the digging to how quickly they were able to melt down the snow. Martine and Jeannot talked idly of tunneling to the village, but what was a short walk would have been a vast, blind distance underneath the snow.

One of the days, Martine took some of the extra water, wet down a rag, and glazed down the walls of the tunnel between the cabin and the mill. It was pitch-black because of the snow above, but she pulled Jeannot in with her, carrying a lantern, just so that he could see the gleaming in the ice. The reflection made it seem like they were walking through the stars.

I'VE BEEN THINKING of heaven recently. Not the heaven of avarice—a heaven full of mansions and streets of gold—but heaven as a real, physical place. There is something about clear nights in the winter, the perfection of snow and ice in the light from the stars and the moon that always reminds me of the existence of God. When it's cold enough, the sky seems to empty, and there is an infinite darkness, a sense that there is something unreachable and never-ending, something past the idea of heaven.

I've been thinking of heaven for the obvious reason—the approaching death of my mother—and perhaps the less obvious reason, which is that if my grandfather were here, if he somehow burst through the doors in a gust of wind, he'd tell me that I was wrong in my conception of heaven.

I think that the tunnel that my grandmother washed down with water, ice smooth enough to make it seem like they were among the stars themselves, is close to heaven. I want to believe that when I die I'll find a place where my mother and my father and Marie are all together, where what we have on this earth does not simply end, but my grandfather would have argued that I already had what I wanted within my grasp. That if I only went deep enough into the woods I would be able to find him and my grandmother, to find my father and Marie and, in a short while, my mother. And yet, if my grandfather were here, I am now old enough that I would have to ask him what he thought of hell, if that was a place that was also within my grasp.

Of course, if my grandfather were to come blowing

through the doors of my stepfather's house again, I know that he'd hover over the body of my dying mother and then look at me and say, you just have to believe.

AFTER NEARLY FOUR WEEKS in the mill, Martine and Jeannot's cheeks sucked in, and they drank water to fill their bellies. Only Gregory, who had started his residency in the mill with his bones already pushing through his skin, did not seem to be melting away.

Still, the tall Russian became less forthcoming with the food in his pack, and once or twice Jeannot woke to the sound of what he suspected to be chewing. He was feeling weak, though he tried not to let Martine see; he had been doing his best to slip her some of his share of food, but still, she spent most of her time lying on the hard wooden bunks that he and Gregory had made during their first days in the mill. Even Flaireur became ill-tempered.

The dog had gone mute again, and my grandfather began to imagine that this was just another prelude for a miracle, that at any moment Flaireur would begin to sing and that salvation would come to them. He waited and waited, but it did not happen. The only time Flaireur opened his mouth was to snap at Gregory when the miner stepped too close to the dog. The first time it happened, Gregory jumped back, but the second time, the miner held his ground, and Jeannot knew that if the man could speak to them he would say that the dog would be put to better use in the soup pot.

I HAD HEARD BITS and pieces of this story before, whispers of
that winter, and knew that my grandfather and grandmother
had spent a winter buried under more than thirty feet of snow,
as had Franklin and Rebecca, as had Pearl and every man and
woman who lived in Sawgamet that winter. But I had not
heard the details, and I remember that even though my grandfather said he had never told anybody this story before, it came
from him easily, as if he told it every morning. It was only that
one moment—when he stopped to touch the stovepipe—that
flustered him.

It was on the thirtieth night, my grandfather said, that he
woke to a small sound. He heard the complaint of wood bend-
ing, and then the shuffle of dirt. He was careful not to shift
his body. He let his eyelashes part only enough to take in the
dimness. He had banked the fire before going to sleep, but it
still cast enough of a flame for him to make out the shadow of
Gregory standing above him. Jeannot did not know how long
the miner stood there watching him, but it was only when
Gregory finally turned and went back to his bunk that my
grandfather saw the pistol in the man's hand. While the miner
settled back onto his slatted bed, Jeannot felt the soft touch of
Martine's hand on his back, and he knew that she had seen as
well.

They lay quietly for as long as they could stand, until they
could hear Gregory's ragged breathing between the occasional
crackle from the fire in the stove. Neither one knew how long it
was before Gregory rose again, this time with a loud groaning

and an obvious stretch. The two of them sat up and watched him move to the stove and pull the pot of water from where they had left it to warm overnight.

"Morning," Jeannot called over, and Gregory gave a wide, tired smile and a quick wave. He took a long splinter of wood and lit the lanterns—an action that seemed to pass for sunrise in the mill—and then walked back to his pack. He pulled out the small cloth sack that carried his limited supplies, and then dropped it on the plank table. He shook his head with a grimace and then turned it out. The tins sounded hollow and sharp, and one by one he picked them up and shook them. Only one gave a soft swish, the last hint of grains or flour. He pointed purposefully to Flaireur and then gave a nod to Jeannot.

Jeannot sat up and then, after a short pause, nodded back, and then pointed to himself.

The Russian took the pot of hot water behind the screen that he and Jeannot had rigged early in their isolation, and Jeannot and Martine heard the splash of his hands in the water.

"Jeannot," Martine said, but she stopped as he touched her mouth.

"Keep your voice even," he said.

"You're not going to . . ." She trailed off.

Jeannot looked grimly down at where Flaireur slept on the floor. "I would, if I thought it would save us," he said. "But it won't. He's skin and air and might keep us fed for another week or two, but with this snow we've got months to go. We need more meat than that." He glanced over at the screen and then took Martine's hand.

She felt her stomach turn, but she was not sure if it was the baby or the thought of the Russian. She stared at her husband, and then, slowly, she nodded.

"He was going to do it to us," Jeannot said, like he was seeking some sort of forgiveness, and then he quietly got to his feet.

Near the corner of the mill, my grandfather touched the handle of the ax. The blade was sunk into a large round from a log that he had been using to split the firewood into kindling. He gently rocked the handle, working the blade from the wood until he held the ax cleanly in his hands. The metal reflected the flickering of the lanterns, and Jeannot looked again at Martine. She closed her eyes.

My grandfather waited until he heard the creak of wood and the sound of Gregory stepping out from behind the screen, and then he swung the ax. The sound of the miner's skull was less clean than that of wood, and he heard the wetness, but Jeannot was surprised at how much it felt like splitting a log. The sharp impact and the cleaving of the blade.

He was sick twice—once immediately after he pulled the ax from Gregory's skull, and once having to bolt away from butchering the man's body—and my grandmother huddled over herself in the bed, keeping her back to the proceedings.

Despite Gregory's thinness, his body proved bountiful, as if another body lay beneath the skin of the Russian. As my grandfather worked the knife, he thought of the wehtiko, men turned cannibals, cursed to grow with every bite of human flesh they ate so that they were forever hungry. Jeannot shivered with relief when he finally finished carving, and then he dug a side tunnel out from where he had already tunneled to the firewood, filled one barrel with bones, and put it behind another barrel that was almost full with meat. Though he knew that he had no worries of scavengers or spoiling, he packed snow on top of the meat.

When that was squared away he shooed Flaireur away from the blood-soaked floor, dug it out clean, shoveling the soil into the snow that covered the creek, and then broke apart the miner's bed and added it to the wood to be burned in the stove. After that was finished, he lay on his own bed and cried, my grandmother trying to calm him despite the smell of the soup boiling on the stove. Finally, he sat himself at the table, but with the first bite of the greasy, floating flesh, Jeannot gagged and began to cry again: something in the taste reminded him of the rotten meat smell of the fish-pale and blind creature that visited him his first night in Sawgamet. It was not the same— it was not a qallupilluit, he knew—but still, he felt as if everything that he feared from the woods rested in the bowl before him, and that with a single bite he had called down a vengeance upon himself.

WHILE JEANNOT AND MARTINE tried to swallow their first meal alone since the fire, Rebecca and Franklin slept late; there was not much else for them to do. They had been busy the first few days after their marriage. Even with the blizzard, the men and women left in the village made their way into the store. A few of them came with ropes tied around their waists, afraid they might be lost in the storm, but most of them just made their way in unencumbered.

For once, they did not buy tin pans or shovels or any of the things that might be used for mining. They bought rice and beans, butter, sugar, tea, even the canned goods that Franklin had despaired of ever selling because of their enormous cost. They bought candles and thread and books, paper and ink, nails and wire. By the end of the first week of their marriage, however, the traffic to the store had stopped. The broad front windows were covered half over with snow, and though at night, during the breaks in the storm, when the snow slackened enough that there was hope of it stopping, they were able to see light from the second-floor windows of a few other buildings—the brothel, Dryden's saloon two buildings down from that, and a well-built house further down the street that glowed from candles and lanterns—all else was a sea of whiteness. They did not mind the privacy.

NINE

Salt

I'VE ASKED MY STEPFATHER to stay on in the rectory—it has been his house for more than four decades and has room enough—but he does not seem convinced that he wants to stay here. He has been talking some of reclaiming the small house beside the church, the one that he lived in for his first winter in Sawgamet, though I suspect he does not know what he wants. He is as adrift as I am at the impending loss of my mother.

It is as hard for me to imagine him living in that small house now as it is for me to imagine him living there as a hopeful young man in a new town.

Again, I'll have to ask forgiveness at what might seem another digression, but it was only last night that my stepfather told me this story. I have to think it was the snow in the first winter of my stepfather's marriage that shaped his faith as much as it was the snow in the first year of my grandparents' marriage that broke my grandfather's faith. And though I know in a village the size of Sawgamet there is little in the way of coincidence, it still startles me the ways—both small and

large—that my stepfather's life and mine have been entwined
from even before I was born.

.The day of my parents' wedding was only Father Earl's
second day in Sawgamet, but his parishioners had insisted
he and his wife come down to the banks of the river for the
picnic. He had marveled at the mass of logs piled at the top
of the chute, sampled as much pie from his congregants as he
could stomach, and much to the amusement of his wife, he
even tried a bit of logrolling, quickly ending up in the water.
He was changed and dry and back at the picnic in time to see
my father dunk Pearl Gasseur, but he had not understood it as
anything remarkable until my father and my mother already
stood before him. My father was dripping with water and
laughing. My mother was laughing herself, blushing, wearing
a simple dress instead of a wedding gown, but radiant despite
or perhaps because of it. I still wonder if that was the day—
though he had a wife of his own—that my stepfather first fell
in love with my mother, even if only a little bit.

He asked my parents if they ought not to wait for Father
Hugo, a little stunned at their casual ability to switch churches,
but my father had insisted, had said they could marry again
after the float; he did not want to wait lest my mother change
her mind. So Father Earl married them, right there, right
then, with my father still wet from the river. The next day,
after Father Earl blessed the float—Father Hugo still sleeping
off his drunk—the men started poling down the river and my
mother came to Father Earl's house to give his wife a pie. A
little thank-you, my mother said.

When he told me this story yesterday, I was not sure if it
was the knowledge that my mother was so close to death or

simply the newness of my return that led to the unsettled feeling between us. My daughters had long gone to bed, and my wife was in the kitchen, starting on her baking for the next day. My stepfather and I shared a pot of tea and alternated between staring silently through the window at the clouded sky and engaging in the sort of small, weightless chatting that characterizes unease. The fire gave off small and flickering light, just enough for me to think that he blushed when he said that he thought the pie my mother had brought over as thanks for officiating at her wedding was the best that he had ever eaten, something that he never told his wife.

When he and his wife arrived in Sawgamet, his parish members told him he was lucky to enjoy the last blush of summer, and then they showed him the small house next to the Anglican church that was to be his until the house in town was ready. They showed him the store, the mill, pointed out the drunks, the degenerates, and the Catholics, told him how to cut and stack firewood, and how to keep his pregnant wife warm. But they did not tell him the most important thing: how cruel and final the winters were.

The day winter arrived, his wife said, "The sky hurts," and my stepfather, who was sitting at his desk, looked out the window and saw what she meant: clouds like bruises.

"It's too early for snow," he said, but his wife laughed.

"Yet I don't think you'll be able to stop it from coming. Even you can't put a halt to winter. You'd best get some wood stacked up on the porch."

Father Earl finished the sentence that he was writing and then pushed the sermon aside. He could complete it later. He had tried working in the church earlier that morning, but the ink kept freezing in the well; it seemed too much of an extravagance to light a fire simply so he would have a place to work outside of the rough-hewn mouse hole of a house. He touched his finger to the glass of the window, happy that they at least had that, had something to let the light in. The house that the congregation was building in town would be much more comfortable, but until that was finished sometime in the spring, this house would be satisfactory enough. It was better than what many men had lived in during winters in the past, he thought; he knew that the first men in Sawgamet, the ones who had come for gold, had lived in dark and brutal, patched-together cabins. Father Earl had not passed on to his wife the stories he'd heard about the original miners, the ways they kept themselves warm in the winters.

The light had already begun to dim, though it was still midmorning. As he stepped outside and looked up, he felt as if the clouds were joining together before him. Holy matrimony, Father Earl thought.

When he was telling me the story he paused and grinned at me for a moment, knowing that I had picked up his habit of thinking of almost everything in a biblical light. He joked that becoming the sort of clichéd pastor that he heard on radio dramas was an occupational hazard, though in truth, I find it comforting both in him and in myself. Maybe that is why I am not worried that my stepfather will be lost and wandering in the woods looking for the ghost of my mother: he has the compass of God to guide him.

That day, however, he had more immediate concerns: he

had a wedding to perform in the afternoon and was worried about the onset of snow and the sudden drop in temperature. He opened the door to the house again.

"Do you think we should light the church fire?"

"Soon enough," his wife said. "I'll put the bread up and then I'll get it lit. The girl ought to be able to wear her gown without having to keep a coat on top of it."

Father Earl smiled at her, but she was already turned back to the table. They were not so old that she could casually call another woman a girl, he thought. He supposed that was her way of playing the role of a minister's wife.

He closed the door carefully, making sure that the latch shot home. The wind's fingers were already clawing at him. He did not want the door to blow open, the cold and sudden gust of air swirling the fire in the hearth, his wife spinning to find the intrusion. At least the house was chinked up solidly; whoever had built it had been meticulous, fitting each log with care, setting the door flush and tight.

As he stepped behind the back of the house, by the wood-pile, he heard whistling and saw my father—though he was not my father yet—moving down the trail that ran past the church and headed toward, as my stepfather's wife often said, "what passed for town."

I AM NOT SURE if I thought of this last night, but now I wonder if part of the reason my stepfather never told me this story before was because of that exact moment. Such a small one, really, this interaction between the man who was to become my father and the man who was to become my stepfather, but it would have been enough to make my stepfather hesitate in telling it to me when I was younger.

And that makes me wonder if I am doing justice by my stepfather, if when I tell these stories to my own children they will understand what a fine man Father Earl was.

It is easy enough with my grandfather and my father. They were, as I've said before, like gods among the forest, a sort of living folklore. Something that I in particular, as a man of the cloth, should know better than to believe in.

And yet. And yet. And yet, of course, how can I not believe in them, how can I separate the raw, natural—supernatural—Sawgamet that was already dying when I was a child from the settled land which I now occupy?

And how do I place my stepfather among that mythology so that my daughters can understand that despite the fact that he did not settle the land, did not work the cuts or run the river, he was, nevertheless, very much part of my own story?

But it is not that simple. Nothing ever is. My daughters can just as easily look at me and see the ways in which I did not follow my stepfather's path, the ways in which I am much more like my grandfather or my father. Or maybe if I can figure out how to untangle these stories, how to tell them properly, my daughters will be able to understand the things that brought me to where I am now: in the study of my stepfather's house, waiting for the moment when my mother will breathe her last.

One of the things I do know is that on that first day of winter in Sawgamet for my stepfather and his wife, Father Earl cannot have known how entangled his life was to become with the threads of my grandfather's and my father's lives.

AS MY FATHER MOVED closer to the woodpile, he looked up and saw Father Earl. "Morning, there," my father said. "How you doing, Father?"

"Well, thank you," Father Earl said, glad to see it was my father and not one of the other Catholics. So many of the loggers kept their distance, as if he could not possibly understand them as men because he did not speak their bastardized French. My father was not that kind of man, or perhaps it was because he thought of Father Earl as the man who had married him to my mother. Either way, Father Earl had found it hard to believe that a Catholic would allow him to perform a marriage; while he knew that it was necessary for survival, the men of Sawgamet showed a certain moral flexibility that he sometimes found to be uncomfortable. He supposed he might begin to understand it with time.

My stepfather told me that, as he looked at my father, he thought that my parents would start having children soon. A presentient thought, though looking back I can count the pages of the calendar and realize that my mother would already have been early in her pregnancy. My stepfather did not know this, of course, but he could read the seasons; in Sawgamet, with the snow and the cold, he thought it would be that time of year, and there would be many families that would have children sometime in the fall.

Now, though, the men were frantic. There was little time between the end of logging and the float and the beast of winter for them to prepare for the months of short days. Father

Earl's own wife had been anxious, canning and sewing, making him a new pair of gloves from thick leather and fur.

He wondered if his wife was anxious enough. When they had left her parents' house, when she had agreed to come to Sawgamet, he could not make her see why she should favor thick-spun cotton over lace, why an extra quilt was more important than an extra gown. She had been pleased when she discovered that Franklin kept some canned foods. She thought Father Earl had been too narrow with their needs: wood, flour, salted meat, and beans. "It will be a longer winter than necessary if you do all our provisioning," she told him.

My father motioned with his ax toward the woodpile. The handle had a burn scar and he gripped the ax with a sureness that my stepfather was beginning to think of as something that was necessitated by the woods and the brutality of Sawgamet. "Would you like me to help you split some more wood, Father? There's a snow coming, that much I'm sure of," he said, and then he raised his ax, as if he were challenging God to prove him wrong.

"Thank you, Pierre, but I'll be fine. I've got plenty of wood split. I just need to move some to the porch. Besides," my stepfather said to my father, trying a clumsy wink, "I can always borrow from the woodpile at the church if I need."

"Keep a lantern lit," my father said.

"Oh, it's not so dark as that, at least not yet."

"In the window," my father said. "If you're going to be out in this, keep a light going so you can find your way home."

"It's only a few feet," Father Earl said.

"Men get turned around easy," my father replied. "Don't let

the qallupilluit call you down. Don't listen to them if they call for you."

Father Earl started to smile, and then he realized that my father wasn't joking. "I thought they lived in the sea ice."

He shrugged. "It's an old tale, and we hear these things only the way we want to hear them. I don't know that they tell us all of it. But you'd best stay away from the river in weather like this. They don't look like witches all the time, the qallupilluit."

"I'm a man of the cloth, Pierre."

"One with a wife," my father said. "Keep a light." He waited until my stepfather nodded in assent and then he gave a brief nod himself and started down the trail again.

MY STEPFATHER TOLD ME that when he watched my father walk away, it seemed as if my father towered over him, though he knew that my father was not a particularly tall man. Perhaps it was the solidness of him, the knotted sinews, the implicit availability of violence. Father Earl finally allowed himself to smile once my father was out of sight. The Indian children's stories that were told throughout Sawgamet did not scare him, though he understood the allure of the qallupilluit; sea witches were more effective than any parent's warnings.

Father Earl carried an armful of wood onto the porch and then looked up at the sky again. It had gotten darker, dark enough that he was not sure how long it would be before he was willing to be tricked into believing it was already night. Through the window he saw the shadow of his wife moving through the house, or at least he thought it was the shadow of his wife; the fire in the hearth cast light and darkness with equal measure. He brushed some bark and dirt off his sleeve and then opened the door. Whatever else he might wonder, Father Earl believed that my father seemed to understand the weather in some way that Father Earl did not.

"That was quick," his wife said. "Would you light the fire in the church for me, then? I still haven't put the bread up."

"No," he said, "I've still to put wood on the porch. I'm just putting a lantern in the window." He did not say why, and as he moved the lantern to sit on his desk, his wife did not ask him. Even after less than a year of marriage, she was used to him by now, understood that he had a reason for everything he did. That's not to say that she did not disagree with him, did not read through his sermons and mark them up. If he was honest about it, he knew that she was smarter than him, had certainly had a more rigorous education, alternating between the tutors and the girls' school where he had briefly taught and she had picked him to be her husband.

"That's fine, then," she said. "I'm thinking I might try to hurry down to DeBonnier's, to buy some sugar. I'd meant to do it yesterday. If this storm is really to be all that we're making it out to be, I'd rather be stuck in here with a pie or two." She stepped over to him and grabbed his open coat with her hands, pulling him toward her. He bent down and let her kiss him lightly on his lips, rubbed his nose against hers. "And that way I won't have to listen to you complain about how bitter the tea is."

They had argued about it once, during the first week or two after they had come to Sawgamet. He did not think it right that they use her father's money. "I'm given enough for us to live on," he said.

"No," she said, "enough not to die on. There's no shame in it. My father came to it honestly, and besides, I don't think an extra sack of flour, a bolt of cloth, is anything to get up in arms about. I said I'd live with you in Christ, but I'm not living with you in rags."

If he were a different man, he would have settled the issue, would have insisted, but if he were that kind of man, she never would have married him. And she was not that kind of woman. She did not say any of it with the bite or malice that he had heard other women use, and he knew that she was right. It was only that she did not limit it to an extra sack of flour or a bolt of cloth. She had bought up much of DeBonnier's expensive canned foods, had ordered a new mattress and bureau to be brought in from Vancouver.

"I saw Pierre just now," he said. "He warned me of the qallupilluit."

"He believes in them?" She shook her head. "Why a Christian would believe in witches is beyond me."

"He says that they'll promise anything to get a man under the water."

"Even sugar?"

"We can go without sugar for a few days," my stepfather said, turning away. The tea they had been able to get was almost unbearably bitter without the soft cut of sugar, but it bothered him that she could not do without it for a short time. "Light the fire in the church and then stay inside the house."

"We need candles, too. I'm happy enough for an excuse to spend time in bed with you," she said, and then paused to smile, though she knew it discomforted him when she spoke so openly. "But I don't relish sitting in the dark and just listening to the wind and the brush of the snow on the roof."

"You can pull your chair a little closer to the fire, that's light enough," he said, but he smiled and touched his finger to her cheek to let her know that he was joking. "After the storm we'll go down to DeBonnier's."

OUTSIDE, MY STEPFATHER looked up at the sky and he thought again of bruises. He wondered if he were only tall enough to touch the clouds if they would split like overripe fruit, if that would make them spill their seed. As he had the thought, the first few flakes started to fall, drifting and lazy. He watched them settle on the ground, expecting them to melt as they hit brush and leaves, but even though this was the first snow it had been cold for a few weeks now. The snow stayed where it fell. He had not said anything to his wife, because he knew that she was dreading this first winter, but he had been waiting. Snow like a Communion. He bent over to pick up wood.

He made several dozen trips from the back of the house to the front. He stopped occasionally to shake out his arms. When he was done, the porch was half filled, enough for a few weeks. Too much, he knew. Father Earl did not want to admit it to his wife, but my father and his talk of witches had taken him aback. The stacked wood and the lantern in the window were things he could understand.

My stepfather took one last trip to the woodpile behind the house, this time for an armload to bring inside. As he pulled wood off the pile he heard the door of the house shut hard. He called out to his wife—he was almost done; he could light the fire in the church before he came inside—but she didn't hear him.

She was already out of sight by the time he came around to the porch. The snow was coming down hard, moving from an idea in the sky to the beginnings of a blanket on the ground with almost no notice. He stomped his feet on the steps before gingerly balancing the wood in one arm while he reached out with the other to open the door. A thin line of snow spilled off the shoulder of his coat, some down his collar and some down his arm, hitting his hand. He shook it off his hand and then opened the latch.

The smell of yeast and cooked meat enveloped him. He saw the large pot hanging over the fire, and he wondered if she intended for him to eat a thick stew for his lunch—hunks of meat and potatoes—or if it was something thinner and meaner, a soup, a few small chunks of venison just to hint at what his wife was capable of cooking.

She had been odd about food the last few days, alternating between cheeseparing dinners of bread and onions and lavish meals that would not have been out of place on feast days, as if she could not decide if the winter was something to be feared or embraced. Since she had realized there was a child growing inside her she had been easy with her father's money. Not only would they not go hungry this winter, they would eat better than anybody else in Sawgamet, he suspected. There were still items that she had wanted to add to their larder in quantity—sugar being not the least—but my great-uncle had assured her that his store would be stocked to last through to the spring when the snow would melt enough for horses to get in from Havershand.

My stepfather had been quiet about his wife's dithering. Perhaps if she kept on with the feast or famine, but for a few days it was almost amusing to him. She was normally so sure-footed, so insistent about what she wanted. He was not sure if it was something else that he needed to learn about her, or if it was a by-product of her pregnancy. Either way, she would settle down once the child was born. He was glad that she had become with child so quickly. She needed it, he thought. She needed the weight of motherhood to teach her what it meant to be a priest's wife. Not that the life of a priest's wife was the same here as it would have been had they stayed in Ottawa, as her mother and father had wanted.

He resisted his urge to peek in the pot to see what was cooking, and instead hung his coat on the peg by the door and settled back down at his desk. He should have time to finish the sermon before he needed to dress for the wedding. He had quickly gotten into the habit of wearing the same rough, heavy work clothes that the other men wore in the cuts, changing into collar only when he was actually in the church.

It took him a few minutes to restart his thoughts, as if he had to rejoin himself in midspeech. He loved delivering the sermon, and knew that was a weakness. He had been told many times by Father Barns that he should not take so much pride in his role as a leader of the flock. He was only given the chance to speak at all because of the words of Jesus Christ. But he could not help himself. He was good at it.

"He giveth the snow like wool: he scattereth the hoarfrost like ashes." Looking out the window at the solid curtain that seemed to have been lowered in front of him, he thought that perhaps Job would have been more appropriate than the Psalm: "Out of the south cometh the whirlwind; and cold out of the north. By the breath of God frost is given: and the breadth of the waters is straightened."

SOMETHING ACRID TUGGED at his nose. The bread, burning, he realized. He wrapped his hands in cloth and then reached in and deftly plucked the loaf out. It was not too bad, just singed on the bottom, nothing that could not be scraped off. He had not realized his wife had been gone so long, though. He thought he had only been sitting and writing for a moment or two.

The house had grown dark. Not much light came in through the window, though the lantern on his desk and the fire helped. It should not have taken her that long to light the fire in the church and then come home.

He threw three more logs onto the fire, fastened his coat around himself, and then slowly pulled on the heavy new gloves that she had made for him. He opened the door and almost staggered back, surprised by how much the weather had turned in the time he had been writing.

Even with the covered porch, snow blew against him, small, sharp pieces, like sand, like sugar, stinging his cheeks and eyes, blurring his vision. He could not see past the bottom of the steps, and the dimness was pervasive. Almost as an afterthought, he stepped back in and took the lantern from the table. He would be no help to her if he could not lead them home, or worse, if he spent the night wandering around like a lost soul. He closed the door tightly behind him, careful once again to make sure the latch shot home. The idea of the fire breathing out heat into the small house cheered him; while it was not the sort of house that his wife had been used to, it would keep them warm; it would be a welcome place to return to from out of this storm.

Squinting, he could barely see what lay in front of him. There, the man-sized boulder beside the path, already covered in white, and over there, the unbroken geometry of the church. The well-worn path between the house and the church, fifty paces, more or less, was gone.

He hunched over, burrowing his head between his shoulders, reaching up and tugging his hat down further over his ears, trying to protect the exposed skin of his face from the biting snow. That was what it felt like, he thought, like a plague of biting insects swarming against him, and as he had the thought, he realized that was also the way the falling snow sounded.

He had always thought of snow as something quiet, as something that drifted silently from the sky and lay in dampening blankets on the ground, the trees. It would make a solid whoosh and whomp as it fell from trees and roofs in sheets, but it was not supposed to sound like this. This snow hissed. It crackled against the small house, against his coat, his pants, against the trees. The snow reminded him of fire, of locusts, of devouring destruction.

He stayed bent over, and when he looked up, he realized that all he could see was trees and whiteness. The church was gone. A magic trick. A miracle. He could see the boulder

ahead of him. Behind him, he could still see the house, but
even though he was barely a dozen paces gone, it was already
shimmering, ready to disappear just like the church. He held
up the lantern, as if that would help, and then lowered himself
into the storm again, confident that his initial line would hold
true. The church was not like the stone and stained-glass cathe-
drals that his wife's parents had envisioned, but it was large
enough to hold a hundred men and women, large enough that
he would not pass by it in the artificial night.

The snow lapped his ankles; he could not understand how
it had come so quickly. It had been cold for days, for weeks,
and they had known that winter was coming, but still, here it
was, like an unexpected and unwelcome visitor. And suddenly
Father Earl had the image of winter circling like a wolf, waiting until his back was turned. He still could not see the church,
and he had to stifle the impulse to run. He could turn around,
he thought, but when he looked behind him, the house had
disappeared.

He looked for the church, and then for the house again, and
as he turned, he realized what he had done by turning around.
There was no front, no back now, just the biting whiteness, the
stinging snow attacking him.

He would not die. He knew that. In one direction was the
church, in another was the house. The other ways were toward
the slope down to the river, which he could follow to town,
or to the woods. If he ended up in the woods, the force of the
snow would be blunted and he would find trails that would
either lead him into the cuts and the quick-built shelters or
back into town. But it was his wife that he was thinking of. He
did not want to lead her purposelessly through the night.

He closed his eyes for a moment, standing straight and raising his face into the storm. He had read a book once that described a sandstorm somewhere in Arabia, and he thought that it would feel like this, the way the snow scraped against him and slipped down his collar. He did not know which way to go, but it was best to move. Best to do something other than stand out in this stinging snow. He opened his eyes again and started walking, purposefully, forcefully, as if he knew which way would take him to the church, as if he were leading his flock behind him, and he felt as if he had been touched by providence when, after a few dozen steps, he saw the broad face of the church in front of him.

He was relieved when he stepped inside the church; though it was no warmer inside the church than out, at least he was given shelter from the biting storm. His relief quickly turned to anger, though. She was not there, and he knew that she had decided to go to town despite his instructions, thinking she would stop in the church to light the fire on her way back. She may have been smarter than him, but she was not as cautious as he would have liked her to be; there were still times when she thought that Sawgamet was quaint, when she did not realize that men died out in the woods. He gave himself a moment to fume and then he touched a match to the kindling. He knew Franklin and Rebecca would not let her leave the store in weather like this. She would have to wait out the snow in town, but she would be safe.

In front of him, the wood quickly began to eat at itself, sending up a welcome light and touch of warmth. He was glad that he had laid the fire out so carefully earlier in the week. He let it take, and then carefully added a few logs. The fire was for him—the wedding would be on another day, a day with better weather, he knew—and he luxuriated before its warmth. Inside the church, the sound of the snow on the roof and the walls was almost peaceful, a lulling comfort, like the river. He could have lain down in front of the fire and gone to sleep. He wanted to. Tiredness had descended on him, had fallen on him, and he thought about it for a few seconds, but then he heard something.

The sound was high and keening, not quite animal, but not like anything my stepfather had heard before. At first he thought it was just the wind, the snow howling at him, or perhaps a leftover, a ringing in his ears from his time outside, but whatever it was, it was not natural. He could not hear words, and he did not know why he was sure, but he knew that it was a voice, that it was calling him. The voice was not human, and it was not ethereal; nobody would ever mistake that voice for anything angelic, Father Earl thought. It was unnerving, and it cut through him, yet he could not stop himself from going to the window. He could not see anything, of course, but he stood by the window and looked anyway, transfixed. He wanted to see the qallupilluit, to hear what the sea witches were promising if he followed them down to the river, to death and destruction. And then it came clear to him, a single note, like somebody had touched a fork to a crystal goblet: he realized that the voice had to be his wife.

He closed the door of the church behind him and stood in the entranceway, carefully aligning himself. He knew that he needed to move, to head home to her, but he was transfixed: two white birds perched on the railing by the door. Doves.

"Lord?" he said, and then he spoke to the doves. "Are you angels?"

The birds did not move, and after a moment my stepfather reached out and touched one. It was dead, frozen. His finger brushed off the coating of snow and ice—it was as if the bird had been encrusted in salt—and he realized that they were a pair of chickadees. He felt a blush of shame. He should have known that they were not doves, that things were always more simple than they seemed. He had to stop looking for signs from God wherever he went, he thought.

As he brushed some of the crust off the bird he heard the voice again and snapped back to what had made him leave the church. He forced himself to step out of the shelter of the porch. Snow or not, it was a straight shot to the house and his wife.

Again, he wanted to run, but he forced himself to stay disciplined, counting his steps. Fourteen, fifteen, and the voice faded, no longer calling him. Thirty, thirty-one, the only sound that of the snow, the only thing he could see the whiteness through the thin squinted slits of his eyes. He squatted down, trying to take some comfort in the shelter of the snow-covered boulder, but even in the lee of the rock, there was little respite. Still, he rested a moment.

He was exhausted. The snow was deep enough to be a slogging. Foreman Martin had given Father Earl and his wife a pair of snowshoes each. His wife had held them out as if they were something offensive, a poorly skinned fur, but my stepfather had smiled and thanked the foreman. He knew that they would need the snowshoes, that by Christmas the snow would sit waist-deep or higher, and they would flounder without them. He wished he had them now. The snow was already near his knees. The thought gave him a rush of fear—how quickly the snow gathered—and he started to walk again.

Forty, forty-one, and he was lost, a white blindness, and then he slipped, falling hard onto the ground. For a moment his ankle burned, and he was afraid that he had broken it, but when he stood, the pain flared away.

Forty-two, forty-three, forty-four, and he stopped, suddenly afraid. He was once again in the lee of the snow-covered boulder, as if he had been turned around, but the boulder was to his left, as it should be if he were headed home. He looked up, as if that would help, and like a little miracle, he saw something, a glimmering, a gleaming in front of him, and he breathed out a small prayer. But as he was about to walk toward the light, he heard the voice again, calling him. This time it came from all around him. He stopped, unsure if he should go toward the light or if he should try to follow the voice. The voice echoed and crackled around him. It had changed. It enticed him, and he knew that if he closed his eyes he would have no choice but to follow it. He was no longer sure if it came from his wife or a witch. He had enough humility to know that he could not tell the difference between an angel and the devil.

He followed the light.

Forty-seven, forty-eight, and he could make out the shape of the house, saw that the light came through the window. He had taken the lantern from the desk—stupidly left it at the church in his hurry. It was his wife who set a second lantern in the window to guide him home. She was a smart one, and he would tell her so. He knew that she would take the storm as an opportunity to ask him to lie languorously with her. She had come into their marriage a virgin, but she was eager to be his wife. He had been hesitant since she had started carrying his child, thought there was something unnatural in it, but he would give in to her now. He would lie in bed with her, grateful to be warm and naked under the covers, and keep his hands on her stretched-out stomach, feeling for the kicks of his child, holding her until the snow stopped.

The door hung open a few inches, and he felt a momentary surge of irritation at the thought of the cold she had let into the house. There was still a blast of heat when he opened the door, however, the smell of the soup boiling. But the house was empty. A glance was all it took—it was not as if there were anywhere for her to hide—and yet he still called to her, still called out her name, hoping she would answer, and as he did so, he realized that he had been right before. She had been the one calling to him, but he had gone toward the light, toward the warmth and shelter of their home, instead of turning back to save her.

HE SPENT THE NIGHT WALKING. He came to the river and followed the bank until he stumbled into the first house in town. He knocked on every door, but she was not inside any of the houses, had not been to DeBonnier's store, the saloon, the whorehouse, the Catholic church. He walked through the woods until he came to the feeble shelters at the start of the cuts, and finally, as the snow started to slow, as the first light of day broke through, he stumbled once again upon their house.

The snow was past his waist and each step burned his legs. He moved slowly, barely able to get himself onto the porch. Even with his new gloves, his hands were cold, frozen, and he struggled with the latch. He remembered the spindrift coming from his sleeve the previous day, saw a glint of ice holding the latch down, and he banged his fist against it a few times until it rattled free.

The fire had gone out, but the heat still lingered. It was welcome. He did not even bother to remove his jacket, his boots. He just collapsed onto the chair in front of the dormant fire. The chair that his wife sat in while she knit or read. He sat for a few minutes, too tired to sleep. The room suddenly brightened, and he looked over to the window, to the burned-out lantern sitting on his desk. Sunlight marked a rectangle on the floor.

He looked again at the lantern and realized that he had not been back to the church. He had left his own lantern there. She would have seen his light like he had seen hers. She was there, in front of the church fire, waiting and worrying for him.

He tried to run off the porch, an awkward sort of shuffling in the deep snow; he was stopped not by his own exhaustion but by the brilliance of the light. The sun bounced against the crystalline snow, and he felt as if he were staring at a million candles in front of a million mirrors. He squinted, tears rolling down his eyes, and he placed his hands in front of his face. Snow was not always this blinding. It was the shape, the grains of snow like sugar, like salt, reflecting the light, beaming it directly at him.

He could not open his eyes all of the way, but after a few minutes he was able to make out shapes against the dazzling whiteness. Trees bent and laden with coats of snow, whispers of green still evident. The church, so close, holding his wife. And there, between the church and his house, against the flattened landscape, beside where he thought the path was buried under the snow, two shapes protruding from the snow.

And even before he took another step, he knew there should only be one shape, knew that there was only one boulder encrusted by snow. He knew then, and he would always know, that if he had had the courage to look back into the storm he would have found her, would have been able to carry her home, would not have left her to turn into a pillar of salt.

MY STEPFATHER STOPPED talking and looked at me, but I felt like I could not catch my breath. He stared and waited, looking almost fearful, but I did not understand what he expected me to say. Was he waiting for me to cast judgment, to blame him for his loss of faith, if that's even what it was? Did he think I would somehow find him at fault for the loss of his wife?

Neither of us moved for a while, and I did not know what to do: I did not want to keep looking at him, but neither did I feel like I could look away.

The sound of crying drifted down to us from the bedrooms. My youngest, waking in the dark of night. Then the sound of my wife's footsteps in the hallway above.

"She looks like her," my stepfather said. "The baby takes after your mother. All of your girls do. I can see her in them."

"You'd best not say that if my wife's parents come to visit us here," I said, though I thought there was little chance of luring them to Sawgamet from Vancouver. "They are insistent that the girls are carrying the looks of their family through and through."

My stepfather looked down at his hands like he hadn't heard my response, and then he let out a sound that could have been a cough, a grunt, or a sob. "I didn't know," he said.

It took me a moment to realize that he had gone back to the story, that he was thinking of his first wife, alone and frozen under the covering of snow.

"I thought I knew," he continued. "I thought I knew what to expect from the winters. I'd taken seminary in Edmonton and thought that meant I understood the cold, that it was my wife who was unprepared for the cold, for the snow, for the darkness. I thought I would be able to watch over her. But I didn't know."

"You couldn't have—"

"When your father and sister died . . ." He cut me off and then let his words trail off. He looked at me and then dropped his head.

He picked up my teacup and placed it in the sink and then leaned heavily against the sideboard, his shoulders slumped, showing his age.

"When your father and sister died, that winter, I went down to the ice sometimes, to stand above them, to visit with them. Did you know that?" He let out a small laugh. "Of course you didn't know that. You were still a boy. What were you, ten, eleven that winter?"

"Ten," I said. "I turned eleven the following summer, after you and Mother married, after Jeannot came back to

Sawgamet." I did not add that I knew, that I had seen him walking out on the ice that winter, and that once I had even seen him kneel and place his palm flat against the ice. "Why?" I asked. "What do you mean, you went to visit them?"

He kept his back to me. "I don't know, exactly. I used to just stand and look at them, the way they were reaching toward each other. Your sister's small hand, so clean and pale, reaching out, and I used to marvel at how trusting it seemed, how much faith she had that your father would reach her."

I wanted to tell him of how, when the ice had broken that year, when the water started to flow, I liked to think of their hands joining under the water, fingers touching as they were washed down the Sawgamet, but I didn't. Instead, I said, "But he didn't. He didn't reach her."

"But he tried. He had—you can't remember what he used to be like, how he was with two hands, before he injured himself—but he was so close, just the thinness of a hair between them. He went after her. He went after your sister. He didn't turn back."

I rose from my chair and walked over to him, unsure what to do with my hands until finally I stood next to him and put my hand on his arm. "You couldn't have saved her," I said. "You couldn't have saved your wife. You tried, and it's better that you survived than that you perished in the snow without reaching her."

He looked up at me, and I was shocked to see that he looked almost angry, something I had rarely seen on his face.

He spoke sharply. "This isn't about my wife, Stephen. Just because I told you about how she . . ." He closed his eyes, took a deep breath, and then started speaking in a more measured tone. "I was thinking about your mother, Stephen. I was wondering if, when your sister and father died, she felt that if only she had more faith, they would have been returned to her."

"God doesn't—"

"Dammit, I'm not talking about God," he shouted, and then pushed off my arm. Heat started to rise in my face. And then I realized that he had begun to cry.

"I'm not talking about God," he said. "I'm talking about the woods, about whatever it was that your grandfather thought he could do so many years ago."

We were both silent, and then my stepfather wiped his eyes with his sleeves and sat back down. "I'm sorry, Stephen. Your mother . . ."

"No. I understand."

"I'm being selfish. She's my wife, but she's also your mother."

"It's hard," I said.

He looked out the window at the clouds that had gathered low in the sky. "It's going to snow soon. Tonight. Tomorrow night. You can feel the way it's aching to snow. Winter's ready to come. Good thing they dug the grave already. Even with the new diesel-powered shovel, digging the grave would have taken some effort. Quicker than the old days, two men with pickaxes, and better still than having to put her body on ice until the thaw."

BUT FOR ALL OF OUR talking last night, we both understand that even if ghosts didn't haunt my mother, memories did.

I've been up in the study most of the night, but near ten, Father Earl came to tell me that my mother had asked me to sit with her. I held her hand for a while, and then read by her side after she fell asleep. When she slept, her breath came in uneven fits and bursts. Despite the blankets covering her and the way the heat of the furnace soaked through the house, she seemed to shiver, so I stoked the fire until the room closed with warmth and my mother's breathing flattened into regularity.

I don't remember falling asleep, but I woke near eleven, thinking I heard Marie calling me. The lamp still angled away from my mother's bed, light spilling over me, my book open on my lap, and it took me a moment to place myself, to remember that I was sitting vigil over my mother. I reached to pick up my book, but I heard my mother cough and realized she was awake, looking toward the window.

"Turn off the lamp," she said, her voice a whisper, and I couldn't tell if she was conscious of the hour or simply unable to speak louder.

"Sorry," I said. "I fell asleep while I was reading. I didn't mean to wake you."

She smiled a little and blinked slowly enough that I thought she was going back to sleep, but then she shook her head. "Look out the window," she said.

As I reached up to turn off the lamp I realized that my hand was shaking. With the room dark, I could see that a mist hung in the air outside, thin sheets of rain icing the trees.

"I want to go down to the river," my mother said.

"You—"

She reached out and took my hand, stopping me from protesting. Her skin felt thin in my hand, and I knew that what I had been about to say—that it was raining, that she shouldn't be outside, that she should rest—didn't matter.

I put on my coat and boots and then bundled my mother the best I could in her blankets. When I picked her up I staggered a little. It was not that she was heavy, but rather the opposite: she was as light as one of my daughters in my arms. I had braced myself for the weight of an adult, but it was like carrying a child, and I wondered if my mother thought of the way our roles had been reversed, how I was the one carrying her.

The street was slick, but the mist fell star-bright, and I walked carefully down to the river. It was a short distance from my stepfather's house, a hundred yards at most. My mother had her arm around my neck, and I think we both expected to see the same thing when we got down to the banks, the same thing we had seen thirty years earlier on the night of the freezing rain: the water frozen, ice shining like the river had swallowed the moon.

But even though there was a scrum of ice against the banks of the Sawgamet, the water ran fast and clear, the river open and dark in the night.

I waited a moment for something to happen, but nothing did. It was just me, standing on the banks of the river, my mother still almost weightless in my arms, the water pushing toward Havershand. I heard a noise and turned to see that Father Earl had crept down behind us, hanging back like he always held back, but close enough so that I could take strength in knowing he was there.

My mother looked out over the river and then, while looking back to me, saw Father Earl. She reached out to him. He hesitated, and then stepped forward and took her hand, and we just stood there, the three of us, on the banks of the Sawgamet, looking out over the water and the first pieces of ice. The mist fell over us, but the cold left us untouched.

BACK AT THE HOUSE, I covered my mother with dry blankets and then added a log to the fire.

I kissed her on the forehead and told her that I loved her. "I'm sorry."

She may have already been asleep, and I said it so quietly that I was not sure if she heard me, but Father Earl did. He touched my elbow but did not say anything, and the two of us sat in the room together, not saying anything together, watching over my mother's body.

She died just past midnight.

TEN

Cinders

M Y GRANDPARENTS THOUGHT A ghost haunted them that long winter. They did what they needed to get through—the meat from Gregory's body was enough to sustain them, though my grandfather swore that every bite made him feel more hungry—but at times they thought they were going mad. Every creak of boards at night, every shifting of the hard-packed snow, every crack of a log in the fire seemed like the miner's footsteps, his voice. They lost track of days, buried alive under snow so deep that there might as well not have been a sun. They subsisted on the flesh of a man they had killed and watched my grandmother's pregnant belly round out as my father grew inside her.

When it finally stopped snowing that year, in July, none of the men or women in Sawgamet, including Jeannot and Martine, knew it; even the three-story buildings in Sawgamet were covered over. But by the seventeenth of July, winter had broken hard. The sun pushed the temperature into weather that would have called for short sleeves had any men or women been unburied.

In the brothel, Pearl was the first to notice the sound of water trickling off the snowpack. He had ended the night of Franklin and Rebecca's marriage by paying for the touch of a woman—a woman who I suspect later ended up becoming Mrs. Gasseur, though that was only whispers—and when he found himself cut off from the rest of the world the next morning, he did not mind his plight.

The women had plenty of food stocked away—the madam ran a restaurant as a side business—and after the first few weeks they were as bored as Pearl was; it did not matter that he had run out of money. By the time the snowfall let up for long enough that he could have seen his way back to his cabin, it had piled high enough that he had no desire to try. Though he worked cutting trees for my grandfather, Pearl still lived at his old mining camp, a good mile away. Even if he had been able to return, he knew what he could expect. The men would be mining and sleeping, mining and sleeping, mining and sleeping. At some point they would slaughter their mules for meat, and if they had any sense—which he was not sure of— they would start digging through the snow in hopes of find- ing town and food. An unlikely miracle, given the distance. A mile of digging was much more difficult to navigate than a mile of walking, but it was worth trying. Anything rather than starving to death in the cold and dark.

In July, though, Pearl finally heard trickling water instead of the soft whisper of falling snow. He opened the window on the third floor and used his hands to dig out enough so that he could see through to the bright, clear sky. It took him nearly a full minute to understand that it had finally stopped snow- ing and that summer had come. He cleared enough snow that some of the light spilled into the room, and then he called for the women in the brothel to join him. They crowded around him, standing in the brilliance of light that did not come with the choking smoke of an ill-trimmed lantern wick or the dim flickering of a candle. Nobody knew who started laughing first, but the mirth infected them, and they laughed for hours, until the sun went down.

IN THE MILL, my grandmother woke my grandfather from a light sleep. A thin lick of water came in through the cracks in the wall, puddling on the floor. They listened quietly to the sound of the snow settling under the new heat. Working carefully from the doorway of the mill, Jeannot broke through the roof of the tunnel and dug upward. He took the cleared snow and packed it into steps, widening the hole as he went so that the snow would not collapse upon him. As he came nearer to the surface, he could first see a dim glow, and then a burning whiteness. It was blinding. Whiteness and light.

The sun reflected against the snow, bouncing the rays until it was so much brightness that he felt like his eyes would melt. With his eyes closed, however, my grandfather realized that along with light, sound had returned. During the snows, he and Martine had firewood and enough of a store of oil to see them through the winter, but still, they spent half of every day in the dark, trying to sleep away the winter. It was a darkness that could only be found underground, a complete absence of light. It was the sound during those months, though, that was harder to get used to. At first they had the wind and the pelting of snow against the sides of the building, but after a while even that had disappeared, leaving them with only a hush and the imagined whisperings of the man they killed; after butchering Gregory, neither Jeannot nor Martine found much to say.

That first day, he and Martine spent several hours simply standing at the top of their snow-packed staircase, but neither of them could figure out how to hoist themselves on top of the snow. Each time Jeannot tried, the snow crumbled under his weight, and he feared being buried. Finally, they simply retreated back inside the mill. By the next day the sound of water came louder, and a thin veil flowed constantly across the floor. Every few minutes the mill crackled and groaned, nails squeaking against the weight of the shifting and settling snow.

On the third day after Jeannot had broken through, the treetops melted clean, and from the top of the staircase they were able to see green pines. They stood on the stairs and watched birds dart from branch to branch, and a squirrel came close enough to the hole in the snow that Jeannot was able to hit it with the shovel. They had a different kind of stew for dinner that night. The sun shone down warmly enough that Jeannot and Martine stripped off their clothing while they stood atop the staircase, until they realized that the sun was baking them red with unforgiving intensity.

Day by day they climbed to the top of the stairs and watched the snow melt, still unable to exit from their burrow. They were not prepared, however, at the end of July, when they heard a voice calling to them. At first they thought they were hearing things again. In the long darkness of the winter, with only each other for quiet company, they had often

imagined the sound of another person's voice—usually Gregory's, though sometimes that of a person who they were less
intimately acquainted with—and though it broke their sleep,
they had mostly learned to ignore the phantom callings. But
this time, at the sound of the voices, Flaireur perked his head
up. The dog, as if he, too, had been hearing voices that he could
not believe, stood warily, and then, with something approaching a great joy, he began to bark.

Jeannot and Martine, feeling like prairie dogs peeking their
heads from the ground, greeted the man at the top of their
staircase. He stood above them, his feet strapped into crudely
fashioned snowshoes that appeared to have been made with a
frame taken from chair backs and webbing from ripped silken
undergarments. He wore only light pants and an undershirt,
but a scarf swaddled his head; they could barely see his eyes
behind the thin slit that he peered out of. Only when he lowered the scarf did Jeannot recognize Pearl Gasseur.

Jeannot brought out scrap lumber to make his own poorly
constructed snowshoes. Pearl hauled him to the surface, and
then he and Pearl together helped Martine emerge from
beneath the snow. They had to move slowly; not only were
the planks unwieldy, but Martine's enormous, pregnant girth
made it difficult for her to keep her balance. The sun beat
down upon them with a welcome warmth. Thin streams of
water ran across the surface of the snow at frequent intervals,
and they could hear a powerful rushing sound.

"It's a river," Pearl said.

"It's unfrozen already?" Though they were in the woods,
Jeannot stopped and tried to peer through the trees, as if he
might see the river.

"No, not the Sawgamet. A new river made of meltwater. It's a churning madness. The water is running over the snow and cutting its own path." Pearl shrugged. "Maybe it is above the Sawgamet, following the same channels, the same furrows in the earth, but I would not be able to tell." He gestured to the trees that they walked through, the tips and branches that lay at their feet. "Even with this furious melting, there is still fifteen, twenty feet on the ground. I would have walked by you if the roof of the mill had not been peeking from the snow, and if I hadn't seen your burrow and your grand staircase."

When they came out of the trees, they stopped to look at the water. Like Pearl, neither Martine nor Jeannot could tell if the raging water followed the path of the Sawgamet, or if it followed some different course of its own choosing. The water ran wide, one hundred feet across, and frothed and churned like they had never seen the river do, even in the violent spring melts. Broken trees and boulders swam by them, heading down and away with no remorse.

"Look," Martine said, taking Jeannot's attention away from the water. They could see hints of the village before them. It appeared as though there were only a half-dozen houses, their third-stories resting on the snow like buildings of only a single floor. They could see two scantily clad women sitting on what must have been a porch roof, and further down, the first appearance of a shelter near the mines.

THEY SPENT SEVERAL HOURS digging and looking for Franklin's store before they finally came upon it, Jeannot's shovel bouncing off the rooftop. He banged the handle of the shovel against the roof several times, and after a short pause he heard a muffled yell and a knocking return. While Jeannot shuffled back to the mill to get his ax, Pearl brought Martine over to the brothel. The whores greeted her with hugs and wonderment at the size of her belly. They made her sit in their overstuffed chairs, bringing her soup with a slice of fresh-baked bread, and rubbing scented lotion into her swollen feet. She was so firmly ensconced in her comfort that she did not even realize Jeannot had returned and was hacking at the roof of her brother's store.

The roof surrendered quickly to the blade of Jeannot's ax. When he smashed through, opening a hole the size of a dinner plate, he saw Rebecca and Franklin's upturned faces. They stood beneath the gap staring up at him, blinking like owls astonished to see the day.

"You put a hole in my roof," Franklin said, a note of confusion in his voice, as if that was all he could think of to say after so many months buried beneath the snow.

"I'm trying to get you out."

"Wouldn't digging have done less damage?"

Jeannot rested the ax head on the lip of the hole and then let out a laugh. "You've got me there, Franklin. I got so excited at the sight of the roof that I didn't even think of trying to find the door. Martine will be glad to see you well. And speaking of which, step back a ways. I've already put a hole in your roof, I might as well make it big enough for you to come out of."

He swung with his ax, smashing and broadening the opening, and then, more gently, smoothing it out. When he was finished, Franklin pushed his counter under the hole, stacked a crate on top of that, and while he pushed from below and Jeannot pulled from above, the men helped Rebecca out.

At the sight of Rebecca—pregnant, though not quite as large as she herself was—Martine broke into tears. She was, she said to her sister-in-law, relieved to not have to give birth while buried under thirty feet of snow. She had been expecting the baby at any moment for the past few weeks, and in the overstuffed chair, with the soup finished and her brother's wife before her and bearing the same bloated belly that she had carried for far longer than she had expected, she felt like she had experienced some sort of salvation.

Jeannot, Franklin, and Pearl decided that it made the most sense for them all to move into the brothel while the snow kept receding. Jeannot did not say anything about the pernicious limitation of the almost-depleted food supply at the mill—though I am sure that he and my grandmother were not the only people in Sawgamet to resort to eating human flesh to survive that winter—but he did agree that it would be nice to have some company for a while. That night, they had a festival of sorts, with cakes and a roasted goose that Pearl brought down with a shot from his rifle.

The next day, Franklin opened the store to Pearl and the women in the brothel, helping all of them crawl through the hole in the roof. They bought thread and needles, silk, bottles of ink, and toilet water. Though it nearly broke his heart to do so, my great-uncle charged them barely more than it had cost him to bring the supplies in, and he freely shared his flour, sugar, canned fruit, and tea with the women of the brothel. In return, over the next several weeks, they cooked for and pampered his sister and wife.

Franklin, Jeannot, and Pearl spent their days helping to dig out the five mining camps that showed signs of life. Where a roof still stood over the pit mines, Jeannot chopped his way through. The men usually came out slowly and warily, pale and blinking like moles, scared of the brightness of the day. Their clothes hung off them and their cheeks were hollowed out, like they had spent the winter carving at their own flesh rather than the ground. The miners were weak and smelled so badly that the madam insisted that they bathe in a large copper washtub set on the porch roof before they be allowed to enter the brothel. Each man took his turn, stripping and adding his clothing to a pile to be burned, then scrubbing himself in fresh hot water that the women from the brothel carried pot by pot up the stairs and passed out the window.

By the time they had dug out all five camps—nearly forty men in all—Jeannot, Franklin, and Pearl had heard the same story many times. The men working to exhaustion in their mines, at first not even realizing the direness of their situations, too excited by the idea of gold. Then, later, after it was too late to flee, rationing beans and biscuits, then resorting to butchering mules—or worse—and sucking on ice to create the illusion of fullness. The miners came out with such little strength that they often allowed themselves to be carried to the brothel like infants, and for the first few weeks the women treated them as such; it was not until near the end of August that they became paying customers again.

Most of the miners came back to health well enough, my grandfather told me, though one man never recovered his sight: He was part of a syndicate of five men who had been kept warm underground by the presence of a hot spring that they had accidently uncovered. They had no fire and only enough candles and oil to see them with light through to January. They had spent nearly six months in complete darkness, eating uncooked beans and hardtack, learning that they could not trust the sound of each other's voices. It quickly became commonplace among them to lay their fingers upon a speaker's face, trying to divine intent and emotion through feel. Aboveground again, the first four men kept their eyes tightly closed against the brightness, only opening them slowly and gradually over the course of a week, but Alfred alone among them had opened his eyes to greet the sun immediately upon leaving the mine. Alfred's eyes, so used to being without light, did not distinguish between the blindness of the dark and the blindness of the sun, and his eyes turned milky and forever sightless. Though he was an agreeable man despite his blindness, my grandfather said he could not stand to be near him, and was glad when the man went east to be with family; Alfred's frosted eyes brought back the memory of the rancid meat smell and the fish-pale flesh of the hag who had temporarily stolen Flaireur's voice on my grandfather's first night in Sawgamet, the gagging taste of Gregory's flesh in his mouth.

They unearthed a sixth mine as well, but there were no men left alive, only a fat and bored mule and the picked-clean skeletons of nearly a dozen miners. Though Pearl suggested they shoot the animal and leave the whole lot in their mine as a tomb, Jeannot convinced him that they might need the animal in the coming months.

After they finished digging out the mines, they saw a wisp of smoke past where they thought any man might be, and they came across the rooftop and stovepipe of a small cabin barely sticking out from the melting snow. When they dug out the door enough to open it, they found Xiaobo, the Chinaman who had been hired to work for Jeannot and my grandmother. He seemed as if he had lost his senses; he was naked and yelled at them, trying to push them away. They forced him into clothing and brought him back to the brothel, and though he calmed down and stopped slapping at them, it was a few days before he spoke English.

While Pearl, Jeannot, and Franklin dug and the women in the brothel took care of nursing the miners back to health, there was little thought of the saloon owner who had treated my great-uncle so poorly, Dryden Boon. Perhaps had Boon been a more likable man he would have been dug out sooner, but as it stood, his body was only discovered in mid-August, nearly a month after the snow had stopped falling. Nobody could figure out how Boon managed to get outside of his saloon, buried headfirst in the snow, but it was one of the women from the brothel who first saw his boots. More people saw his calves and knees stick into the air as the snow melted around him. After my grandfather, Jeannot, and Franklin dug him out, they put his body on ice in the empty stables behind the blacksmith's shop with the bodies of the other men—and even a few women—that they had found in the snow, in crude cabins, and in one collapsed tent. They did not know how many others had been swept away by the floods, but in the stables, as the snow continued to melt and the sun returned with the fury of a lover scorned, like it was trying to recapture the winter glory that it had lost, every few hours one of the men had to shovel more ice and snow onto the corpses.

AS THE SNOW MELTED and settled, men began to return to Sawgamet in a trickle, five or six a day. The snow had been light elsewhere. The miners said that even a few hours' walk away the ground had been clear since May. Downriver thirty miles, a new gold strike had created the town of Havershand almost overnight, and the men who came to Sawgamet were those who had come to Havershand too late or who did not remember that Sawgamet had seemed on the verge of playing out even before the snows came.

The runoff from the melt scoured Sawgamet clean, taking whatever gold remained from the ground, removing the abandoned tents and poorly built or half-finished cabins, taking the detritus of the men who had fled, sweeping it into the river. Miners working the banks downriver in Havershand fished out useful bits, picks, shovels, and tin pans.

When Jeannot tried to return to the mill to gather a few tools, the meltwater turned him away. The water ran so swift and cold down the slope and through the woods that he could not make his way through it for fear that he might be swept away along with the debris that raged along the new-formed river. Ultimately, after waiting for a few days, Jeannot hiked through the snow and up into the hills behind the meadow before coming down from above. Standing on the slope, he could see that the mill had remained untouched, but the melting snow had taken away the ashen remains of their house, it had taken all of the old cabin except for a few logs, and most importantly, the floods had removed the barrel of bones that had been buried in the snow. Alone among the wreckage he found an embarrassingly dry copy of a Bible.

It was, he and Martine agreed, glancing nervously at the Bible, a message, and they began to believe that Martine's extended pregnancy—extended beyond reason, beyond the counting that was normal—was part of some punishment for the way in which they had survived the winter. At the brothel, Jeannot went downstairs and knocked on a few doors until he found the room where Xiaobo slept, thinking the Chinaman might have some herbs that would bring about the child's birth.

"You should not be sitting, sitting, sitting," Xiaobo said to Martine. "Look how fat you are. You should be walking if you want this baby to come out."

So she walked. Most days Rebecca accompanied Martine on her walks. Franklin kept himself busy. He patched the hole in the roof of the store and spent the mornings tending to customers. In the afternoons he worked with Jeannot to get the sawmill running again. The two of them had partnered on the lumber operations, Franklin providing the gold to hire men, and Jeannot driving the operation.

Martine did not ask Rebecca to come on her walks, but Rebecca could see that it gave her comfort to have company. Martine was clearly past the time when she should have had her child, and though the Chinaman insisted that the baby would come when it was ready, Martine was anxious. The two pregnant women walked slowly through the woods. The streets of the village, though cleared of snow, were impassable. What had once been dirt ruts with a line of boards for walking was now an impossibility of mud. A mule had sunk into the muck and when the miner had not been able to pull it out—even with a dozen men pulling on ropes—he had to shoot the animal and leave it to rot. That same day, one of the women from the brothel had accidently stepped off the boardwalk, and had been stuck in mud up to her knees until Pearl rescued her.

They did not always talk on their walks—both women found it difficult to keep their breath with the added weight of their stomachs—but they enjoyed each other's company. Most days they saw small animals, squirrels and birds, though occasionally, if they were quiet enough, they would come across caribou. One of the days they saw a ram that was inexplicably wandering through the woods instead of up on the mountain.

They did not stray very far from what was left of the village. My grandmother kept her hand on her stomach, as if that would tell her when the baby was ready to come, and if they were gone for more than an hour or so they would usually hear Jeannot's voice calling to them, carrying across the air.

After a few weeks of walking like this, Xiaobo shook his head and gave Martine a thick, foul tea to drink. "Your baby is too happy in there," he said to Martine, and then he turned to scowl at Rebecca, too. "And where is your baby? You must drink some tea as well." He passed Rebecca a cup of the tea and she obligingly drank. "Come out," he said with a mock sternness, speaking to Martine's stomach.

Martine tried to force a smile as she drank down the tea. "Perhaps he's waiting for Rebecca to have her baby so that he'll have somebody to play with."

"He?" Xiaobo lifted his eyebrow.

"It's going to be a boy," Martine said.

Xiaobo put his hand firmly on Martine's belly and felt jabs

of the baby pushing against the skin. He shook his head. "It's a girl," he said to Martine.

"What about me?" Rebecca asked.

He straightened and turned away.

"Wait," Rebecca said. "Can't you use your magic to tell me?"

Xiaobo paused with his hand on the doorknob. "It's not magic," he said. "Not the sort of magic that you think of when you are walking through the woods." Still, he relented and returned to touch Rebecca's stomach as well. "A boy. Now finish your tea."

XIAOBO WAS RIGHT about the herbs, but wrong about which woman would have a boy and who would have a girl. Martine had my father, and despite the extra time that he claimed in my grandmother's womb, he was no bigger than any baby should be. Rebecca's daughter, Julia, was small and anxious, rooting fiercely at her mother's breasts.

The children grew fat and happy, though they saw little of their fathers: Franklin and Jeannot kept at the mill. They were certain of their new venture. The trees downstream in Havershand did not amount to much, and they thought they could make money by floating wood down the river. They worked logs into lumber and stacked it beside the mill, hiring Pearl and a few other men to join them. Franklin even promised Rebecca that he would build them a house the following summer, once my grandparents replaced the one that had burned down during the winter.

At the end of September, when Jeannot, Pearl, and Franklin launched the rafts made from the rough-cut lumber, my grandmother, holding my infant father, and Rebecca, holding the baby that was to become my aunt Julia, watched the men take to the river.

The men lashed the lumber together in the shallows, making large and solid rafts for them to ride to Havershand. Jeannot and Pearl—and Franklin, when he was not in the store—had worked the mill hard, using the daylight for all it was worth. They had hired a few men at first, and then a few more, until they had nearly a dozen men bringing down trees and working them through the saws. With the gold seemingly gone from the ground, Franklin's ability to pay men cash on the barrel trumped work in the mines. Franklin talked of adding a grindstone to the mill wheel, but for now they focused on cutting. The wood piled as the snow had piled only a few months earlier, and Martine said that she could not imagine such use for the wood that the men had milled.

"They don't have the same trees downstream," Jeannot said, "but they have men and mines, and they will buy as much lumber as we can bring to them."

"And what are you setting aside to build a house?" Martine asked. "I'm not going to spend another winter in the mill."

"After we float the wood down the river," my grandfather promised. "Wood enough for us, for your brother and Rebecca, and money enough for us to buy beddings and whatever else you need for the house to see us through the winter." He paused, both of them clearly thinking of the way Gregory's flesh had stuck in their throats. "And food. Money enough so that we won't go hungry."

MY GRANDFATHER HAD BEEN practical about the floods. He had returned to the clearing in the woods, half hoping the golden caribou would be there to guide him again, but whatever magic was still there was only an echo. The only thing left was a small dip in the ground and some antlers. He picked up the antlers and angled them in the sun, but there was not a trace of gold. What he and Martine had left was the mill, and he made use of it. He had no more expectations of sudden wealth, none of the same certainty that he had only a few years before when he had arrived in Sawgamet, but he was sure of his own ability to work.

I wonder if a different sort of man would have spent the rest of his days trying to find the golden boulder or dangling a hook in the water for a fish with a belly full of gold. Though a different sort of man would have fled after that first night in Sawgamet, gold or no gold, the qallupilluit chasing away any thoughts of riches.

For my grandfather it seemed as simple as this: He had decided to stay in Sawgamet, and he believed that nothing could drive him away. It did not matter if he was wrong or right. He did not think of the woods in terms of good and evil. He saw the magic as a reality, not as a benevolence or a punishment, and he realized that the only thing he could count on was himself.

THE RAFTS FLOATED down the river with much more speed than Jeannot had expected. They had taken care to lash the lumber tightly, but still it shifted a little beneath his feet. He was comfortable enough, but wary. More comfortable certainly than Franklin. He could see Franklin on another raft, looking unsure of his footing, but he was glad that his brother-in-law had come along. He knew Franklin would be able to drive a better deal than he himself would. Along with Pearl, he had hired on five of the other men who had been working the mill to help bring the lumber down the river. They had cut long poles to help move the rafts, and each raft was tied to several others, but he hoped they would not encounter much difficulty. As the river turned and he lost view of the banks of the village, he thought that he did not want to be long gone from my grandmother and my father.

They learned quickly that the river was dangerous; they did not even reach Havershand before they lost their first man. The rafts kept getting caught in eddies and against the banks, each time requiring them to pole hard to get the wood moving again, and it took them three days to float the lumber down the river to Havershand. On the third morning, with no warning, with no sound, with no alarm at all in the night that had passed, they realized that one of the men was missing. It was only when they pulled the rafts from the water in the slow, broad shallows of Havershand that they found his body, swollen and wrinkled, fully dressed and caught among the lashings underneath the cut lumber. His eyes had been eaten clean by the fish.

Despite the man's death, Jeannot had found himself captivated by the swirling growth and industry in Havershand. While Franklin saw to the sale of the wood, Jeannot walked through the streets. He stopped in a jury-rigged store that sold goods at prices so inflated that it put even Franklin to shame, and watched a butcher working the skin off a moose. He strolled past a row of tents that served as brothels, the whores lingering outside in the last of the summer heat, each and every one of them equipped with a scale to measure the gold that their customers paid. He saw the stripped-away banks where men dug for gold, and hiked up into the hills above the town where silver had been discovered. From his vista, he could see out over all of Havershand. He saw where the river opened enough for docks, the rough shape of a steamboat being built, and the well-laid lines that the city seemed to be growing upon. He saw men mining, men sawing, men hammering, men walking the streets with a brisk purpose. He saw a creek that emptied into the Sawgamet River and the first signs that somebody had taken it upon himself to build a mill in Havershand. Jeannot also saw the sick, stick, scraggly trees that dotted the slopes, and he knew that as long as men kept coming to Havershand he would be able to earn his living by floating logs down the river.

They did not linger long in Havershand. By midafternoon they were already walking back to Sawgamet. Two of the men that Jeannot had hired thought about staying in Havershand, but as they talked to the men already working the banks, they decided to return to Sawgamet; gold offered rewards, but cutting trees offered certainty. The hiking was not difficult, and it was made easier by the fullness of their wallets. Franklin bought roasted chicken and bread for all of the men despite the dearness of their cost, and they walked well past supper-time and into the gloaming. They spread their bedrolls on the bank and built a fire, but they had need of neither. Even in the darkness, the temperature stayed such that Pearl said he was grateful of the cooling breeze that pulled off the river.

BACK WITH MY GRANDMOTHER in Sawgamet, my grandfather saw the village growing again, though not like it had during the boom of gold. Every day men who had taken ships around the coast passed down through Sawgamet on their way to the new goldfields of Havershand, and every day some of them decided to stay and make their way in Sawgamet instead. Some men came the other way, as well, those who had traveled from Quesnellemouthe or further east, and had found the land in Havershand leaner than they expected. Franklin spent time with his ledgers and with the new goods that he paid to bring in, restocking the shelves that had been laid bare by the savagery of the previous winter. He gave Rebecca and my grandmother dispensation to take from the store as they would, encouraging his wife and his sister to lay into the canned fruits, sugar, and any other notions they might want.

When he was not in the store, he worked the mill with Jeannot. Though the men who came into Sawgamet clamored for wood, Jeannot set aside lumber first for himself and Martine, and then for Franklin and Rebecca. The house that they built for Jeannot and Martine was more modest than the one that had burned to the ground, though they built it with the intention of adding a third story the following summer. Martine insisted that this house be in the village—she did not want to have to worry about another winter cut off from all others, she said—and she said she would barely let the last hammer fall before she planned to shoo the men down the street toward Franklin's store, so that they could build a house there.

By Christmas the mud of the streets had frozen into brutal ruts, and the men had to walk carefully so as not to trip. Jeannot and Martine's house, only a few doors down from Franklin's and finished just the week before, was ready for a companion; the men had seated the foundation to Franklin's house early in November, before the ground froze, and Jeannot said that the day after Christmas he and the men would be set to build enough of a house to get Franklin and Rebecca through the winter at least. Franklin did not mind the cabin behind the store, but he had begun to realize how close it was at nights, how little space there was for him and Rebecca to share with the baby. But at least they had no need to worry about food. Franklin and Jeannot—as had every man and woman who had seen the world covered with snow—had set aside more food than was necessary, but still it was reassuring for Franklin see the barrels of dry goods, the canned food.

And, of course, they need not have worried; spring broke early that year, as though to try and make up for the previous winter's passion for snow, and the melt, more gentle this time, smoothed the streets of Sawgamet into something passable. A few men, of the type that preferred to work alone, kept at mining claims that were picked clean, but the tin pans on the shelves of the store stayed neatly stacked. Most men took to homesteading or migrated to the woods, cutting trees for Franklin and Jeannot or working for the new outfit from Havershand. The mosquitoes swarmed in the dimness of the woods with particular vengeance, and more than one man split his skin trying to shoo away the biting insects while holding an ax.

THE MILL COMPANY MEN from Havershand brought a cook with them, and except for a few nights a week when they would visit the new saloon or the brothel, they mostly stayed in camp. They started with two dozen men and hired more—it seemed like for every man from Sawgamet who cut wood for Jeannot, there were five who cut for the Havershand crew—and the sound of trees falling carried through to the village. Every month, the other company floated huge rafts of uncut logs down toward Havershand.

Franklin thought that they should send their logs down the river as they accumulated near the mill, but Jeannot argued the wood would be worth more in the fall.

"Once we saw it and raft it down the river, we'll be able to name our price. The sawmill downriver will go through all the logs the other company has sent, and when we come in with our boards, men will be feeling the pinch of winter coming. Good wood for building houses is scarce enough in Havershand, and no matter how fast they run their mill, they won't be able to meet all the need there is for lumber. Besides," he added, "if we float it down uncut, we'll have no choice but to sell it to their mill at their prices."

While Jeannot kept a crew of ten working in the woods, widening the circle of stumps around the mill, Pearl supervised the cutting, stacking, and stickering of the fresh-cut boards.

More men and even a few families trickled in to Sawgamet, keeping Franklin busy in the store. As June wore on, the sun seemed to meet itself, setting and rising so close together that it was difficult to tell if the day ever ended, and during the few hours that they slept, the men who lived in windowless hovels were thankful for the darkness that they cursed throughout the winter. My grandfather did not sleep easily, however, even with the heavy curtains that Martine made for their new bedroom.

The logging camp of men from Havershand had swelled to more than two hundred. They had started making the half-hour walk to the village more often, and they had not been content to leave well enough alone. Their foreman, Jonah Feed, had been eating away at Jeannot's men. He offered higher pay, and bragged of paying cash outright, rather than the combination of pay and credit at Franklin's store. Feed spoke French with an outsider's bastard Texas accent, but that had not stopped him from keeping his crews running tight. There were enough holdouts who stayed with my grandfather, though. The Rondeau brothers had run into Feed in town and they told him they were not interested in working for the son-of-a-bitch boss of his that owned the Havershand mill. A few of Feed's crew had taken exception to the Rondeaus' comments—six men for the two Rondeau brothers—and Giles Rondeau spent several days laid up in bed.

Feed himself was not supposed to be a terrible fellow, no rougher certainly than my grandfather himself, but the owner—the man behind Feed—seemed to inspire an almost unnatural fear and devotion. Pearl had talked briefly with him once, had been offered a job, and he told Jeannot that the man carried a stink with him, an unworldly foulness that made it difficult for Pearl to remember even his own name.

AND HERE AGAIN, my grandfather paused as he had paused when he burned his hand on the stovepipe. He told me the story of the long winter in one push, and I had not said a word. I did not want to interrupt him as I had interrupted my father the winter before, asking him whether or not he missed the float when he was telling Marie and me the story of my parents' marriage.

"You'd think I would have known," my grandfather said, but he didn't really say it to me at all.

In some ways it has been the same for me this past week. I read aloud to my mother as much as I could bear, and I realized that it did not matter if she was listening or not as long as I could fill the silence.

MY GRANDFATHER HAD NOT much wanted to speak to Feed before, but after the beating that the Rondeau brothers took he thought he had no choice. He rose early that morning, checked the mill, and then whistled for Flaireur. The sun already burned over the mountains, sending a glare off the permanent tops of snow, and Jeannot was pleased when he reached the line of trees. Even the short walk from the village had left him sweating. Flaireur lunged into the thin trickle that passed for a creek and drank with loud, lapping urgency. Jeannot kept walking, knowing the dog would catch up.

He had thought of taking his rifle, but had decided against it. He was just going to talk. He carried his ax and ate the rest of a muffin that Martine had pressed upon him as he left the house. The ax felt a comfortable weight in his hand, more comfortable than it had been his first few days of cutting in the spring. That winter, though short, had been long on time by the fire with Martine and the baby. He spent a few days working traplines with the old Indian and his young son—who, of course, turned out later to be my uncle Lawrence, Julia's husband—but he worked the trapline just enough to understand the beauty of the woods in the winter and his own lack of desire for collecting furs. Mostly he slept late. The snow had been light, but the cold had been such that he needed little encouragement from Martine to spend the days inside. When he had started cutting again in the spring, his hands had been pink and tender for the first week or so, until a hardened layer of flesh turned them into something as rough as the wood he took down.

Though the trail was well trampled by the Havershand men, Jeannot did not walk as briskly as was his wont. He occasionally stepped off the trail to move into the woods, thinking he saw the glint of something golden in a clearing. Each time, however, he realized it was simply the sun flitting through the openings in the trees, not the boulder that he and Martine had come across. Flaireur stayed alongside him, tail held high and nose to the ground, but the dog gave no signs of warning. Soon enough, the trail came out along the banks of the Sawgamet, where the trees pulled back to reveal an open gravel sweep of shoreline. The river was wide and slow, and aside from the incredible swath of forest that might run forever, Jeannot could understand why Feed had picked this spot to stack wood.

He could see men working teams of horses, dragging trees to the shore, stacking and laying them to prepare for the next float down the river. A small gang of men worked taking down trees, expanding the cuts that other men had already made, and Jeannot thought he saw a distant rustle and heard the yells of another crew working further in. Flaireur bounced across the smooth stones of the bank and into the river, dunking his head beneath the water and then shaking it. The spray flashed against the sun, and Jeannot thought for a minute of joining the dog. During the coldest days of winter, when he could stand only a few moments outside and even trying to cut firewood sent a jolt through his hands, he had wished for a day like this, but with the sun's full fury upon him, Jeannot realized that he now wished for the winter's return.

As he walked through the tents set along the riverside, he caught the smells of food and remembered talk of camp cooks, a pair of Chinamen. He had not seen a Chinaman himself before coming west, but had seen plenty since, and even though Xiaobo's baking seemed like some sort of punishment, Jeannot enjoyed the meals that Xiaobo cooked. Martine was happy with the Chinaman instead of having to hire one of the few rough women in town, and my infant father seemed to have taken to him, quieting every time Xiaobo picked him up. There was something off in the man, my grandfather said, some sort of distance or disappointment that Jeannot could not understand, but he did not want to question the happy balance of his household.

He had not passed fully through the camp before he heard his name.

"Vous me cherchez?" Feed asked.

"I can speak English," my grandfather said, turning around and deciding not to comment on Feed's poor French. The Texan was younger and taller than Jeannot had thought. He had only seen the foreman from afar, and though the man's face showed the lines of a man who was used to working, he wore a suit, neat and pressed, like he was going to church rather than into the woods.

"Good," Feed said, "because my French isn't the best thing about me. I've been expecting you," he said. "He told me you would come."

"Who?"

"My boss."

My grandfather glanced over toward the water. Flaireur stood on the banks watching the current, and then, for no reason that Jeannot could see, the dog lunged into the river and snapped at something beneath the surface. "A few of your boys laid out two of my men yesterday," Jeannot said.

"You'll have to talk to the boss."

"Aren't you the foreman?" my grandfather asked.

My grandfather told me that he was not sure if he smelled the rotting meat first or if he felt the man's appearance behind him, but he turned to see a tall menace standing beside him. When he saw the sunken cheeks, the deep grooves of hunger, he stumbled backward, trying to get away from this ghost. The man opened his mouth, and though he had the same voice and face of Gregory, he spoke with a clear, quick French that showed no hint of Russian. "I've been waiting to see you," he said to Jeannot.

My grandfather held the ax in front of him like a talisman, and he felt Flaireur lean wet and shaking against his leg.

Gregory turned to Feed and the Texan's body suddenly drooped, hanging in the air like an oversized marionette. My grandfather said that he thought he could see a dull glaze pass over Feed's eyes, and when Gregory motioned at the man with his hand, Feed loped away toward the crews of men taking down trees, his body lurching awfully across the ground.

Gregory turned back to my grandfather with no apparent hurry. "I see that Flaireur made it through the winter just fine," Gregory said, his voice slow and supple.

Again, Jeannot caught a whiff of the rotten meat smell and he felt himself begin to gag, the taste of the miner's flesh rising in his throat. He blinked away a few tears and then forced himself to look at Gregory. "I'm sorry," he said. "We didn't have a choice."

"That's an ugly dog you've got there," Gregory said, like he had not heard Jeannot.

Jeannot reached down and touched Flaireur's head, remembering the wet softness of the ax swinging into Gregory's head, the bloody mess of carving his body. Flaireur's rough hair matted under his fingertips. Despite his swim, the dog still panted in the heat of the day. "What do you need?" Jeannot said. And then, almost as if he were in prayer, "What can I do?"

"I can't sleep. Do you know that?" Gregory turned his head to look out over the water. "I haven't been able to sleep since you killed me. You didn't even bury my bones." He took a step forward and then reached out to put his hands on the handle of the ax. My grandfather could not move. He could only watch as Gregory pulled the ax from his hands. The Russian was oddly gentle with the ax, like it was something alive, something that needed to be cradled. And then, with a sudden, stunning violence, Gregory reared back and swung the ax, slamming it into the top of Flaireur's skull.

There was no slowness, no moment of impact, just a before and after: Flaireur standing next to my grandfather, and then the dog's carcass lying heavily on the ground.

Gregory pulled the ax from Flaireur's head and then, slowly, placed the handle back into my grandfather's hands. "You should have killed the dog. And you should have buried my bones. It's the least you could have done."

He turned away, took a few steps, and then stopped to look back at my grandfather. "Ax, and then fire," he said, and then he disappeared inside one of the canvas tents.

MY GRANDFATHER SAID that he did not look behind him as he walked into the woods, though that is the only part of his story that I found difficult to believe. Even at eleven, as he told me this story, I knew enough, had seen enough, to believe that ghosts and monsters lived in the woods, to believe in the wehtiko, but I could not imagine having the will to resist looking back. And yet, if any man could have done so, it would have been my grandfather. I am not that sort of man. I am the sort of man who always looks back, which may be why I'm so well suited to life leading a church. But my grandfather. If my grandfather had been Orpheus he still would not have looked behind him.

My grandfather stopped along the path by the creek to clean some of the blood and hair from his leg, and then he washed the blood and gore from the blade of the ax. He wanted to go tell Martine of encountering Gregory, but he knew that he had little time. Ax and fire. Flaireur dead and to be mourned later, but for now he had to see to the wood before it was set ablaze by this unholy creature.

"We're floating the wood tomorrow. Whatever we've got is going to Havershand in the morning. Have the men stack it up," he told Pearl.

They helped the men carry the planks down to the banks of the river, stacking them in neat piles so they would be ready for morning. Franklin spoke of building a chute to send the wood sliding down, but Jeannot shook him off and bent his back to the task of getting the wood by the water. They finished before supper, the lumber piled high just past the tents of a group of American miners scratching futilely in the dirt and rock, and Jeannot told his men to be ready to go soon after dawn.

During dinner, Jeannot was quiet. He told Martine that Flaireur had been swept away in the river. He ate little, though this meal contained no meat. Though my grandmother's eyes were red from crying over the dog, she watched him, and my grandfather could see that she had questions she wanted to ask. He wanted to tell her, wanted to say that it would be fine, but he thought there was no reason to tell her. He would float the wood and then he would search downriver until he found Gregory's bones. He would give the man a proper burial. It would all be settled then. The Russian was right. He could at least have done that.

That night, Martine slept with a heavy breath, but Jeannot could not sleep. He kept thinking of the cruel thinness in Gregory's cheeks, the way light cut through them, as if he had continued to starve even in death. He thought of how Gregory had materialized from the snow, as if he were a creature from the woods, and then my grandfather rose from the bed and looked out through the curtains. He saw a glow from the riverbanks and struggled to make out the sound of the voices that called through the darkness. And then he realized. He pulled on his pants and shirt and sat heavily on the bed to lace his boots.

"What is it?" My grandmother's voice was slurred with sleep.

"Fire," he said. "It'll be the wood we've stacked along the river. You go back to sleep. I'll take care of what needs taking care of," he said.

Martine sat up. Her voice came through with less haze. "Jeannot? What are you doing?"

"I'm going to try to get the fire out," he said as he pulled on the boots. "Past that, we'll see," he said, like he might do anything other than try to find Gregory's bones.

My grandfather ran down the steps, his boots hitting the wood loudly. As he stopped to take the bucket from the kitchen and pull his rifle from the shelf, Xiaobo poked his head out of his room. The Chinaman did not say anything, but he looked carefully at the rifle in Jeannot's hands.

"Stay with Martine and the baby," my grandfather said.

Even out the door he could smell the smoke, the acrid,

familiar tinge of heat and ash. He heard shouts in English and French and in other languages that he did not recognize, but they were all saying the same thing. The orange glow of the flames hovered beneath the stars, and even in his running Jeannot was able to recognize the strange, hellish beauty of the fire.

More than a dozen men were already in a bucket line by the time my grandfather reached the fire. Each bucket of water seemed like a woefully small impediment against the devouring of the fire, but Jeannot directed the men who came running after him to form a second line. He stood at the front, bearing the brunt of the flames. He could feel his hands begin to blister and even his eyebrows seemed to be on fire. He glanced over and saw that Pearl was at the front of the other line. Something seared the back of his neck, and he realized it was the barrel of the rifle pressed up against his flesh. Jeannot slid the strap off his shoulder and tossed the rifle to the side.

"The river," my grandfather heard someone shout behind him. He turned to see the priest yelling. "We've got to push the wood into the river," Father Hugo yelled.

Jeannot threw the bucket of water he was holding onto the fire, and then another and another, before he realized the priest was right. "Grab what you can to push," he yelled. "Into the water."

The men followed his lead, picking up branches or what pieces of lumber were not burning, and used them as prods and levers, pushing at the inferno. As the men strained, the piled lumber started to break; what had seemed a singular institution showed itself to be individual logs burning and glowing against the darkness of the night. As the wood fell into the river, the water hissed against the heat, but a smear of burning water moved with the current, a slick of oil spreading.

Jeannot heard a few men shout with surprise at the evidence of arson, but he paid no mind, frantically pushing what remained on the shore toward the river. His only surprise was that Gregory's ghost had done such a poor job of starting the fire. They would be able to salvage at least half the wood, he thought as he tumbled more lumber into the water. Though the branch that he was using had caught fire, and he could feel the heat against his hands, he did not stop until all of the burning wood was in the river.

The cool water felt like a salve against his hands and on his arms, his face. He touched his fingers gingerly to the backs of his hands, the blisters already forming on the tender flesh. The same men who had helped to fight the fire waded out in the water with him, trying to bring as much of the swirling, floating, half-charred wood back to the shore as they could. Even in the darkness of the night, there was enough light from the moon and the stars to see wood floating down the Sawgamet, out of reach.

"Some of it might catch along the banks or get caught up in eddies," Pearl said to Jeannot. "We'll get it in the morning, and we've managed to keep enough of it here. The priest was right to tell us to drop the buckets."

"Well enough that he thought of it," my grandfather said. "I'd have kept pissing to put out hell otherwise. We'd be still with the buckets."

Pearl paused and leaned down to splash some water on his face. "I can feel patches already gone from my beard," he said.

Despite himself, my grandfather laughed. "You were already ugly before the fire. This can't have made it worse."

Pearl smiled and took a few steps to grab a piece of wood. He reached for another and then stacked one on top of the other. "You see, Jeannot, this is why the men like working for you. You show us such respect." He started pulling the lumber to shore and then stopped. His gaze went past my grandfather's face. He raised his hand and pointed toward the village. "Jeannot."

Jeannot turned. It took him a moment to understand what he was seeing. He thought that it might be some sort of echo, something burned into his eyes from standing so close to the fire, but then the image resolved itself. He could see the same orange, flickering, jumping glow from the village. The men around him stopped what they were doing and looked toward the village as well. As he heard distant shouts, Jeannot realized that he had been wrong about what Gregory intended to burn.

MY GRANDFATHER RAN PAST the tents and the Americans who had been watching the men fishing for lumber in the river. Running down the street, he pushed his way past a few women standing in front of the brothel, and then started screaming for Martine. He could feel the heat and the smoke still in his lungs, the ache of his hands.

He stopped in front of the house, almost as though he wanted to marvel at the flames. The porch was completely engulfed, the roof already shot through with fire. The crackling heat seemed to come in waves toward the street. On the second floor, from the window of his and Martine's bedroom, the glass was already broken, fire licking out the sill and up the siding. He heard his name from someone beside him.

"Jeannot." Franklin's voice cracked weakly. He stumbled forward, a strange bundle in his arms. "Jeannot." He thrust his arms out, and my grandfather instinctively took the package. It was not until he was already holding it that he realized it was a baby, my father. The child was quiet and sleeping.

"Where's Martine?"

Franklin shook his head. "She didn't . . ." He gulped air and my grandfather saw that Franklin was crying.

Rebecca touched Jeannot on the shoulder. Her voice was strangely calm. "She threw the baby just now. To Franklin."

My grandfather shoved my father back into Franklin's arms and turned to the house. He had taken only a few steps when Pearl brought him to the ground.

It took Pearl and three other men to hold him, Jeannot punching and screaming and writhing under their weight. The flames threw themselves into the house with a stunning fury to match Jeannot's, the fire shooting into the sky like it wanted to ravage the stars. Even the men who stretched in a line to the river, passing bucket after bucket, moved back from the blaze.

Twice Pearl and the men relaxed their grips on my grandfather, and twice my grandfather tried to rush into the house despite its devastation. They held on to him until even Jeannot gave up hope that Martine might still be alive. The bucket line had long turned toward dousing the neighboring buildings to keep them from being taken under by fire as well. Franklin hectored several men into helping him wet down the store, though it was far enough away to clearly be out of danger.

Once the men released him, Jeannot stepped as close to the edge of the house as he could stand. He saw his ax lying on the border of dirt and ash, a burning piece of wood lying across the handle. He reached for it and grabbed the blade in his hand, not thinking of its proximity to the fire, and my grandfather held the metal for a moment after he felt the searing pain of the heat. The top of the blade struck a rock as it fell from his hand, ringing into the night. He shook his burned hand, and with his other hand he carefully touched the handle of the ax. Though it was hot and scarred, he was able to pick it up from the ground and carry it over to the steps of the brothel.

The madam cleaned and bandaged my grandfather's burns. Inside, she told him, some of the women were busy tending to Xiaobo. They had thought the Chinaman would die: he had been pulled from the edges of the destruction, badly burned over half his body. The fire had neatly bisected him, carving a straight line up the center of his body, burning the right side, but leaving the left side untouched, the skin smooth and undamaged. His right side was devastated, however, his hair burned to his scalp, his breath coming ragged like his mouth was held underwater.

BY DAWN, MY GRANDPARENTS' HOUSE was only embers. A cabin next door was partially burned, a few logs eaten through by flames so that the curious could peer through to see the owner—a saloonkeeper who had spent the night hauling buckets of water—sleeping inside. On the banks of the river, Pearl and a few of Jeannot's men worked to sort through the lumber. In the standing eddies and where the gravel met the river, soot and ash stained the water. The men's clothing was blackened and in some cases sparked with holes. Many of them had beards or hair that had been eaten away by the flames like Pearl's.

Rebecca came to the brothel, neatly dressed and wearing a silk faille dress trimmed with white velveteen and blue satin, as if nothing had happened, as if she were headed to a party, though she had a child in either arm. She stood above my grandfather, who was slumped in a low chair, and in the gentlest voice she could manage, my great-aunt said, "Franklin and I will watch Pierre as long as you need, Jeannot. You know that." Jeannot looked up wordlessly and simply stared at the woman before him, looking from Julia to Pierre, like he did not know which was which, until the madam stood up and shooed Rebecca away.

Father Hugo, wearing his boots and thick gloves to protect him from the lingering, buried heat in the ashes, sifted through the wreck of the house with a shovel. He occasionally stopped to remove something from the fire—a partially melted clock, an oddly untouched painting of a bowl of fruit, a full place setting that rested on the ground—but seemed to be searching for something more specific. After a while, he stopped, left his shovel on the edge of the lot, and went down to the river. He returned with Pearl, both men carrying planks, and together they hammered together a small, neat box. Father Hugo returned to the fire, and with Pearl's help brought out what was left of my grandmother's blackened, heat-split body, still smoking from its ravages, dropping it into the box with a sickening finality. They carried the box over to the building owned by the rat-eyed farrier who passed for an undertaker.

THEY DID NOT HOLD the funeral that day or the next, or even the third day after, because they could not find my grandfather. He had left his ax on the steps of the brothel, but no other sign of him remained. Finally, on the fourth day, Father Hugo decided that they would wait for Jeannot no longer, and he presided over the interment of the sealed box.

The smell of smoke and burned flesh hovered over the cemetery. Franklin came to the funeral dumb stumbling drunk and mumbling, crying furiously like he was not a man. By the end of the following week, however, Franklin seemed to be the same shopkeeper that he had been before, working furiously to fill orders for the new Havershand lumber company—cobbled together as a patchwork concern, the previous owner disappearing as surely as Jeannot—and fussing over Julia and his nephew and ward, my father. He directed Pearl and the other men asking after the half-burned lumber on the banks of the Sawgamet to leave it alone. He had sold it to the Havershand Company, he said, and they would take it from there.

"AND YOU," I ASKED my grandfather when he finished speaking, "where did you go?"

"Where do you think I went, Stephen? You may only be eleven, but even you are old enough to know. I went after Gregory. Man or ghost or monster, I tracked him down and killed him a second time, but this time I kept the bones where they could not get away from me."

ELEVEN

Sweet Like Water

I CANNOT REMEMBER ANYMORE if my grandfather told me the story of that long winter and the death and burning that followed before or after he found me on the banks of the river, barely escaped from the monsters in the water. Which came first, I wonder, the qallupilluit dragging me under the ice, my grandmother begging for my life and then telling my grandfather to bring her light, or my grandfather telling me the story of my grandmother's death? Does it matter?

What I know for sure is that only a few days after my grandmother told Jeannot that she needed him to bring her light he disappeared again. He left Sawgamet sometime during the night and did not return for a month, until only a few days before Christmas. He came back on foot, as he had first come to Sawgamet.

"I've what I need," he told my mother and stepfather the night he returned, over dinner. "And for you," he said, looking at me and my cousin Virginia, who had joined us, "I have a surprise."

The next day, while my mother walked an afternoon snack over to my stepfather at the church, Virginia and I sat around the fire with my grandfather.

"But why won't you tell us why you left again?" Virginia asked, handing my grandfather a cup of tea. Steam poured from the cup into the air, a sign that I should add another log to the fire. I cut the wood for my mother—which might have been why she was so generous with its use—and when she returned from the church she would be disappointed if I had let the house grow too cold. Truth be told, I liked chopping the firewood, enjoyed the chance to handle my father's ax.

My grandfather's hands trembled a little as he took the cup and saucer from Virginia. I did not think he was so old—I knew several men who were older than my grandfather who still worked in the cuts, rode the float to Havershand—but something seemed to have been sapped from him in the month he was gone.

"Have I told you of the night you were born?"

Virginia sat down and looked suspiciously at Jeannot. "You weren't here then. How do you remember that?"

"Ah, perhaps you're right." Jeannot grinned. "Why don't you tell me about the night you were born, then?"

"Really? But how am I supposed to remember the night I was born?" Virginia turned to me. "He's joking, isn't he?"

"Of course he is," I said, though I was never sure with my grandfather.

"Yes, Virginia, I'm teasing at you. How about, instead of talking about why I left, I tell you why I came back?" He grinned. "They are one and the same. Would you like to know what surprise I've brought back for you?" He stood quickly and stepped over to the mantel, pulling one of a pair of lanterns down. He peeled a string of wood from a log and dipped it into the stove and then touched it against the wick of the lantern, watching the flame burn for a moment before setting the lantern down at the end of the table.

"Are you going to play with the shadows, like my mother?" Virginia asked.

"No. Look here," my grandfather said. He nested his hands into a round and then placed them against the glass of the lantern. "What do you see?"

"A wick," I said.

"A flame," Virginia said.

"No," my grandfather said. "What I've brought back is none of those things, though you are close."

"Jeannot," my mother said, her voice surprising all of us. Despite the cold air that must have leaked in through the door with her, we had not heard her enter. She stomped her feet and then loosened the shawl that covered her hair. "I thought we agreed that we'd save that for Christmas night." She turned to Virginia and me. "You can wait four more days, can't you?"

My grandfather looked abashed and then put out the lantern, trying to turn our attention instead to the story of a moose that hunted wolves, but of course, my mother's words had only stoked our curiosity.

THE NEXT DAY, SATURDAY, he took us from the house after a late breakfast. He made us bundle ourselves tightly against the snow, told me to take my father's ax, and asked my mother to prepare a parcel holding lunch for the three of us.

As soon as we started walking, we began with the questions, trying to ferret out his surprise.

"Have you captured a fairy?" Virginia asked.

"No," my grandfather said. "But I've seen them out in the woods. Don't let anybody tell you differently, and don't believe that all fairies are friends. There are many that will lead you into danger."

"Is it a spun-sugar castle? Is that what you have for us?" I asked. "Tommy Rondeau saw one in Havershand last winter, and he said it shone like there was a fire inside."

"I knew his grandfather. Good man."

"Is it spun-sugar? Is it?" Virginia bounced against him as we walked through the trees.

Jeannot looked back at her and shook his head. "Now, stay behind me or you'll be worn out." He broke trail through the snow—knee-high for him—and we followed. We had been walking for near an hour already, and I thought it would have been easier to walk along the river itself. The snow was scoured clean off the ice from the wind, but then again, that same wind cut hard like knives across the open floor of the valley. Though we had to wade through the snow, the trees grew like a wall toward the river, opening to let us pass but keeping tight enough together that the wind was dampened. "No," my grandfather said, glancing back at us. "How could I carry a spun-sugar castle without it breaking?"

"Is it—"

Jeannot cut me off. "It is what it is and you'll see it in a few days." He turned abruptly to face us. "Enough now. All morning you've been asking, and all morning I've been not answering." He gave a sly grin. "Besides, I think we're here."

Virginia and I looked around, staring at the ground and turning in circles. Finally, Virginia looked at my grandfather. "Where?"

"May I have the ax?" Jeannot reached out to me and I reluctantly surrendered it.

"See this?" My grandfather reached up with the ax and pointed high up on a tree where a pair of deep gashes rode near each other. "That blaze used to be near my knee last time I was at this creek." He looked down again and shuffled his foot, feeling for something, and then he used his foot to brush snow back from the ground. "Stand back," he said, and then he swung the ax against the ground.

When it hit, the ground shattered and buckled. Virginia and I both gasped at the violence before we realized that my grandfather had smashed through ice, not dirt and snow. He stumbled a little, and for a moment he looked like he was going to pitch forward into the hole that seemed to be growing at his feet, but then he scrambled back to where Virginia and I stood.

"Hadn't expected it to buckle so easily," he said, and as the words came out of his mouth the hole suddenly elongated and the ground opened like a thread pulled from a seam, racing in both directions through the woods. The sound of the ice breaking and crashing into the running water below was a cracking shock that made Virginia cover her ears.

We stood and watched, and even my grandfather seemed impressed with what a single swing from the ax had wrought. "Here's your ax," he said, handing it back to me.

"My father's ax," I said.

My grandfather glanced down at me and then nodded. "Of course."

We watched as chunks of ice washed clear, until a creek seven or eight feet across flowed before us. The water moved quickly, urgently, rushing down through the woods and to the river below, though I wondered what it would do when it reached the Sawgamet. Would the water spill over the surface of the frozen river, or would it find its way beneath the hard covering and add to the dark swirling below?

My grandfather pulled a polished wooden bowl from one of his coat pockets and then crouched by the river. "Come here before it starts to freeze up again," he said, and then he dipped the bowl into the water. He took a sip, laughed, and then handed it to Virginia.

"It's sweet!"

"I told you it would be sweet," my grandfather said. Virginia handed the bowl to me and I took a sip for myself.

"But it's like syrup," I said.

My grandfather rocked forward so that he was kneeling and shook his head. "I know. Do you think I would have had us walk for an hour through the snow just for the same water we could have taken from the river by your house?"

He dipped the bowl in again and drank it down, and then filled it for Virginia and then again for me. My cousin and I started to laugh, and so did Jeannot. We drank and laughed, making so much noise that at first we did not realize that the laughing excitement we heard from behind us came from something else.

My grandfather pulled the ax from my hand as he turned, and the creature stopped, only a few steps away. I felt the sharp fear of my cousin's hand pulling on my coat and heard my own gasp.

The creature's laugh turned into a maniacal giggle. Its blue eyes, looking through thin, greasy hair hanging over its face, were almost as pale as its ice-colored skin. Tattered scraps of cloth hung from its waist, and it stood barefoot in the snow. It tapped its fingers against its legs, calling attention to its hands. I—and I was sure my grandfather and my cousin—fixated on the gleaming fingernails that jutted from its long, thin fingers.

I heard my grandfather's voice, a low whisper, speaking to us. "A mahaha. The tickler."

Virginia let out a quiet sob, and I knew that she was thinking of the stories her father had told us of the mahaha.

It took a step forward and started to reach for Virginia until my grandfather's voice caused it to stop. "The water," my grandfather said. "It's sweet. You should taste it."

Jeannot handed me my father's ax and then pushed Virginia and me behind him, moving forward and spreading his hands in a gesture of munificence. "I'm just trying to be fair. I brought the children all the way out here just so they could taste this water. It would be a shame if you didn't try it yourself." Keeping his eyes on the mahaha, he knelt down, cupped a hand in the water, and then brought it to his lips. "Cold," he said, "but it's sweet. Like syrup, like candy." He rose to his feet again and motioned to the water. "You should try some."

It gave a low cackle and then stepped toward the water. As it bent over, it placed its hands on the ice that rimmed the edge, the claws sending up shavings of white.

My grandfather waited until the creature's lips were almost touching the water before he gave it a hard shove. It let out a laughing scream as it fell into the water, and almost immediately it was swept along in the current and disappeared into the trees.

My grandfather touched me on the head and then picked up Virginia. She was crying, hard, gulping sobs, and he held her tight against his chest. "There, there," he said. "As long as you know how to handle them, they're more stupid than scary, really. Ask them to take a drink, give a little push, and away they go. Your father's father told me plenty of useful things about what comes in these woods."

I spun the ax handle in my hand, the blade turning and catching the midmorning light that filtered through the tops of the trees.

Virginia slowly stopped crying, and my grandfather put her back on the ground.

"There used to be more of them," my grandfather said. "There was a time when mahahas were almost common, but like I said, they pan out on the dumb side. They're a kind of snow demon. They tickle you until all your breath is gone. Leave you dead, but with a smile."

Virginia started to sob again, a loud howling, and Jeannot gave me a look of surprise and then he tried to quiet her. "Hush," he said. "It's gone and won't be back, I promise."

He wrapped his arms around her and offered her a jam-filled biscuit, more of the sweet water, tried singing to her, rubbing her back, but she would not stop crying, and as his coat stained with her tears and snot, he shook his head. "Don't cry, Virginia. If you stop crying, I'll show you tonight what I brought with me. No need to wait until Christmas, yes?"

She took a few heaving breaths and then wiped her nose on

her sleeve. She looked at me and then back at my grandfather. "Promise?" He nodded, and then she did, too.

Virginia started walking in front, covering the same ground we had trod on the way here, and as I began to follow her, my grandfather put his hand on my shoulder and stopped me.

"Tonight," he said, "I'll show you what I've brought back. I'll show you that there are more things than scary stories in these woods, that there are miracles out here."

"My grandmother?"

"I told you," he said. "I came back to raise the dead."

TWELVE

The End of the Most Beautiful Village in the World

FATHER EARL AND I TALKED for a short while before he headed off to sleep. Neither one of us could bear to wait; the funeral is to be held in the morning. And now it's time for me to go to bed, myself. It's gone past two in the morning, the house long silent.

I do understand that on this night, the night of my mother's death, the night before my mother's funeral, I should be thinking of her, not these stories of my grandfather and grandmother, of my father and sister slipped below the ice, hands nearly touching, of the woods and witches and ghosts. But my mother, more than anyone, would have understood. Though she was not born in Sawgamet, she understood the nature of the cuts, the ghosts that can tie you to a place—as they did for her—or drive you away—as they did for me.

It's fair to say that these ghosts are what have kept me away for so long. A funny sort of providence, my stepfather said, but that is not why I have finally returned to Sawgamet after more than two decades away. I would not have returned if Father Earl had not asked me to, if he had not said that Sawgamet needed me—that he needed me—to come back. I am not like my grandfather—I don't have the faith, or the strength, to raise the dead—but I have come to believe what my mother began to believe soon after my father and Marie went through the ice on the river: memories are another way to raise the dead.

WE RETURNED FROM the woods with my grandfather, and though we did not collude or set out to deceive my mother, neither Virginia nor I saw fit to talk about the mahaha or the stream filled with sweet water. My grandfather must have said something, however, because that evening, after my mother finished the last of the dishes, my grandfather brought his contraption out of the bag and neither my mother nor my stepfather seemed surprised that we were not waiting until Christmas night, a more traditional time for miracles.

A crank ran from a metal box that was attached to a polished board. A series of wires connected the box to a glass globe, and when my grandfather first started to turn the crank, the globe sputtered and glowed weakly.

"That's it?" I said, trying not to display my disappointment.

"It's an electric lantern," my grandfather said. "Just wait."

My stepfather had banked the fire in the stove and screened it off, snuffed the candles and the lanterns, and the darkness in the cottage was encompassing. As my grandfather turned the handle harder and faster, the glass ball began to shine with a startling and flickering brilliance, a tiny sun contained in glass upon the table.

My mother glanced over at me and then took my hand, and I thought of the way she had so often held my father's mangled hand.

And then, for some reason, my grandfather slowed, the sound of the turning crank dimming in concert with the light, and we were all left in the dim whisper from the stove, the memory of light dying in the glass globe.

"Jeannot?" My mother leaned forward. "Jeannot?"

My grandfather stared out the window and then turned slowly to me. "I thought—" His voice caught and then he looked down at his hands. "I wasn't sure. I thought I might need more than one of these lights to chase off the darkness that candles and lanterns couldn't break. I didn't think . . . With all my searching it can't be as simple as this."

He looked at me. "I just thought I would show you the light. Show you what is coming to Sawgamet. Lights like this, trains, moving pictures, what is set to replace the darkness of these woods. But I didn't think . . ." He trailed off and then touched the crank with his hand. "I didn't expect it to be tonight."

And then he clapped his hands together and stood up with a sudden energy. "It's time," he said. "She's out there. She's waiting for me."

"What are you talking about?" my stepfather said.

"My grandmother?" I asked.

"Haven't you been listening to me?" my grandfather said, his voice soft and gentle, a small smile on his lips. "Yes, of course it's your grandmother." He glanced at me and then back to the window. "She asked me to bring her light, and now she's waiting for me." He slapped his hand on the table and then stood up. With a quavering voice, he said, "It's time for me to go. I'll not be coming back this time."

"Do you have to?" I asked.

Jeannot looked pityingly toward me, at my mother, and then at my stepfather and Virginia in turn. "Have you no idea what love means, how long you can carry it with you? What your grandmother meant to me, what I have done and would do for her? Why do you think I came back here? To where I could never forget her? Where I see her in every rock, every tree, every bird?"

He stared at me again. "I see your grandmother every time I look at you. Why do you think I fled and left your father behind? Do you understand?"

He was quiet then, and I nodded, though I was not sure that I did understand.

"Virginia," my grandfather said. "You saw what I was doing, yes? Can you turn that crank and keep turning it?"

She nodded solemnly, and then I rose to my feet. My mother and stepfather rose as well, but my grandfather put out his hand.

"No. Just Stephen. He'll come with me. He needs to see his grandmother. You two stay here with Virginia. Make sure she keeps the light burning."

My grandfather pulled his coat from the peg by the door.

Even in the near dark of the cottage—the fire banked, the candles snuffed, the crank handle still for the moment—I was struck by how shrunken my grandfather finally seemed.

"Once we're outside, Virginia," my grandfather said to my cousin. She nodded grimly and put her hand on the crank.

The door shut firmly behind us, and I could hear the grinding sound of the handle beginning to turn in circles.

Outside, my grandfather and I stood in the street. Candles and lanterns flickered fitfully in the houses around us, but the light from my mother and stepfather's house seemed to flood through the windows, white and burning.

Suddenly, around us, floating in the air, a dozen lights seemed to spring forth from the cold nothingness of the night.

"This is what it was like," my grandfather said. "That day on the river, when we canoed back through the snow, the miners like angels, your grandmother near dead from cold and in my arms, the way the house had been lit from within by your great-aunt, and I felt like there I was, in the midst of salvation." He touched me on the shoulder, and I thought of all the stories he had told me of my grandmother, of himself, of Sawgamet. I thought of the fires, the snow, the woods. I thought of the river and my father and Marie trapped below, my mother chopping with the ax on the night of the freezing rain, when the ice shone from below.

The floating lights momentarily dimmed as the light in the house became weaker, but then, as if Virginia had only needed to regrip the handle, the lights began to glow and shine again. They doubled and then redoubled in their radiance, glowing like the air itself was on fire. Each light cast widening circles of luminescence until darkness was banished from the entire street, until the moon seemed to disappear from the sky and even the stars began to suffer from the light. And then, in the midst of this unbearable brightness, I was able to see a form, a movement.

My grandmother stood like a shadow, and then she dissolved into solidness, standing before us as she should be, as she would have been had she not died nearly thirty years before. She wore a wedding dress and carried nothing but happiness. She stepped in front of me first, raising her hand to my face and whispering her fingers against my cheeks before she turned to my grandfather.

I watched the two of them move into the brilliance of the light. I had to cover my eyes with my fingers, like I was staring into the sun. They rose into the air together, weightless, floating beside each other, suspended against the burning light. My grandmother extended her arm toward my grandfather, and he turned to her, reaching out with both hands.

The light pulled at both of them, and I could see my grandfather stretching and fighting, until little more than the width of an ax blade separated my grandfather's two hands from my grandmother's one. And then the light thickened and blurred, leaving shadows and dark shapes so that all I could see was their hands, my grandfather's large and rough, reaching for my grandmother's small, smooth fingers.

And then, they touched.

At that moment, my grandparents, joined again as one, seemed to rise in a magnificent burst of light, and I could hear the shattering of glass before the light blinked away into darkness.

IN THE MORNING, I helped Pearl make a coffin for my grand-father's body. We placed the electric light—the glass globe bro-ken and melted into something unrecognizable—into the box, and then Pearl, my stepfather, and several other men helped to carry the box to the church.

At the funeral, my stepfather asked me if I wanted to say anything, but I mutely shook my head.

Afterward, because of the snow and the frozen ground, the coffin was sealed and stored in the church's woodshed, to lie undisturbed until the winter broke.

THERE ISN'T ANYTHING more to tell about my grandfather. When the ground softened we buried him beside my grand-mother in the cemetery.

A few summers later—after Pearl and Mrs. Gasseur died in the fire that burned down the mill and the company house—the railway linked into Sawgamet, wires brought elec-tricity and light to all the houses in the village, and I knew that I would never get a chance to join a float like my father had.

Near the end of the July that I turned sixteen, I walked down the banks for an hour or two, toward Havershand, to no end in particular, just getting distance from Sawgamet. I had already spent many of the days that summer by myself, down by the river, fishing and picking wild blueberries. The rocks had stopped holding their heat past the setting of the sun, and the following morning I was expected to board

the train to start my journey to school. I was going to the seminary in Edmonton, the same seminary where my stepfather
had studied.

Everywhere I looked I thought of a story that my father
or grandfather had told me, the implausible details Jeannot
had insisted upon, the moments where my father had always
paused, and I wondered how it was that the rocks and the
river were not crushed under the weight of so many ghosts.
How long would I have to ride the train, how far gone would
I be toward Edmonton before I stopped seeing my father and
grandfather's words spilled across the land?

I walked further, for another hour, and then, at midday,
I stopped and ate my sandwich while sitting on a small rock,
my feet splayed in the cold shallows of the river. I finished, and
then leaned down and pulled a flat oval stone from the water,
and threw it out into the whitewater. The stone disappeared
without a trace, and when I reached down again for another
rock to throw, I saw the skate.

Even with the blade rusted through, the black leather eaten
in places, it was clearly a child's skate. I turned it over in my
hands, water dripping onto my legs. There were no markings
on the skate, and I held it awhile, looking out into the water.

I wondered if their hands had met, if the breaking ice,
the tumultuous destruction of winter, had pushed Marie and
my father together, or if it had torn them apart. I wanted to
believe that my father had taken hold of Marie's hand, that as
the water roared down the Sawgamet, my father's hands, both
of them made whole again, held Marie's hand tightly against
the current.

I put the skate back into the water, in case Marie should need it again, and started home, thinking of my father as a young man, walking back from Havershand after the float, walking to Sawgamet, of my grandfather, coming from Quesnelle-mouthe accompanied by Flaireur and knowing nothing of his destination. I walked until I saw the chute and stairs that ran from the water up to the ashes where the foreman's cottage and mill had once stood.

I scrambled up the steps, pausing for a moment at the top. I had been to the mill and the cottage many times since it burned down, but for the first time I ventured into the ashes, push-ing aside charred logs and treading carefully on the uneven ground. I did not know what I was searching for, and after a while I left the ruins behind and washed off as best I could in the creek. The water was stunning with cold, and though it had none of the same sweetness, it reminded me of the day in the woods with my grandfather and Virginia. Nervously, I looked back over my shoulder, but the only thing behind me was the open meadow and the collapsed and hollowed build-ings that I had once been so familiar with.

I thought to walk out to the cuts for a while, but I did not want to face the chips and flying dust, the breaking weight of wood and branches. Instead, I stood and turned to go through the woods to the village. As I walked, I wondered if this was the same path that my grandfather had trod, or if that par-ticular path had been overgrown and lost as so many of my grandfather's stories had been lost.

I stopped in the thick of the trees. The light filtered down to me and I could see motes of dust glimmer like specks of gold, like fairies. I closed my eyes and thought of the weight of the skate in my hand earlier that day, and then I tried to think of the sound of my father's voice, but it did not come to me. I was not sure if I stood there with my eyes closed for only a few seconds or if it was longer, minutes, an hour, but I opened my eyes again when I heard footsteps.

The boy that came toward me was the same age as me, loaded down by a heavy pack and carrying an ax and a rifle. A dog came trotting from behind him and then raced past the boy and to me. The dog sniffed at me, circled me once, and then kept moving up the path. It was lean and panting, and looked, I thought, as if it would not go much further.

The boy did not seem to see me. He was intent on moving forward, and though I did not know what was in the boy's full pack, I could see the strain and weight. The boy himself was as lean as the dog, but carried himself with such a tight violence that I did not have to think before stepping aside.

I stared at the boy. Sawgamet was not the sort of village that had strangers come with any frequency, and the boy showed none of the same curiosity that I did. He focused furiously on the ground in front of him and brushed past me without any sort of acknowledgment.

I wanted to stay quiet, feeling as if I were somehow intruding, as if, for the first time in my life, I did not belong in these woods. It was only when I saw the stray beam of sunlight catch the blade of the ax that my eyes widened and I called out.

"Jeannot." I said the name softly, and when the boy continued to walk, I called it louder. "Jeannot."

The boy hesitated and then stopped in his tracks. He showed his profile and then turned in a slow circle, as if he had not quite heard something, and then the boy continued walking, following the dog.

I stood and watched for a moment and then I turned back toward the village and began to run. I ran down the gentle slope and through the start of the village, passing by a few curious children who played with a ball in front of the store. Even as my chest began to hurt I kept running until I reached the front of my stepfather's house. I burst through the door and called out for my mother, and it was only when she stepped from the kitchen that I allowed myself to bend over and gulp for breath.

I was startled for a moment at what I took to be a sudden streak of white in her hair, but then I realized it was flour, and I stepped forward and embraced my mother, kissing her on the cheek.

"You've not even left for seminary yet and you miss me already?" she asked.

"I just thought . . . I was . . . I wanted to see you," I stumbled. I stepped back and she took my hands in hers.

"Dinner won't be for a few hours still," she said, "but if you want to sit in the kitchen with me, you'd be welcome. Your stepfather is up at the church, and he wouldn't mind spending time with you, either."

"I'll sit with you," I said, and followed her into the kitchen. I sat on a stool and took the cookie that my mother handed me.

"I shouldn't," she said, "but I won't be able to spoil you once you're in Edmonton." She turned back to the dough on the counter and sank her hands into it. I watched the rhythm of her kneading, and for a moment I lost myself. "What's wrong?" she said.

"Nothing." I had a sudden panic and then looked up to the peg by the back door and let out a small breath when I saw the ax still hanging there. I glanced over at my mother and saw her watching me.

"What did you see?"

I stuffed the last bite of the cookie into my mouth and stood. "I'll bring in some more wood for the stove," I said. I reached out and pulled the ax down from the peg. "And I'll cut some kindling for you."

"You've stacked enough to get us through this winter and the next already. Besides, Earl does know how to use an ax." She paused and then added, "I think."

I did not look back over my shoulder to see the smile that I could hear in her voice.

"Can never have too much cut wood," I said as I pushed through the door and out into the cooling air.

The woodshed bulged with split wood in neat stacks, but I had already started another stack, three layers deep, leaning up against the back wall. I took a large piece of wood and balanced it atop the stump that I used for a cutting platform. I swung the ax down hard. The blade smashed cleanly through, splitting the wood into two smaller pieces. I picked one from the ground and then split that again, and then took those smaller pieces and added them to the pile of kindling.

I worked like this for an hour or more, settling into a reassuring pattern, until the thought of the boy in the woods—the ghost of my grandfather—fled from my mind. I did not waste movement, keeping the ax biting into logs and adding to the pile of cut wood. I worked hard enough that I stayed warm even though I noticed an odd chill in the air. Occasionally I stopped and looked up at the sudden roiling black clouds that pulled in across the sky, like darkness against the roof of heaven.

Despite the dropping temperature and the change in the sky, the light stayed clear and steady. Still, I was not surprised when I saw the first few flakes of snow drift down before me.

The late summer snow melted as it touched my skin, and I had no worries that this snow had come to stay. At most, I knew, it was an early visitor that would be gone by morning, and I welcomed it. There would be snow and cold in Edmonton, but not like this, not like what I knew from Sawgamet. Though I had never even been as far as Havershand, I was afraid that the streets and buildings of Edmonton would be as foreign and frightening to me as the dark and woods of Sawgamet were to men and women who came unprepared to the north.

I paused for a moment and then took one last piece of wood and placed it on the stump. I rested the ax on the ground and pushed my palm into the solidness of the handle. When I picked it up again, I was struck by the weight of the ax and the history it carried. The dents and dings in the blade, the marks and grooves, and, of course, the scar of a burn worked into the handle, each blemish a story that my grandfather or father told me, stories that I did not yet realize I would tell to my own children.

I lifted the ax behind me, and as I swung it down into the waiting wood I felt something shift. As the ax struck the wood, the handle broke and sent the blade twisting into a knot in the log. I saw the blade buckle and heard the groaning shriek of the metal give. The blade cleaved in two, one piece lodged in the wood, the other shearing into my leg.

As I fell to the ground, I did not see the future, did not

hear the stories of my own life that I would tell my daughters—Marie, Martine, and Nathalie—when I returned to Sawgamet and the winter snows kept us in for days on end, did not even see far enough ahead to know that I *would* return to Sawgamet.

Neither did I think of the present, of the way the metal burnt a bright suffering in my leg, of how I had ruined my pants with blood, of how I would be forced to take to my bed for a week before I could leave for Edmonton.

Instead, as the shattered blade entered my leg, as I fell heavily to the ground, I thought of the stories that my father and grandfather had told me, just as I think of them now.

I thought of how my grandfather had crossed a continent to stop here, in Sawgamet, and how with that very ax he had cut saplings and branches to make a lean-to, the first marks of destruction to visit these woods. I thought of how my grandfather must have thought that the ax would be passed down from son to son to son, keeping on as long as Sawgamet kept on.

I lay under the purpling sky and watched the snow falling gently down upon me. My leg hurt, but I did not worry. I knew with utter certainty that at this moment something both terrible and wonderful was happening in the kitchen or in the church, and that any moment my mother or stepfather would come rushing to me. It was a shame, I thought, that the snow was not falling hard enough to give me one last taste of the fury that Sawgamet could bring to bear, but as I had the thought I realized that maybe this snow was something else: maybe the soft, fluttering flakes of snow were a sort of tenderness, an

offering of love, a benediction to see me safely off to Edmonton
so that one day I would be able to return to Sawgamet.

OR PERHAPS THE SNOW was just snow that day, and perhaps
the snow is just snow on this night, the night before I bury
my mother. But it is hard not to ascribe some meaning to it. I
look out the window now, and think that the snow is falling
with reverence, slow and spinning, great pieces of white drifting through the lights of the train yards.

It is the same Sawgamet that my grandfather knew, that
my father knew, that I knew as a boy, and yet it is barely rec-
ognizable. It is not the town that has changed so much as the
woods. The cuts are just a place to work now. Horses and
sleds and axes and saws are still used, but so are machines and
motors now. They've driven out the ghosts and terrors of my
childhood.

I'm tired, and I know I need to sleep before my mother's
funeral in the morning, but I can't stop thinking about what
happened to my grandfather, my grandmother, my father, my
sister, even Pearl and his wife, as if the woods have tried to
reclaim what is rightfully theirs.

Perhaps tomorrow, after the funeral, when my wife takes
the baby home, I'll walk along the river or into the woods with
my two oldest daughters, Martine and Marie, and I'll tell them
the rest of the stories that they have yet to hear. Maybe I'll
convince them to look for their namesakes, my grandmother
and my sister, and maybe, in turn, they'll be able to convince
me that if we walk far enough into the woods we'll find my

grandfather, young again, with my grandmother, that we'll find my father and Marie holding hands, my mother looking over them.

THIS ONE LAST THING before I go to sleep. I keep the broken halves of the ax head on my desk, but tonight I decide to take them down to the river. They are the most physical part of Sawgamet that I carry: Jeannot's ax, my father's ax, good for little more than paperweights since the day the blade cleaved in two.

I scoop them from my desk and creep down the stairs, conscious of not waking my wife or daughters. I pull on my coat and shut the door behind me. In the morning I'll walk to the graveyard and speak over the body of my mother—the same graveyard where my grandfather and grandmother are buried, where my father and sister would have been buried if we had found their bodies—but for tonight, it's down to the river.

The snow seems to carry me the short distance to the water, and even though there is a part of me that is expecting it, I am still stunned at what is before me: the river frozen over, the ice shining from below, as if the river had swallowed the moon. I think for a moment of flinging the pieces of blade out onto the ice, of the sound the broken ax head would make when it hits, like metal on metal, or how the halves might break through the ice and leave a dark hole of water, but instead, as the light under the ice fades, I slip them back into my pocket and turn toward home.

And once there, back in the house, I take a last look at the sleeping forms of my daughters nestled into their bedrooms before I pad down the hall and slip into bed beside my wife. She stirs a little at the comfort of my weight. I fall asleep listening to the snow continuing outside. I can hear its soft whisper on the window and against the trees, the quiet it brings, and I think it is fitting that tomorrow, when I wake, Sawgamet will be made clean for my mother's funeral.

ACKNOWLEDGMENTS

I WOULD LIKE TO THANK: Bill Clegg, a wonderful agent and reader, and his assistant Shaun Dolan. Jill Bialosky and her assistant Alison Liss at W. W. Norton & Company, Michael Schellenberg at Knopf Canada, Juliet Brooke at Chatto & Windus, and all editors and assistants everywhere who deserve thanks. Téa Obreht and Jared Harel, best friends and best writers. Marie Mockett, Maud Newton, Kaytie Lee, Matt Grice, Seth Fishman, early readers, extra eyes. Michael Koch, Stephanie Vaughn, J. Robert Lennon, Alison Lurie, Sigrid Nunez, and Ben Fountain, teachers and encouragers. Ben George, who picked me out of the slush.

To my family: my mother and father, who despite everything else, always encouraged me to write. My brother, Ari, and his family. The Rhéaumes. The Willicks. And always, to my wife, Laurie Willick, and my daughters, Zoey and Sabine.